Emma Ch4 *Today* bestselling
author wand passionate"
(Katy Eva, turns her award-
winning talents to the sizzling escapades of lawyers in love,
lust, and compromising positions . . . the Legal Briefs series!

Raves for Emma Chase and her sexy bestsellers

Sustained

"Emma Chase is a master at writing sexy bad boys turned
good, and *Sustained* is one of her best!"

—Jennifer Probst

"TEN STARS! Emma Chase's unique writing style sizzles in
this funny, meltingly hot romance. I laughed, sighed, and
swooned nonstop. *Sustained* is not one to miss!"

—Katy Evans

"Emma Chase does it again! Full of humor, emotion, insanely
hot chemistry, and a chaotic family that absolutely stole my
heart, *Sustained* is one great read."

—S. C. Stephens

"Laugh-out-loud funny and with surprisingly poignant
moments, the title is perfect for romance."

—*RT Book Reviews*

Overruled

"Chase has proven, once again, that she creates heroes who
are grounded, successful and lovable . . . There are funny,
appealing characters introduced, and watching their love lives
unfold is fun."

—*RT Book Reviews*

"*Overruled* is even more proof as to why I have come to look forward to every single book Emma Chase releases."

—*Harlequin Junkies*

"*Overruled* was sexy, fun, and a good read."

—*Fiction Vixen*

Tied

One of PopSugar's Best Books for Women 2014

"Sublimely irreverent, massively sexy, and so frigging perfect, readers will be bursting with giddy smiles. This, praise Emma, is the ending we all wanted."

—Christina Lauren, *New York Times* bestselling author of *Beautiful Secret*

Tamed

One of PopSugar's Best Books for Women 2014

"Witty, endearing, laugh-out-loud funny. Emma Chase doesn't disappoint."

—K. Bromberg, bestselling author of *Driven*

Twisted

"A great escape."

—Katy Evans, *New York Times* bestselling author of *Real* and *Ripped*

"A delicious treat . . . funny, witty, and very sexy."

—*The Book Bella*

"Emma Chase grabbed me from page one and put me through the wringer."

—*Caffeinated Book Reviewer*

"Is emotional whiplash considered a sickness? I am more in love with this series than I was before, my heart just took a severe beating along the way."

—*The Geekery Book Review*

Emma Chase was chosen as the
Debut Goodreads Author in the Goodreads Choice
Awards for 2013 for her sensational novel

Tangled

Also a Goodreads Best Book of 2013!

"Addictively entertaining. If you're looking for witty, laugh-out-loud insight into the male psyche look no further: it's *Tangled*."

—*Miss Ivy's Book Nook*

"Total stop, drop, and roll reading. . . . Oh, and the sex . . . completely and utterly scandalicious."

—*Scandalicious Book Reviews*

"I give *Tangled* . . . Five Spectacular, Swoony, Fun, Laugh-Out-Loud Stars!"

—*A Bookish Escape*

"I seriously enjoyed this book; any erotic romance that you can laugh out loud while reading and then be turned on in the next paragraph is an exhilarating book to read."

—*Schmexy Girl Book Blog*

APPEALED

EMMA CHASE

G

GALLERY BOOKS

New York   London   Toronto   Sydney   New Delhi

G

Gallery Books
An Imprint of Simon & Schuster, Inc.
1230 Avenue of the Americas
New York, NY 10020

First Gallery Books trade paperback edition January 2016

GALLERY BOOKS and colophon are registered trademarks of Simon & Schuster, Inc.

For information about special discounts for bulk purchases, please contact Simon & Schuster Special Sales at 1-866-506-1949 or business@simonandschuster.com.

The Simon & Schuster Speakers Bureau can bring authors to your live event, For more information or to book an event, contact the Simon & Schuster Speakers Bureau at 1-866-248-3049 or visit our website at www.simonspeakers.com.

Manufactured in the United States of America

10 9 8 7 6 5 4 3 2 1

Library of Congress Cataloging-in-Publication Data

Chase, Emma
Appealed / Emma Chase.
First Gallery Books trade paperback edition. | New York :
   Gallery Books, 2016. | Series: The legal briefs series ; 3
LCSH: Man-woman relationships—Fiction. | BISAC: FICTION / Romance
   / Contemporary. | FICTION / Contemporary Women. | GSAFD: Love stories.
LCC PS3603.H37934 A87 2016 | DDC 813/.6—dc23

ISBN 978-1-5011-0209-7
ISBN 978-1-5011-0210-3 (ebook)

For all the girls next door—and the boys who love them.

Acknowledgments

I've always enjoyed fairy tales. Their timeless magic, their innocent simplicity, the soul-stirring idea that love can overcome any obstacle—vanquish the villain, save the princess, break all the evil spells.

The idea for *Appealed* began, for me, as a fairy tale. A simple story about a handsome prince, a good-hearted princess, and their sweet love. From there it evolved—and the evolution was really fun. Now it's hilarious and passionate, a battle of wills—a story of how young love grows into something stronger, something unbreakable.

I love this story. I love these characters—their resilience, their wit, and most of all their laughter. I hope you come to love them too, that their story will leave you with that warm, satisfied feeling and the knowledge that true love really can conquer all, and the dream of happy ever after is within reach for all of us.

I'm so grateful to have been able to work with the best, most talented people on the Legal Briefs series. My editor, Micki Nuding—thank you for helping me see how to make the impossible totally doable. Brainstorming with you is the best!

My agent, Amy Tannenbaum of the Jane Rotrosen Agency—thank you for always being in my corner. I've said it before, but I really would be lost without you!

My publicists, Kristin Dwyer and Nina Bocci—I adore you both forever—thank you for making work fun and for being so awesome at all you do. My assistant, Juliet Fowler—thank you for staying on top of everything, for your innovative ideas, and amazing energy. So much gratitude to Sullivan & Partners for their impeccable *Sustained* campaign. So much gratitude to Molly O'Brien for your tireless work and support.

My thanks to everyone at Gallery Books, including Sarah Leiberman, Liz Psaltis, Paul O'Halloran, my publishers Jennifer Bergstrom and Louise Burke—it's a joy and honor to work with all of you.

I have so much admiration and love for Katy Evans, Jennifer Probst, Kyra Davis, Alice Clayton and Christina Lauren—thank you for your smiles and amazing support!

I'm so very grateful to all the blogs who read and review my work and who make the romance community vibrant and wonderful.

Again, to my lovely readers—thank you for staying on this journey with me, for loving, laughing, and enjoying these characters and their antics just as much as I do! I adore every one of you!

And to my family, thank you for your patience, your ridiculousness, your love—you are my own love story come to life. xoxo

APPEALED

APPENDIX

1

"**Y**ou rotten bastard!"

Kennedy sits up and stares at me like she doesn't even recognize me. Which is pretty weird, considering we're bare-ass naked in my bed. Every inch of us is intimately acquainted.

But it's the tone of her voice that bothers me most—flat with tightly controlled anger and breathy with pain. Like I stole the air from her lungs—like I punched her in the stomach.

The words don't worry me. Insults are our flirting. Arguing is our foreplay. One time, she was so worked up she hauled off and took a swing at me—and my reaction was a boner that wouldn't be denied.

It's not as twisted as it sounds. It works for us.

At least it did up until ten seconds ago.

"Wait. What?" I ask, genuinely surprised.

I thought she'd be grateful. Happy. Maybe offer me a blow job to demonstrate her supreme appreciation.

Her eyes glitter dangerously, and thoughts of letting her

anywhere near my dick flee like tiny fish in a big aquarium. Because she's not a woman to be taken lightly; she's a force to be reckoned with. A breaker of hearts and a buster of balls.

"You planned this all along, didn't you? Screwing me silly, lulling me into a false sense of security so I'll drop my guard and you can win the case," she hisses.

She moves to hop off the bed but I grab her arm. "You think my cock is powerful enough to turn you stupid? Aw, precious, that's really flattering, but I don't need to whore myself out to win my cases. You're freaking out over nothing."

"Fuck off!"

I used to have a way with women.

If the word *fuck* came out to play, it was always followed by *me* and then words like *harder, please, and my friend, more.*

Those were the days . . .

She jerks out of my grasp and scrambles off the bed, furiously gathering clothes that are strewn across the hardwood floor. And because she's doing it naked, bending down, jiggling in all the best places, I have to watch. There are teeth marks on her ass—*my* teeth marks. No broken skin, just dark pink indentations. It's possible I got a little carried away last night, but her ass is just so damn sweet and round and bitable.

I grab the prosthesis sleeve from the bedside table and slide it onto the stump on my left leg. Yes, part of my leg was amputated when I was a kid—a transtibial amputation if you want the technical term. I'll get into that later, because she isn't waiting. I actually like that about her—she doesn't give an inch. Doesn't even think about making special concessions or treating me any differently than the fully capable man I am.

Or the prick she apparently thinks I am at the moment.

I snap the pin of the sleeve into my prosthetic leg and stand up, just as she finds her shoe in the corner, adding it to the pile in her arms.

"Calm down, kitten," I try, my voice level.

"Don't call me that!" she snaps. "We said we wouldn't discuss the case—that was our agreement."

I move in closer, palms out, the universal sign of *I come in peace*. "We agreed to a lot of things that no longer apply, sweet-cheeks."

Her nostrils flare at the trial nickname. Guess I can add "sweet-cheeks" to the *no* column, which is a damn shame. It suits her.

"I only brought it up because I'm trying to help you."

It's official: I'm a fucking idiot. Of all the wrong things I could've said, that's the wrongest of them all.

"You think I need your *help*? Condescending cocksucker!"

She turns for the door, but I grab her arm again.

"Let go. I'm leaving."

I want to respond with a good old *Like hell you are* or the more direct *You're not going anywhere*. But they both have a psychotic, it-puts-the-lotion-in-the-basket-or-it-gets-the-hose kind of vibe. And that's not what I'm going for.

Instead, I snatch the clothes from her arms and head to the window.

"What are you—? Don't!"

Too late.

Her designer skirt, sleeveless silk blouse, and red lacy underthings float on the air for a fraction of a second, then fall to the sidewalk and street below us. Her bra gets snagged on the antenna of a passing car and waves majestically down the street like the flag on a diplomat's vehicle from some awesome country named Titsland.

Feels like I should salute it.

I close the window, cross my arms, and smile. "If you try to leave now, poor Harrison may be scarred for life." Harrison is my butler. Again—later.

"You son of a bitch!"

And her fists come flying at my face. All those years of ballet classes have made her quick, gracefully agile. But as fast as she is, and as mighty as her disposition is, she's only five foot one at best. So before she can land a punch, or thinks to knee me in the balls, I easily toss her onto the bed. Then I straddle her waist, leaning over to press her wrists into the mattress above her head. My cock brushes hot and hard against the smooth skin just below her breasts, which gives him some fabulous ideas—but that's gonna have to wait until later too.

Pity.

I gaze down at her. "Now, peaches, we'll continue our conversation."

That nickname fits too. Her silken skin is all peaches and cream. And the way she smells, *Jesus*, the way she tastes on my tongue—sweeter and softer than a ripe peach on a summer day.

Strands of blond hair dance across her collarbone as she bucks beneath me, giving my dick even more fabulous ideas. "Fuck you! I'm done talking."

"Good. Then how about you shut that beautiful mouth and listen? Or I could always gag you."

I may gag her anyway, just for the fun of it. Probably should've held on to her panties.

"I hate you!"

I chuckle. "No, you don't."

Her brown eyes burn into me, the same way they branded me decades ago. "I never should have trusted you again."

Keeping her wrists pinned above her, I lean back a little to enjoy the view. "Bullshit. Best decision you ever made. Now listen up, buttercup . . ."

And I start to tell her all the things I should've said weeks ago. No—*years* ago . . .

• • •

4 weeks earlier

"I had a weird dream last night."

I pace behind the couch with a racquetball ball in my hand. When I get to the end, I bounce the ball against the wall, catch it with one hand, then turn around and head the other way. I talk easier, think better when I'm moving.

"I was on a beach . . . at least I think it was a beach, I don't remember any water. But there was sand, I was digging in the sand."

Bounce, catch, turn.

Some people think it's weak to see a therapist—but they couldn't be more full of shit. It takes some big brass balls to bare your thoughts to another person. Your fears, faults, down-and-dirty desires. It's like a workout for the soul. It forces you to see yourself—the real you.

And I think that's the problem—most people don't want to see themselves. They prefer to believe they're actually the person everyone on the outside thinks they are—not the selfish, deviant asshole who's really calling the shots.

"The grains were rough—white, beige, and black, and I kept digging deeper. I didn't know what I was looking for, but I knew it when I found it."

Bounce, catch, turn.

"It was a ruby. A ruby in the sand. But here's the weird part—when I tried to pick it up, it kept slipping from my hands. No matter how hard I tried, how much I tightened my grip, I couldn't hold on to it. Fucking creepy, right, Waldo?"

My therapist's name is Waldo Bingingham. He's a softspoken, contemplative kind of guy a few years shy of retirement. All his other clients call him Dr. Bingingham, or Dr. Bing for short. But I like Waldo—it's pretty much the most awesome name someone could be named. If your kid's name is Waldo, at some point in his life, you're gonna have to say, *Where's Waldo?* And that's hilarious.

He gazes at me patiently. He removes his dark, thickrimmed, 1960s Walter Cronkite–era glasses and cleans them slowly with a tissue. It's a strategy he's used often in the years I've been coming to him. He's waiting me out—giving me time to answer my own question.

Bounce, catch, turn.

But this time, I'm genuinely determined to hear his professional opinion. What the fuck does it all mean, Waldo?

He finally blinks first. "I thought this week we had decided to discuss how you use sexual intercourse to avoid intimacy."

I roll my eyes. "Sex, sex, sex—that's all you Freudians want to talk about. Is that all I am to you—a piece of meat? A cock

with legs? Well"—I chuckle, tapping my prosthetic limb—
"leg, anyway. Is the wife holding out on you again?"

He writes a note on the pad in his lap. "We can also add
how you use inappropriate humor to deflect conversations
that make you uncomfortable to our list of topics for future
discussions."

Bounce, catch, turn.

"No, I'm just a funny guy. Life's too serious—it's not
gonna weigh me down. Besides, I think you're way off base on
the intimacy theory. Screwing is by its very nature intimate."

"Not the way you do it."

"Are you judging me, Waldo?"

Yeah—I just get a kick out of saying his name.

"Do you want me to judge you, Brent?"

"Do you think I *should* want you to judge me?"

I've been in therapy since I was ten years old—I can go
around and around like this all day.

"I think you're using this dream to avoid discussing how
you use sex to avoid intimacy."

"No—it's just messing with my head. I want to know what
it means."

Bounce, catch, turn

Waldo sighs. Giving up and giving in. "Dreams are a
reflection of our own subconscious. The expression of feelings
and desires our conscious mind doesn't want to acknowledge.
It doesn't matter what the dream means—only what it means
to *you*. What's your interpretation?"

My first thought is my subconscious is telling me I need a
vacation. Somewhere warm and tropical, with umbrella drinks
and hot women in small bikinis.

Or even better—no bikinis.

But that's too simple. The dream was different. It seemed . . . important.

"I think it means I'm looking for something."

Waldo puts his glasses back on. "And?"

"And when I find it, I'm afraid I won't be able to keep it."

He nods. Like a proud papa. "I think you're right."

Bounce, catch, turn.

This is why therapy rocks. With those four approving words, I feel a sense of empowerment—solid self-awareness and competency. I may not know what's coming around the bend—but I sure as shit will be able to handle it when it gets here.

"Now . . . back to your intimacy issues."

I make a complaining sound in the back of my throat— grumbling like a kid who's been made to sit at the table to do his homework. I settle on the couch, resting one arm across the back. "Fine. Hit me, sempai."

He suppresses a smile and glances at his notes. "You mentioned Tatianna was coming to town last week. Did you see her?"

Tatianna is an old friend. In the biblical sense. She's also a real live princess. If Disney ever decides to go naughty, Tatianna could be their muse. She's a couple of dozen relatives away from the throne but her blood is as blue as it gets. And if there's one thing royals know how to do, it's party.

"We got together, yes."

"And how did that go?"

I stretch my arms over my head, cracking my neck. "She came. She left."

We both came actually. In the bed, the kitchen, the hot tub in the backyard. It was a nice visit.

Waldo nods. "You said Tatianna is engaged now?"

"That's right. The next time she comes to the States she'll have *Duchess* in front of her name."

The last real duty of today's nobility is to make sure the fortune stays in the family—by producing little heirs and heiresses who can inherit it. Which, sadly, means no more fun times for me and Tatianna.

"Your business partner, Mr. Becker, he's engaged also?"

"Yep, three months out and counting. He hasn't officially lost his mind, but he's damn close."

Few things in this world are funnier than watching Jake Becker—a big mountain of a guy—being forced to contemplate flower arrangements for the table centerpieces in his upcoming nuptials.

"And your other partners, Mr. Shaw and Ms. Santos, they're expecting their first child soon?"

I nod again. "Yes, a boy. Little Becker Mason Santos Shaw."

That's the name of our law firm—where we're all partners, criminal defense attorneys. I think it's only fitting the first child born to our firm be named after it. Haven't convinced Stanton and Sofia yet, but I'm working on it.

Though now that I think about it—I wonder if they'd be more open to Waldo?

"How do you feel about that, Brent? That so many in your inner circle are getting married, having children, moving forward in their lives."

"I think it's great. I'm thrilled for them. I mean, up until last year, Jake was a hard-core bachelor—a Dark Knight in a lonely Batcave without a Vicki Vale. But now he's got a gorgeous woman and a house full of kids. He's happier than I've ever seen him."

Waldo scribbles on his notepad. "And is that something you want in your life? Marriage, children?"

I narrow my eyes. "Has my mother been calling you again?"

"Every month." Waldo sighs, rubbing his forehead. "But you know I don't discuss our sessions with her."

My dear mother should probably schedule some sessions of her own—considering last month she asked their butler, Henderson, to make inquiries into her adopting a grandchild. Since I—her only son—have been so very derelict in my duty to give her one. Cue the guilt trip.

I lean forward, bracing my elbows on my knees. "All right, here's the thing—I'm happy for them, of course. But there's a part of me that thinks now they're trapped. Tied down with all that responsibility. I, on the other hand, have my work to keep me busy—but I can still jet off to Switzerland to go bungee jumping, or fly-fishing in New Zealand. With one phone call I can fuck two hotel heiresses six ways to Sunday, then watch them go to town on each other while I recoup for round two."

FYI: there is no TMI in a therapist's office.

"If I'm jonesing for a family fix, I can swing by my friends' houses for dinner and be the favorite uncle to their kids." I open my arms to emphasize the brilliance of my theory. "All the perks, none of the obligation. Life is short—I want to live it. And I really like living it free."

He regards me for a moment and says, "Mmmm."

Then—nothing.

"*Mmmm*, what?" I ask. "I think we're past '*mmmm*,' don't you, Waldo?"

He taps his lips with the end of his pen. "Well, it's apparent that you believe what you say. That you *think* you want this self-focused, low-responsibility lifestyle. The way Pinocchio wanted to cut his strings so he could be a real boy."

"But?"

There's always a but.

"But I wonder, deep down, if you've outgrown that philosophy. If you actually crave something more profound in your life. Commitment isn't always a burden, Brent. It can also be the source of unimaginable joy and satisfaction."

I clear my thoughts and search my mind—the way Luke Skywalker did when Obi-Wan was teaching him the ways of the Force.

Nope—I got nothing.

"You're barking up the wrong tree on this one."

He shrugs. "Then ask yourself this: As "tied down" as your friends may be, do you think any of *them* are dreaming of rubies in the sand?"

Have I mentioned that Waldo can also be one shrewd son of a bitch?

2

I've seen my last name inscribed on libraries, hospital wings, and the like, but there's an extra thrill seeing it on the Law Offices of Becker, Mason, Santos & Shaw. Because it's mine, not my family's, something *I* did on my own. When you grow up in the shadow of all the accomplishments of those who came before you, that's a big deal.

Jessica, our summer minion—also known as an intern—welcomes me with starry eyes and a stack of messages. "Good afternoon, Mr. Mason."

I take the messages and avoid eye contact, keeping my face neutral. It's a well-practiced move. Because interns are hungry, enthusiastic, willing to bend over backward.

And that's particularly true of Jessica.

The way she stares, the way she accidentally brushes her tits against my arm, the way she walks by my office when I'm working late, says she's willing to let me bend her any which way I want. And Jessica's not your average-looking minion—

tall, redheaded, with hips every man would imagine holding onto doggie style. She's hot.

She's also twenty-four.

I don't know when twenty-four became too young—I just know it is.

"Thank you, Jessica."

I walk up the stairs to the top floor. Dark-wood floors, original crown moldings, and bold-toned window dressings give the area a professional, historical elegance. Two desks— one occupied by our secretary, Mrs. Higgens, and one for our paralegal—are stationed along opposite walls, with two long, brown leather sofas facing each other on the remaining ones.

I nod to Mrs. Higgens and head into my office to work the rest of the afternoon.

• • •

At four o'clock I stick my head outside my office door to collect my client, Justin Longhorn. He's a typical millennial slacker—brown messy hair, beat-up skinny jeans, a retro Nirvana T-shirt over a lanky form, his thumb busily sliding over the latest iPhone.

Before I can greet him, sixteen-year-old Riley McQuaid walks down the hallway. She's been working here a couple of hours a week this summer. Riley is the oldest of the six McQuaid kids.

Jake's McQuaid kids.

If you don't understand the significance of that, you will in a second. Because what happens next feels just like watching a car crash in slow motion.

Or the mating dance of pubescent ostriches. There's some really weird stuff on YouTube.

Their eyes drag over each other, head to matching-Converse-sneaker-covered toes.

Justin lifts his chin. "Hey."

Riley pushes her curly brown hair behind her ear. "Hey."

No good can come of this. And I'm not the only one who thinks so.

"Heeey," Jake says—in a low growl from his office doorway—where he looms large with crossed arms and quicksilver gray eyes.

Jake Becker is a hell of a guy, one of my closest friends. He can also be a scary overprotective motherfucker when he wants to be. The scowl he's sending my client's way has reduced older, larger men to tears.

But Justin doesn't see it—because he's too busy checking Riley out.

"I have some filing for you to do, Riley." Jake jerks his thumb over his shoulder. "In my office."

"Okay. Coming." But she doesn't—at least not right away. Not until after she bites her lip Justin's way and utters the classic, "Later."

Justin nods. "Definitely."

Huh. Never would've pegged Justin as the suicidal type. But I guess you just never know.

After Riley slips past Jake into his office, he continues to hold Justin in the grip of his icy glare. And the kid has shit self-preservation instinct, because he nods his chin with a clueless, "S'up man."

Jake's face is as friendly as a rock.

I feel some responsibility for Justin. He's my client; it's my job to keep him out of jail and—you know—*alive*.

"Jake, I got this. I'll . . . explain things."

"I'd appreciate that," he tells me darkly. Then, without another glance at Justin he disappears into his office.

I usher the teenager through my door and shut it behind him.

"Who was—" he starts to ask.

"Don't," I warn. Then I point to the chair. "Sit."

"But—"

"Stop." My voice rumbles—grabbing his attention. Because I'm a happy guy. Carefree. Easygoing. Until I'm not. When those moments come, it gets a reaction. Justin sits.

I face him from across my desk. "Do you watch *Game of Thrones*, Justin?"

"Yeah, sure." He answers, brows drawing together.

"Do you remember the episode where the one guy crushed the other guy's head with his bare hands?"

"Yeah . . . ?"

I point toward the door. "You keep thinking about *that* girl the way you were thinking of her a minute ago—that's what's in your future."

He sits back, considering my words—and probably imagining the terrifically brutal scene that can never be unseen by viewers all over the world.

But the boy's persistent—gotta give him that. 'Cause he still tries, "But I—"

"*You're* a seventeen-year-old hacker who's being prosecuted for theft, wire fraud, and a host of other federal charges. And let's be honest, Justin—you're fucking guilty." I point to the door again. "That girl is the daughter of my partner. His old-est daughter. You get me?" I hold my hands out over my desk, then slowly clench my fists. "Squish—just like a grape."

Justin's not a bad kid. He's smart, funny. He reminds me of Matthew Broderick in *WarGames*—didn't realize he was in deep shit until he was already at DEFCON 1. But Riley's like a niece to me, so any kid who's been "charged as an adult" at any point in his life just isn't gonna make the cut.

I drive the point home with a final warning. "And before you get any ideas about The Fault in Our Star-Crossed Lov-ers, remember, *Romeo and Juliet* isn't a romance. It's a tragedy. They die."

He glances at the door one more time, then gives me a solid nod. "Gotcha, boss."

"Good." I pull up my chair. "Now, let's talk about your case. Where's your mother?"

Justin raises one slouchy shoulder. "She got a call from her lawyer and had to take off. I'll catch the bus home."

Justin's parents are getting divorced. Like, *really* divorced. Forget being in the same room—they can't even be on the same conference call. His mother's bitter and his father's a dick. They're both totally self-absorbed and astoundingly uninter-ested in anything that has to do with their son.

Which is likely how he ended up hacking into an inter-national banking computer system in the first place, because Smart Kid + Shitty Parents = Trouble.

And even with his trial coming up in just a few days, their heads are still completely up their own asses. It's sad.

"Your case has been assigned a new prosecutor." I look at the file on my desk. "K. S. Randolph. I've never heard of the guy, but I'll be scheduling a meeting with him to discuss a plea deal."

Justin nods, hands folded across his waist. "Probation, right? Because this is my first offense?"

"That's right. And because you didn't spend any of the money you took. I don't want you to worry, Justin. You won't even see the inside of a courtroom, okay?"

"Thanks, Brent." He lets out a breath and leans forward. "Really. If I haven't mentioned it before, you're like . . . a superhero to me. Thank you."

My father was the one who bought me my very first comic book. He gave it to me in the hospital—after the accident that took the lower half of my left leg. It was a Superman no. 1— worth almost a cool million at the time. He showed it to me, ripped off the plastic covering that ensured its value and we read it together.

Because, he said, being able to read it with me was worth so much more to him than a million.

I became an avid reader after that—and a collector. In those early months, comics made the time go faster, gave me something to focus on besides the pain and all I'd lost. And— between you and me—the heroes in the comics spoke to me. I got where they were coming from. Because every one of them had had something terrible—awful—happen to them. And they came out the other side, not just okay, but better because of it.

And that's how I wanted to be too. How I decided to look at the loss of my limb. It'd be the thing that would make me better—more—than I ever would've been if it'd never happened.

So, though Justin has no idea how much those particular words mean to me, they mean a hell of a lot.

"It's what I'm here for, buddy."

• • •

Even when I was a kid—even after the accident—I had an overabundance of energy. Growing up, the worst punishment my nanny could inflict was making me sit still in the corner. With nothing to look at. Nothing to *do*. Used to make me feel like a lab monkey in a cage—batshit crazy.

That trait followed me into adulthood. It's why I run ten miles a day, why the first thing I do every morning is a long set of push-ups and sit-ups. It's why I have a set of hand grips in my office drawer that I squeeze while I dictate a motion or take a call. It's left me with a strong, rock-hard body and stamina to spare.

Women really enjoy both, and boy, are they appreciative.

It's also why, although I have a butler at home who doubles as my driver, I walk to my office every day.

It's dark by the time I stroll through the door of my townhouse. The house itself is professionally decorated, and though dimension-wise it's a fraction of just one floor of the beast I grew up in—on a high-end street, filled with young professionals who drive BMWs and hybrid Lexuses—it's the perfect size for a bachelor.

Well . . . a bachelor and his trusty sidekick.

I'm secure enough in my manhood to call, "Honey, I'm home."

Just to mess with him.

Because, British or not, Harrison is more serious than any twenty-two-year-old should ever be. He's the son of my parents' beloved butler, Henderson. When he decided to go into the family business—and because my mother still breaks out in hives at the thought of my living alone—I was more than happy to take the kid under my wing. And now that I've got him, I hope to corrupt the hell out of him.

Harrison takes my briefcase. "Welcome home, sir."

I raise an eyebrow—feeling like a parent who's had the exact same conversation with his teenager a hundred times. Because the day I become a "sir," just fucking shoot me.

His brown eyes pinch closed, then he forces out, "Brent. I meant, welcome home, Brent."

With fair skin and a hearty dose of freckles, Harrison looks younger than his age—something we have in common. It's why I decided to grow my beard, a full jaw of neatly groomed dark hair.

Women appreciate that too—these bristles have all kinds of creative uses.

"How was your day?"

I smack him on the back. "It was great. I'm starved—what's for dinner?"

"Chicken cordon bleu. I've set the table up on the back patio—it seemed like a lovely night to dine outside."

Harrison's chicken cordon bleu rocks.

My small backyard is professionally landscaped. A white privacy fence frames the property, which is only considerate because it's rude to force your neighbors to watch you screw. And the screwing happens a lot back here due to the large, fantastic hot tub that holds a place of honor on a raised, lighted platform in the center. A small patch of grass, a scattering of evergreen bushes, a few Japanese maples, and a fragrant lemon tree complete the setting.

I sit down at the round, cloth-covered table and Harrison removes the silver lid from my warm plate.

"Your mother phoned today," he mentions, moving to stand just behind me. "Your cousin Mildred is hosting her daughter's first birthday celebration this Saturday, at the Potomac estate. Mrs. Mason's exact words were: 'I insist he attend, and I will personally come to retrieve him if he does not.'"

That's my mother for you—Jacqueline Bouvier Kennedy on the outside, Dirty Harry on the inside. When a direct order comes down, you really don't want to disobey—unless you're feeling lucky, punk. And punks are never lucky.

Before I dig in, I look over my shoulder, "Would you like to join me, Harrison?"

It's not the first time I've asked recently, but his answer is always the same.

"The invitation is greatly appreciated, but if I accept, my father may disown me. And I'm rather fond of my father."

I nod. "Go enjoy your own dinner, then. I won't be needing anything further."

With the slightest bow, he goes inside.

After a few minutes and a few bites, the quiet settles in—not even the crickets are out tonight. I don't like silence any more than I like sitting still.

The four of us used to go out a lot after work. Dinner, drinks, sometimes dancing. But these days there are cribs to put together, kids to drive around, and wedding plans to make. There are other people I could hang out with—acquaintances, old school buddies, women who'd be thrilled to get my call. But those options just don't seem worth the effort.

The silence feels stifling—itchy—like a heavy wool blanket.

So I stand up, grab my plate, and head inside. Because as awesome as my backyard is—dinner in front of the TV seems even better.

3

On Saturday, I have Harrison drop me at my parents' estate about an hour after the party starts. He has some errands to run, so I tell him to go—with strict instructions to pick me up in exactly three hours.

It's not that I don't like my family, they're great. But only in small doses. If I spend too much time with them . . . well, you'll see.

My steps echo through the immense marble foyer. I pass the music room, the front parlor, the conservatory, the library where a portrait hangs of me at five years old, dressed in blue overalls and a cap—looking like the pansy-ass kid in the Dutch Boy paint advertisements but with dark hair. I've offered my mother the firstborn child I'll probably never have to take it down—but she won't budge. If Stanton, Jake, or Sofia ever lay eyes on it, I'm screwed.

At the back of the house there's a bustling energy coming from the kitchen that you can feel more than hear—servants shuffling, refilling trays of champagne and caviar and carrying buckets of ice to keep the lobster and oyster table fresh.

Outside, there are tents and tables, a band, and a fully stocked bar with two bartenders. What there isn't are streamers or shiny balloons, no clowns or magicians—even though this is supposed to be a kids' party. Because in reality, this kind of party is for the two hundred adults milling about, chatting, shaking hands, kissing cheeks, and stabbing backs.

Yes, I said two hundred—just friends and family.

See, my father is the youngest of eight. My mother, the youngest of twelve. And both sides are in excellent health— they all live for fucking ever. Which means there's nieces and nephews, aunts and uncles, great nieces and nephews, and cousins galore—and the gang's all here.

Besides good health, there's another trait that's strong in my family. One might say they're . . . eccentric. Crazier than shit-house rats works too.

Let's take my Aunt Bette, for example. She's the woman in the tan dress, looking up into the branches of that maple tree—talking to the birds like a homeless woman in a park. She has four kids and she doesn't speak to any of them—not for years. She prefers the company of her racing pigeons. I think she's won awards.

It's important to have a purpose in life. Boredom has killed more in my social class than cancer and heart disease combined. Because most people work for things like food, a house, and clothes, and working for those necessities instills drive and ambition. It gives you a reason to drag yourself out of bed in the morning.

But when your necessities are covered—when you literally don't have to wipe your own ass if you don't want to—what the hell do you do with yourself?

If you're stupid, you do drugs, drink, or gamble to occupy your time. Boredom is a disease. Either you cure it doing something you love—or you die trying.

"Hey, cuz."

Then there's my cousin Louis, a smarmy, short guy with a bad comb-over. Wealth turns some men into assholes, but even if he didn't have two pennies to rub together, he'd still be an asshole. He was just born that way.

"Louis." I shake his hand.

Notice, I don't ask him how he's doing—'cause he's gonna tell me anyway.

"I'm doing great, man. I just closed this sweet real-estate deal. Prime location. I'm gonna tear the building down and turn it into a parking lot. My guy is serving an eviction notice to the old tenants—nuns and orphans or something." He guffaws like an evil villain. "But that's business, amiright?"

"Not really."

He doesn't hear me—the roar of his narcissism drowns out everything but the sound of his own voice.

I notice his gaze settle on the ass of a brunette to my right. "Wow, Cynthia Beardsley grew up nice." Then he glances at me. "Aunt Kitty get you married, yet?"

"Nope."

He chortles again. "We all have to walk the plank someday. I'll bet you a bottle of Royal Salute 50 she has you engaged by the end of the year."

"You're on." I hold out my hand again and we shake on it. Louis may be a twat, but I'm not above taking a ten-thousand-dollar bottle of scotch off his hands.

I spot my father a few yards across the lawn and head in his direction. Looks-wise I take after him—tall, thick dark hair, blue eyes, and a face that appears fifteen years younger than his actual sixty-five.

We shake hands and he pats my shoulder affectionately. "Son."

"Hey, Dad."

He sips his brandy. "How are the criminals these days?"

And here we go.

My father was never a fan of coasting by on the clout of one's last name. During my teen years, family dinners were like the Spanish Inquisition: *What have you contributed today? How have you distinguished yourself? What will you be remembered for?* When I started law school, he got it in his head that I should go into politics—become Prosecutor Brent Mason, then Attorney General Brent Mason, eventually Senator Brent Mason—after that it'd be to infinity and beyond.

Instead, I became a criminal defense attorney. And I don't think the old man's ever gotten over it.

"They're defendants, Dad. Not criminals."

"Is there a difference?"

"I'm sure it makes a difference to the innocent ones."

Okay, almost none of them are innocent. But people rarely do illegal things just for the sake of doing them—there's always extenuating circumstances. Evening out the playing field for those who weren't born with a silver spoon up their ass is what gets me out of bed in the morning.

"I play racquetball with a higher-up in the DOJ," he says.

My father plays racquetball with everybody. But he's not a name dropper. Because to him, money and connections are like *Fight Club*—the first rule of having them is you don't talk about them.

"They're always looking for good men—keep it in mind, Brent."

I tap my temple. "It's in the filing cabinet."

"Brent, sweetie, you're here," my mother says in that soft, breathy voice as she walks up beside me.

Everything about my mother is hushed, gentle, delicate. Like a rose whose petals will fall off if you blow on it. She's never cursed, doesn't raise her voice—not even when I was seven and they had to take me to the emergency room because I jammed popcorn kernels up my nose just to see how many would fit. (Twenty-three, in case you were curious.)

"Hi, Mom." I lean down and kiss her cheek.

She runs her hand over the fabric of my light blue polo shirt. "This is a very nice color on you, dear."

"Thanks."

Her gaze drifts over me adoringly. "Walk with me, Brent."
Oh shit.

My mother saying *walk with me* is akin to a woman you're dating saying, "we need to talk"—it never ends well.

She loops her arm through mine and we stroll across the grass, away from the crowd.

"I've been reading a lot recently," she begins. "And thinking. You're thirty-two years old, darling—you're handsome, you're a fine dresser, you dance well—you've always been very clean."

The last comment has me looking at her funny, but I let her go on.

"Talula Fitzgibbons's son is about your age, and he recently told her that he's become a homosexual."

Oh boy.

"Not only that, he's also hired a lovely surrogate and she's expecting triplets. Isn't that amazing, Brent? Triplets!"

"Mom—"

But that train has left the station.

"So I wanted you to know, if you are a homosexual, your father and I will love you every bit as much as we do right now." She pats my arm and amends, "As long as you have children."

"I'm not gay, Mom."

She looks disappointed. "Are you sure?"

"Mom, I'm as not gay as a man can possibly be."

Her dainty finger taps her lips as she thinks it over. "Well, all right. Then I'd like you to chat with Celia Hampshire's granddaughter. She's here and she's a lovely young lady."

"Celia Hampshire's granddaughter is in high school."

"No—she graduated last month."

I pinch the bridge of my nose. "Okay . . . I'm gonna go to the bar. Now. Can we talk about this later?"

"Of course, sweetie. I'm so happy you're here."

And because I love her and I'm a good son, I lie, "Me too."

My mother glides back toward my father and I head to the bar. It really should've been my first stop.

I make it three steps and then an arm coils around mine and my hip gets bumped hard. "But are you *sure* you're not a homosexual? You realize you're keeping Aunt Kit out of the in-crowd?"

I pull my cousin Katherine into a tight hug. "Thank Christ you're here."

Her dark eyes sparkle as she laughs. "Why, because I'm your only normal relative?"

"Yes, that's exactly why."

Katherine's also my favorite cousin. Boisterous and loud— with the kind of smile you can't help but return. When we were young and my other cousins said I was too little—too annoying—to play some stupid game, Katherine made sure I was included. When I turned twenty-one, she showed up at my college and took me out for my very first legal beer. You don't get to choose family, but if you did—Katherine would be my first round draft pick.

Her four-year-old son collides with my leg, followed quickly by his two-year-old sister.

"Uncle Brent!" she squeals.

I scoop her up. "Annie, baby."

I look down at Jonathon. "What's up, dude?"

He tilts his head back, still gripping my leg. "I go poops on the potty now."

"Welcome to manhood." I give him a high five, which he jumps to return.

Annie squirms in my arms, so I set her down and they run in circles around us. I glance behind Katherine. "Where's Patrick?"

She shrugs, and the sparkle in her eyes dims. "He's in Portugal, on 'business' with his secretary."

Patrick is Katherine's husband, whose ass I'm going to kick hard the next time I see him.

"Come on, don't get angry," she soothes. "It is what it is."

"What it is, is fucked up. Why do you put up with that?"

She shrugs. "Because when he's around, he's actually a good husband and father. Because the kids love him—and so do I."

"You deserve better, Kat. A lot better."

"He's what I want."

I shake my head as Annie pulls on the leg of my jeans and points toward some bushes. "Uncle Brent, I wants da butterfly, but it won't come."

"Okay, let's you and me and Jonathon go get us a butterfly."

I get a grateful smile from Katherine, then I hoist the boy over my shoulders and the three of us go hunting.

• • •

Two hours later, I look across the yard at the crowd of chattering, monochromatic people. All of them so eager to clone each other, to not be labeled as too flashy or ostentatious. It's a sea of beige—tan slacks, taupe summer dresses, and one pair of light brown Ray-Ban sunglasses after another.

Until a burst of red steps out from under the white party tent.

Maybe this afternoon won't be a total loss, after all.

The dress is tastefully alluring—knee-length, sleeveless, a corded neckline that loops around the collarbone and ties in the back. But the body within it is the real highlight. She's tiny but unmistakably womanly—warm peach-hued skin, an elegant neck, delicate arms, a slight swell of cleavage, a tight waist, and toned legs with the sweetest hint of muscle. Her hair is thick, a multifaceted blond—pale, almost white strands grace her dainty jaw—but there's shades of honey-gold and caramel leading back to a low bun.

She's fucking stunning. I have no idea who she is—but finding out just became my number-one priority.

She spots me as I approach. Bright turquoise eyes, sharp and appraising, rake me over from head to toe. *Enjoy the view, baby.* I'll be happy to give her the extended tour later on.

"Hi," I say, smiling when I reach her.

She raises her chin, straightening her shoulders. "Hello."

There's something familiar about her. It tickles the back of my brain and stirs my cock. I wonder if she's a friend of my cousins'—possibly a bridesmaid I hooked up with at one of their weddings?

"Enjoying the party?"

Her gaze turns toward the crowd as she sips from the crystal flute in her hand. "Yes. I'm sure the birthday girl is ecstatic. Caviar and champagne—what every one-year-old wants."

Sarcasm. I like sarcasm. It suggests intelligence. Confidence. I like her ass even more—which I've discreetly checked out.

"Word around the country club is you've gone into business on your own," she comments casually. "Got yourself a law firm with your name on it."

Her tits are pretty phenomenal too. A little on the small side, no more than a B cup—but I just bet they're firm and perky and magically delicious. The kind that can forego a bra, so her nipples poke against her shirt when she's turned on. I love that look on a woman.

"Yes, almost two years now. We've built quite a name for ourselves."

"You must be so proud."

"I am."

She lifts one shoulder. "I think it's pretentious as hell."

My eyes snap to her face. "I beg your pardon?"

"It's a farce. The brave young defense attorney, giving up the big-paycheck firm to serve the little people." Her voice turns derisive. "It's easy to be brave when you have Great-Grandpa's money behind you."

My brow furrows. "That's pretty presumptuous of you."

"No, what's presumptuous is thinking you can walk over here, ogle my tits and ass, and assume I won't call you on it."

Guess I wasn't as discreet as I thought.

"Is ogleable a word? Cause if it is—you're it. A lot of women would take it as a compliment."

She faces me head-on. "A lot of women are idiots. And not as knowledgeable as I am about what a selfish, immature little prick you can be."

Little? I resent that—particularly in such close proximity to the word *prick*.

"Who the hell *are* you?"

She stares at me for two beats. Then she throws her head back and laughs.

"My God. Of all the ways I pictured this going, I never considered you'd totally forget me. But I guess I shouldn't be surprised—I was pretty forgettable back in the day."

"What does that even—"

A woman's voice calls "Kennedy!" cutting me off—and knocking me on my proverbial ass.

Mitzy Randolph, one of my mother's oldest friends and our next-door neighbor, walks up and plants two air kisses on the blond beauty at my side.

"I've been waiting for you to arrive," she tells her.

"I've been here for twenty minutes, Mother."

Holy fuck.

Mrs. Randolph turns to me, her arm around her daughter's back. "Isn't it wonderful that our Kennedy has come home, Brent?"

And all I can do is parrot like an idiot. "Yeah . . . wonderful."

Mitzy steps back, takes her daughter's hands, and holds them up at her sides—looking her over, judging and evaluating—just like the good old days. "I'm so happy to have you out of Nevada. All those nasty casinos and dust and desert." She caresses her cheek. "That dry air has wreaked havoc on your skin. I'll make you an appointment with my esthetician this week—she's a miracle worker."

Kennedy gives a resigned sigh. "Thank you, Mother."

"Now I'll let you two get reacquainted. I see the Vander-blasts are here and if I don't spend at least ten minutes with Ellora she'll work herself into a snit."

When we're alone again, I can't stop staring. Once upon a time she was my best friend. For a hot minute she was more. After that, she hated me. And then she was just . . . gone.

I haven't seen her for fourteen years, and the last time I did, she sure as shit didn't look like this.

"Kennedy . . . ?" I whisper, still not entirely convinced it's her.

She regards me with a tilted head, a cocked hip, and a disdainful smile. "Hello, Dickhead."

Okay. Now I'm convinced.

4

It takes a few seconds to recover from the shock, but when I do, I hit the ground smirking. Because if there's one thing I know how to do, it's give as good as I get.

"Kennedy Randy Randolph."

Her smile drops like a barrel over Niagara Falls.

"My middle name is Suzanne."

"I know, but I never did come up with a nickname for you. Though we already considered Randy, didn't we? It wasn't a good fit—I'll keep working on it."

I shake my head, checking her out all over again. Because now that I know who she is, we're talking a whole other level of depraved interest.

"God*damn*. You look—"

"Yes, I know." She sighs, then gazes at her manicure in that bitchy way women do. "Thank you." There's not a shred of sincerity in her tone—like she's heard a million compliments before. Which, with her level of hotness, is possible. Except for one thing.

"What'd you do to your eyes?" I lean in, frowning.

"They're called contact lenses."

"Well, take them out. I don't like them. Your real eyes are incredible."

Breathtaking, actually—deep, warm brown with flecks of gold. I'd know Kennedy's eyes anywhere.

"What'd you do to your face?" she asks, folding her arms.

I touch my chin. "I grew a beard."

"Well ungrow it. It looks like a vagina from a 1970s porn film."

My lips twitch—because, *fuck*, the things that come out of her mouth.

That always did.

"I'm starting to get the impression you don't like me anymore, sweetness."

Challenge rises in her eyes. "You're assuming I actually liked you to begin with. You know what they say about people who assume, ass."

I square off against Kennedy. *Game on.*

"You definitely liked me. Remember that summer you flashed me your boobs? That has to count for something."

"I did not flash you my boobs." She scowls.

"You totally did. They were the first I'd ever seen—made an indelible impression."

She grinds her teeth. "I jumped in the pool and my bathing suit rode up."

"I think it was a Freudian Nip Slip. Subconsciously, you meant to do it, because you liked me."

"I think you're a pompous bastard. Possibly a sociopath."

I grin. "Doesn't mean you didn't like me."

Over Kennedy's shoulder, I catch my mother's eager gaze on us. She'd be less obvious if she had a spotlight and binoculars aimed our way.

"My mother's watching us."

Kennedy places her empty glass on the tray of a passing waiter and picks up a full one. "Of course she's watching us. For years, her greatest wish was that I'd grow up to bear your spawn."

I snort. "That's ridiculous." Then I glance sideways at Kennedy, gauging her reaction. "Isn't it?"

"Completely." She looks me straight in the face. "I could never be with someone like you—you have the maturity of a twelve-year-old boy."

I raise my glass. "And you have the chest of one."

I expect her to come back with a clever, biting retort, but she just gestures to me with an open palm. "I rest my case."

Ironically, my first instinct is to stick my tongue out at her. But I won't give her the satisfaction.

"Besides," she adds with a haughty smile. "I'm seeing someone. Maybe you've heard of him? David Prince."

David Prince is a junior senator from Illinois with his eye on the White House. He's a rock star, the second coming of John F. Kennedy. I bet the entire Democratic Party and a good percentage of Republicans have his picture hanging on their office wall—the same way that poster of a feather-haired Jon Bon Jovi hung on the bedroom walls of all sixteen of my girl cousins'. And two of the boys.

"You're dating a *politician*?" I say it like it's a dirty word, because in my experience politicians are rarely clean.

She raises a perfectly manicured eyebrow. "*You* were almost a politician."

"Only in my father's wet dreams," I volley back. "Although, you always said you were going to marry a prince. Sounds like you're on your way."

"My mother said that—not me."

I smirk. "Then she must be ecstatic. You're finally everything she always wanted you to be."

Game. Set. Match.

Something shifts in Kennedy's eyes, and I suddenly get the feeling we're not playing anymore. "Not everything. Mother wanted me to be a ballerina."

Years ago, I'd heard she was doing undergrad at Brown University. But other than that tiny detail there's been nothing. Her father is a talker, her mother a bragger, but when Kennedy dropped off the grid after boarding school, information on her locked up like Fort Knox.

"Is that what you were doing in Las Vegas—dancing? Kind of short for a showgirl, aren't you?"

Though I'd be sitting front and center for *that* show if I could.

She nods slowly, smiling way too smugly.

"Yes, too short for a showgirl . . . but just the right height for a federal prosecutor."

That stops me cold. And I suddenly feel a strong kinship to Ned Stark's bastard son because: *You know nothing, Jon Snow!*

And apparently neither do I.

"You're a . . . ?"

"The Moriotti case, the mafia capo? That was me. I transferred to the DC office last week—and I can't wait to start playing on your home field."

Over the last fourteen years I've thought a lot about what

it'd be like to see Kennedy Randolph again—but I never thought it'd be on the opposite side of a courtroom.

"You realize this makes us mortal enemies? You're now the Lex Luthor to my Superman, the Magneto to my Professor Xavier."

"With your comic book obsession obviously still in full effect, I'd say I'm more the Wendy to your Peter Pan complex."

I ignore the dig because I'm too busy connecting the dots. "Wait a second—your middle name is Suzanne."

"Thought we covered that, already."

"*You're* K. S. Randolph?"

Her smile goes wide—two rows of pearly white evil. "Yep. That's my professional moniker."

"*You're* the prosecutor on my Longhorn case?"

She golf claps. "Right again."

"I've been trying to get a meeting with your office—so we can talk."

Her features crumple with mock confusion. "What would I want to talk to you about?"

"Uh, pleading the charges down?"

Ninety-seven percent of federal criminal cases end in plea bargains. If you want a real feel for jurisprudence today, forget *Judge Judy*—watch *Let's Make a Deal* instead.

She chuckles in a distinctly not-nice way. "Brent, Brent, Brent—I don't make plea deals. Ever. It's kind of what I'm known for. Oh, and I've never lost a case. I'm known for that too."

I was wrong—this match isn't anywhere near over. It's just getting started.

"Justin Longhorn is seventeen years old," I argue.

"Exactly," she practically spits. "More than old enough to have known better."

"It's his first offense."

"And he made a hell of a debut. I'm going for the maximum. Your boy is looking at twenty years."

When we were young, Kennedy was intelligent, funny as hell, socially oblivious—but she was never spiteful. But looking at her now, there's a ferociousness about her that's new. Like a sharp-toothed Chihuahua that's been stepped on one too many times.

Part of me finds this scorchingly hot. She's not a girl anymore—she's a fierce, strong, fully self-possessed woman. The kind whose hair I'd love to fist tight and pull while she's deep-throating my cock. The kind who would moan for more while I pounded into her rough and hard against a wall.

But another part of me mourns that sweetness. The brave, innocent, beautifully wild creature who sat on a bike's handlebars and trusted me to keep her safe while I was at the pedals. The one who took my hand and told me to dance with her wearing my unpracticed fake leg, because she thought she was strong enough to catch me if I stumbled.

Then there's the professional in me who's just straight-up pissed off—because she's gonna be a pain in the ass about a case that should be an easy close.

I step in closer. "What the hell, Kennedy? The money's been returned. It was a mistake. He's a child."

She raises her chin and looks at me, all fire and fight. "He's a criminal. And a bully. He screwed with the life savings of a dozen innocent people. He messed with their heads and sense of security, just because he could. He willfully and knowingly stole thousands of dollars—returned or not—and I'm going to make sure he pays for it."

"Wow. Hello, Inspector Javert."

Kennedy shakes her head and chuckles. "You were always clever, Brent. So adorable. I hope for your client's sake you're packing more than cuteness these days."

I bend my head, leaning down, just inches away from her shiny lips. "I haven't had any complaints about what I'm packing so far."

She stares at my mouth for one beat too long.

Then she blinks, shaking off her stare. "Good. Then I'll see you in court, Counselor."

"Bet your sweet ass you will."

Kennedy brushes past me and struts away—leaving me no choice but to watch her go.

• • •

We don't talk again after that. But I discreetly keep tabs on Kennedy the rest of the afternoon—where she's standing, who she chats with. Tension prickles my skin if she's out of my field of vision for too long, but when I find her again, relief detonates in my chest. For a long time—years—I wondered what she was doing, where she was, wanted so fucking badly to see her—the way an alcoholic craves just one more taste.

It wasn't easy, but eventually I went cold turkey, gave up on her completely—because wondering and wanting are lost causes. So, as good as it is to be able to watch her now, I'm not thrilled to fall off the wagon just yet.

"I don't want to go, Mommy!" Jonathon cries, yanking at his mother's hand, trying to dig his heels into the grass.

Because Katherine just told her kids it's getting late—time to head home.

Annie adds her own plaintive wail. "I wants da fireworks."

I step up beside my cousin as her children join forces against her.

"We're gonna miss the fireworks, Mommy!" Jonathon yells.

"Settle down, little man." I tell him. "There aren't any fireworks tonight. We only have them on New Year's Eve."

Every year, my parents go all out throwing a huge, formal New Year's Eve party—they have since before I was born. There's tuxedos and gowns, dancing, fountains of champagne . . . and fireworks at midnight that light up the sky and bathe the Potomac River in bright, sparkling color. Young kids in the family, like Jonathon and Annie, aren't allowed to stay at the party all night. They're sent to bed in one of the dozens of upstairs rooms before midnight. But Jonathon and Annie obviously know about the fireworks. They probably slip out of bed and watch the show through the window. That's what I did every year, when I was their age.

Only—I didn't watch from the window. And I didn't watch alone.

"I'll go first," I tell Kennedy at the base of the ladder. "So I can open the hatch."

Even though we're both nine, she's a lot smaller than I am. This is the first time we've gone up to the roof—and I'm the boy, so I should definitely go first. There could be rabid birds up there, or bats.

We're in the big attic, where trunks, old books, paintings, and

plastic-wrapped dresses get stored. It's dark and dusty, with shad-
owed corners that look like they're moving if you stare too long.
Kennedy loves it up here.

"Come on, it's going to start soon," I tell her. "We'll come back
here tomorrow."

Her eyes are still wide behind her thick-lensed, yellow-framed
glasses as she gazes around the room, but she nods. "All right."

I head up the ladder and push open the access door in the
ceiling. Then I climb through and reach down my hand. Kennedy
grabs it as she climbs through and then we're standing on the flat
peak of my house. Sometimes Kennedy calls it a castle—Mason
Castle—because of the ballroom. Her house is just as big. They
don't have a ballroom, but they have a home movie theater, which
is a thousand times cooler.

The icy wind cuts right through my robe—it's freezing this
year, cold enough to see every breath. The sky is a black blanket
above us, and the stars are so bright, it feels like I could reach up
and grab one—as easily as picking an apple off a tree. Kennedy
spins in quick circles, her long brown hair fanning out. "You were
right—this is the best!"

She's smiling, and the metal line of her retainer shines in the
moonlight.

I grin back—until she gets too close to the edge of the roof. I
grab her hand and pull her back. "Watch out!"

We sit down close to one of the five chimneys, to block the
wind. When Kennedy's teeth start to chatter, I put my arm around
her. She snuggles against me, warming us both up a little. We talk
while we wait for the show to start.

". . . So they let me quit fencing and start lacrosse instead," I
tell her. "It's awesome."

"You're so lucky!" Kennedy cries. "Mother said I couldn't stop ballet even if my leg was broken. She said I'm going to marry a prince, and no prince wants a princess who doesn't know how to dance."

Music floats up from the band downstairs. "I wonder if Claire is dancing with your cousin Louis," Kennedy tells me. "She said she's going to kiss him at midnight."

I feel my face scrunch. "Why?"

"She said that's what you do at midnight. Kiss the boy you like."

My face stays scrunched—because I can't imagine anyone liking Louis—let alone kissing him.

Then a chorus of voices surge from the veranda below. "10, 9, 8 . . ."

A few seconds later, the band begins "Old Lang Syne" and the sky explodes with color. Bursts of reds and blues, slashes of silvery purples and swaths of sparkling greens light up the night and reflect on the river's surface.

While I watch the fireworks, Kennedy turns under my arm. And then she kisses me on the cheek.

"Happy New Year, Brent," she whispers.

I look at her and smile.

"Happy New Year, Kennedy."

As I shake off the memory I scan the yard, searching for that red dress. But when I find her, it's not just relief I feel—it's something else. Something rougher, hotter, hungrier.

Because Kennedy is staring at me.

She doesn't notice that I've noticed. Her gaze is too busy trailing over my chest, my arms, my ass. Her eyes are eager and her cheeks are flushed pink—and I don't think it has anything to do with the afternoon sun. I turn her way, holding my arms out, so she can get the full viewing pleasure—and her eyes snap up to mine.

I smirk and lift an eyebrow.

Her lips part and her cheeks go from pink to red.

I lift my hand and wave.

She lifts her nose and turns away from me.

And you know something? I think this is going to be fun.

5

A week and a half later, I walk into court for the first day of the Longhorn trial, wearing my best navy suit and lucky silver cuff links. Ready to rumble.

Little Miss *I-don't-make-plea-deals-ever* made it pretty clear she's looking for a fight. And if that's how she wants it, that's how I'll give it to her. But when I fight in court, I fight to win. If she's not going to play nice—I'm down for playing dirty. That applies to outside the courtroom too.

I set my briefcase on the defense table. Justin is already here, looking very young and respectable in a gray jacket and burgundy tie. He was understandably freaked when I told him there'd been a change in plans—that he *was* going to be seeing the inside of a courtroom. His father's here today, sitting behind his son in the front row of the galley, staring at his phone, barely sparing his kid a glance. We've worked out an attendance plan for his parents with alternating days. I just hope they stick to it, because the last thing I need to worry about is the two of them keeping their shit together.

Kennedy strolls in, dressed to kill.

Literally—she looks like a smoking-hot, badass business-woman assassin straight out of one of my comic books. A black leather, knee-length pencil skirt, a shiny silk black blouse that clings to her torso in all the right ways, open at the neck, show-ing off an onyx necklace set in silver. Her hair is pulled back into a high bun and her makeup is subtle, accentuating the beauty of her features.

She takes her place at the prosecution table, turns delib-erately my way—and smiles. And my cock reacts like she's a snake charmer, stirring and thickening, rising in the presence of that breath-stealing smile.

It's the perfect combination of sweet and evil. Delicious but deadly. A smile that says *I'm going to destroy you—and you're going to love every fucking second of it.*

She's still wearing the turquoise contact lenses, and I'm kind of relieved. Because her natural eyes would do me in—and I'd be drooling.

She turns slightly to place some files on the table and my eyes drift down over her exquisite form. *Fuck me*, she's got that line up the back of her stockings—that sexy dark thread that glides over her calf, up the soft skin of her thighs, beneath her skirt to the promised land. I run my knuckle over my chin, just in case.

Nope, no drool. We're good.

The bailiff instructs us to rise and the Honorable Judge Phillips enters the courtroom, taking his place behind his bench. He checks to make sure all the primary parties are here and accounted for. I expect him to call the jury in next, so we can begin our opening statements—and I admit, I'm looking forward to seeing Kennedy in action.

But that's not what happens.

Because Kennedy stands up. "Your Honor, we'd like to submit a motion to disqualify the defense's forensic computer expert from testifying."

A forensic computer technician examines data left behind after cybercrimes. My expert is the best in the business and he's going to testify that the evidence of the bank hack and theft that the prosecution says traces back to Justin's computer is faulty. That, sure, Justin's computer *may* have been used in the crimes—but there's a slim chance it wasn't. And slim is all you need for reasonable doubt.

If this were chess, my computer expert would be my rook—not the most powerful part of my defense, but still an essential piece in the grand strategy.

I stand up. "On what grounds?"

Kennedy's eyes cut to me. "Because he's not permitted to testify or be currently employed. A hearing will bear that out."

The judge agrees to a hearing on the motion, and two hours later the judge disqualifies my witness. On a technicality. Because he's based out of London and didn't bother to update his work visa—which is now expired.

Looks like Kennedy came ready to rumble too. And she's damn good at it.

• • •

After the hearing, once our opening statements are given to the jury, Kennedy starts with a forensic computer expert of her own. Her questions are quick, to the point, and emit a heady scent of confidence. The tech's answers are detailed and boring, as most technical aspects tend to be—but he's polished. He breaks things down for the jury to a level they'll understand.

Which doesn't bode well for Justin.

In a short time, the judge calls me to pose my cross-examination questions. Which would be great except—Kennedy barely lets me ask one.

It goes something like this:

"Can you explain—"

"Objection!"

And this:

"How can you be sure—"

"Objection!"

And then:

"When you determined—"

"Objection!"

Most of her objections are overruled, but that's not the point. It's a strategy. She wants to break my rhythm, keep me from finding the zone where I can bait the witness into saying what I want him to, and then throw his answer back in his face.

She's trying to annoy the fuck out of me—and it's working. Did I actually say this was going to be fun? I was wrong. I start envisioning what my hands would look like wrapped around her pretty little neck—and not even in a hot way.

So when I ask, "What are the odds—"

And Kennedy pops to her feet with, "Objection!"

I shout back, "Objection!"

The judge peers down at me through his glasses. "You're objecting to your own question?"

"No . . . Judge." I stammer. "I'm objecting to her object-ing."

He raises an eyebrow. "That's new."

"Am I going to be allowed to question the witness? At this rate, my client will be collecting social security by the time this trial is concluded."

"If Mr. Mason framed his questions correctly, I wouldn't be forced to object, Your Honor," Kennedy says serenely.

"There's nothing wrong with how my questions are framed," I growl.

The judge chides us, "Let's keep the arguments directed my way. And Miss Randolph, let's refrain from any frivolous objections going forward."

"Certainly, sir."

"And on that note, let's call it a day. Court will reconvene tomorrow, 9 a.m. Adjourned."

After the judge exits, I reassure Justin with a back pat and a pep talk. Then I pack up my briefcase and turn to head out the door. And who should end up walking out at the exact same time, beside me, but the Hot Bitch herself.

"Certainly, sir," I mimic in a high-pitched voice. Then lower, "Kiss-ass."

"I'd rather be a kiss-ass than a dumbass. I didn't realize you got your law degree from a Cracker Jack box Daddy paid for."

"Hey." I swing around in front of her, pointing to my chest. "I buy my own Cracker Jacks."

She lifts one unimpressed shoulder. "If you say so."

I let her go ahead of me, because that's the gentlemanly thing to do—and so I can watch the sway of her tight ass as she walks. It makes me feel a little better.

Halfway down the hall, Tom Caldwell calls Kennedy's name and she stops to talk to him. Tom's a straight-laced prosecutor who has faced off against our firm before. He's not a bad guy, just irksomely upstanding—like overly sweet apple pie. I heard he got engaged recently, to a pretty schoolteacher named Sally.

Stealthily, I crouch down to tie my shoe a few feet away from them—listening. Don't judge me.

"A group of us are walking over to the Red Barron for happy hour," Caldwell tells her. "You should come."

"Sounds like fun! Thanks, Tom—I'm in." Her voice is cheerful, friendly. She hasn't spoken to me with that voice in years. Spiky jealousy claws at my gut like a horny porcupine. I watch them walk out together. *Fucking Caldwell.*

Then I take my cell phone out of my pocket. And call Stanton.

"Goose." I tell him when he answers. "Suit up—I need a wingman. You, me—happy hour. Like the old days . . . last year."

His voice is thick with sleep. "Sorry, man, I can't. We're nappin'."

"Napping?" I check my watch. "It's fucking five o'clock!"

"Sofia's heavily pregnant if you haven't noticed."

"Yeah, but she's not eighty! And *she's* pregnant—what's *your* excuse?"

He yawns. "We headed home early. She'll only rest if I lie down with her, and then we both end up fallin' asleep. Then I'm wide awake all goddamn night catching up on work. This kid is turning me into a vampire."

I shake my head. "Feel ashamed, dude. You're letting the team down."

"Where's Jake?"

"Regan's ballet recital dress-rehearsal. He was bitching about it this morning. That's punishment enough."

"Sorry, Brent."

"Yeah, yeah—go back to your nap, grandpa. Don't forget to take your teeth out."

He chuckles. "Fuck you."

I hang up and blow out a breath. Looks like I'm flying solo on this mission.

· · ·

I don't go straight over to the Red Barron; that would be too obvious. I loiter for forty-five minutes or so—then I walk into the small, one-room bar. It's old school—beer, wine, and whiskey. There's a dartboard in the back corner, a small television behind the bar, and a couple of tables and chairs that have seen better days squeezed along the mirrored wall. Even though it's run-down, the place is packed. I weave between a few patrons, and spot Tom Caldwell's tall frame among a group of suit-clad men and women clustered at the bar.

Tom turns when I tap his shoulder and his eyes register surprise, but he smiles. "Hey, Mason."

I shake his hand. "How's it going, Caldwell?"

"Good. Just stopping in for a drink after court."

"Yeah, me too."

Over Tom's shoulder, I spot Kennedy. Those thick-lashed turquoise eyes narrow for a moment—like she's preparing to tear me a new one—but then she snorts to herself and shakes her head. A sign that just maybe, she's prepared to throw in the towel on giving me a hard time. At least for the time being.

I step through the group, nodding to a few familiar faces, until I'm standing in front of her. So close she has to look up to keep eye contact. One corner of her mouth quirks. "You realize stalking is a crime?"

"Stalking?" I scoff. "Someone has a pretty high opinion of herself. I come here all the time."

"*You* come *here*? To this bar?"

"Yeah." I shrug. "Don't be paranoid."

She stretches up, her breath tickling my ear. "It's not paranoia if it's true. Look around."

I do. And that's when I realize why she doesn't believe me. Because the place is filled with police officers—some in uniform, some plain-clothed with their guns and badges still visible. It's a cop bar. Cops and prosecutors flock together—because they're generally on the same side.

You know who's *not* on their side? Criminal defense attorneys.

Kennedy's eyebrows lift. "Care to rephrase your statement?"

"Nope. That's my story and I'm sticking to it."

She chuckles.

"Hey, Brent. I haven't seen you in forever!"

Michelle Lawson—a delectable brunette prosecutor I dated briefly a few years back—wiggles up to my side and kisses me hello on the cheek. She's a nice girl, we had a few good times—and I mean that exactly like you think I do—and then it ran its course. No hard feelings.

"Hey, Michelle. How are you?"

"Same old, same old. You look good, Brent."

"Thanks." I wink. "You too."

An unhappy shadow falls over Kennedy's face as she watches our exchange.

Interesting.

"What are you drinking?" I ask her, after Michelle moves on.

Kennedy's tongue peeks out, wetting her plump bottom lip. "Pinot grigio." She puts her hand on my bicep—deliberately—almost possessively. And she leans in so close I can smell the sweet wine on her breath. "Get me another, please?"

I don't really know what's going on here. I'm not sure how we got from her calling me a dumbass in court an hour ago, to her flirting with me now. But hell if I'm going to question it—I get the lady her drink.

• • •

We spend the next half hour talking, teasing, laughing—about absolutely nothing that matters. Sometimes with the people around us, but mostly each other. Kennedy looks me up and down. Boldly. Seductively. She touches my arm, my chest. She leans in close and speaks softly into my ear.

I'm hard as a rock the entire fucking time—but I'm not complaining.

I just want to know what her game is. Why the sudden change in attitude? I plan to ask her as soon as we're alone, but she beats me to the punch.

"You want to get out of here?" she asks, with one hand on her hip, the other rubbing up and down my chest. Driving me insane.

"You took the words right out of my mouth."

Her smile is slow, secretive. "Then maybe you'll have to put something in mine—to make it an even trade."

Did she just really say that? Holy shit, if this is a dream—put me in a goddamn coma.

My heart pounds a little harder. "Sounds like a plan."

She hooks her thumb behind her. "I'm just going to hit the ladies room first."

As she turns I down the rest of my beer, wishing it was something stronger. I have to play this just right. I have lots of questions, there's so many things I want to know—and so many positions I want to screw her in.

A mug crashes off a table in the back, drawing my head in that direction. Toward two big, drunk, numbnuts talking shit and shoving each other, ready to brawl. There's a narrow hallway to the bathroom, and Kennedy doesn't have a lot of room to make it past them.

I know exactly what's going to happen—and there's no fucking way I'm going to let it.

A second later I have my arm around Kennedy's waist, lifting and turning her, putting her safely behind me. Then I shove the back of the dickhead who would've collided with her.

"You want to beat the shit out of someone, do it outside," I growl.

The jerk-off forgets about the original guy he wanted to pound on and turns on me. "Who the fuck are you?"

I get in his face, my voice low and lethal. "You almost knocked into my girl. If you had, you'd be in a world of fucking hurt right now. So I'm the guy who's telling you to stop being an asshole. If that's gonna be a problem, I can step outside too."

He stares at my face—probably trying to figure out if I'm serious. I have a few inches on him, my jaw is rigid, and my eyes are hard—I'm totally fucking serious. After a moment, he senses that and backs down.

"I don't have a problem with you." He shrugs, swaying unsteadily.

"Good."

After he walks away I turn around to Kennedy. I slip my hand behind her neck, gently cradling the back of her head, searching her face. "You okay?" I don't like her color. She's pale, her eyes hollow looking. "Hey, what's wrong?"

She blinks, looking away from me, shaking her head. "Nothing's wrong. I'm just . . . I'm gonna get a cab home instead. Alone."

"What? Why?"

"Because I can't . . ." She stops herself and she goes stiff in my arms. Defensive. "Because I changed my mind."

Kennedy slips out of my arms and slides between the patrons toward the front door.

She's a lot tinier than I am, so she gets through faster than I can keep up. By the time I get out the front door, she's got a cab hailed.

She opens the door—but I push it closed. "Where are you going?"

"I'm going home, Brent."

She tries the door again—but I push it closed—harder this time. "Not until you tell me what spooked you in there."

She doesn't look startled or scared or confused now. She just looks pissed. At me.

"Don't tell me what to do! *You* don't get to tell me what to do!" she yells.

"Everything okay, guys?" Tom Caldwell asks from nearby. His voice is friendly enough, genuinely concerned. "We, ah, called a car service. They'll be here in a minute. Are you riding with us, Kennedy?"

She brushes back her hair, composing herself. "Yes, thanks, Tom. I'll ride with you." Her expression is chilly when she turns to me. "I'll see you in court tomorrow, Brent."

I tap the top of the taxi hard, frustrated because this isn't a battle I can win tonight. "Yep. See you tomorrow, Kennedy."

• • •

Only later that night, around 2 a.m., I'm awakened by the sensation of electricity shooting from the end of my stump up my thigh. I break out in a cold sweat, my entire body locked up, every muscle contracted in agony. It happens occasionally.

In the beginning it was phantom limb pain, the feeling of an ache in a limb that no longer exists. Back then, it was just a cramping in my foot. I wanted to rub it, wiggle and twist it until I got comfortable, but of course that wasn't possible.

Nowadays it's different. Nerve pain.

It's the reason your uncle's knee aches when it rains, even years after the replacement surgery from that old football injury. Some nerves just don't know when to quit—they want to fire, and they're fucking pissed off that they can't.

My thigh spasms when another jolt comes—this one burning and sharp. I grunt and call for Harrison to get my wheelchair. Wearing my prosthetic is out of the question, and so is going back to sleep.

I've been to many specialists and they all have explanations—weather, stress—but no definitive answers. One wanted me to go back under the knife, but he couldn't guarantee it would cure the flare-ups, so I declined. Instead, I try medical massage, acupuncture, and just plain old sucking it up.

After I wheel myself out to the living room and tell Harrison to go back to bed, I send a text to Sofia, telling her to count me out at the office tomorrow. And at court.

• • •

In the morning, my masseuse comes to the house—an aging Asian woman with sure, strong hands who curses like a sailor. The pain is less after she leaves, but only slightly. I spend the day in my wheelchair, wearing a T-shirt and sweatpants.

Later in the day, I get a surprise. There's a loud knock on the door and Harrison goes to answer it. He comes back into the living room with Kennedy right behind him, looking fantastic in a white skirt, fitted black blazer, and shiny high heels, her hair down, thick and wavy.

She also looks mighty ticked off.

"Miss Kennedy Randolph," Harrison announces.

She pulls up short. "You have a butler?"

I shrug. "My mother worries. To what do I owe the pleasure?"

Kennedy unleashes her pointed finger. "If you think you're going to pass this case off to your partner like a chickenshit, you're out of your mind!"

"I don't know what you're talking about."

"I'm talking about the fact that you weren't in court today. But your barracuda of a partner was!"

I chuckle, even as razor-sharp pain slices across my leg. "Barracuda—Sofia will like that. I'll be sure to pass along your compliment."

"Don't even try to bait and switch this, Brent. I'll file a complaint with the court, I'll contact the bar association, I'll—"

As entertaining as her tirade is to watch, I cut her off. "The case is mine, Kennedy—the client is mine. I wasn't up to making it into court today and Sofia was free. That's all." My eyes drag over her and I force a wink. "Though it's good to know you missed me."

Her mouth snaps shut, and her brows draw together as she regards me. "You don't look sick."

"I'm not sick," I counter.

She glances at the wheels of my chair, then my face—and I know she's noting the circles under my eyes, the clenched jaw, the perspiration on my forehead.

"Is it your leg?" she asks quietly.

I force a grin, but it feels bitter. "I'm one of the lucky few who experience chronic pain years after amputation. It makes wearing my prosthetic leg pretty fucking unbearable, and I don't like to use the wheelchair in court. It distracts the jury."

She takes that in, then her voice goes even softer. "A year and a half after your accident, my parents and I went to your house for dinner. I snuck upstairs because I wanted to see you; I needed to know if you were okay. I made it halfway down the hall to your room—and then I heard you crying. Henderson was with you, but it sounded . . . horrible."

I duck my head. "It was worse then. And I was young—didn't know how to deal with it. Now I do."

I take my time raising my eyes to hers. There's a difference between pity and compassion, and I've had twenty-two years of practice in noting the distinction. Pity is feeling sorry for someone, while being glad you're not them. Compassion is a shared pain—you hurt *with* them; their pain becomes your own.

I can accept curiosity, unease about my leg—they come with the territory. But I can't handle pity.

Not from her.

When I drag my gaze to her face, relief loosens my chest. Because her eyes crinkle with hurt—mine and hers.

"Is there anything I can do?"

I smirk. "Now that you mention it, blow jobs always make me feel better. Don't suppose you're interested?"

She actually laughs—it's low and sweet and beautiful. And it makes the pain just a little bit easier to ignore.

"Sorry, not interested."

"Damn it." I snap my fingers. "How about a drink, then? Drinking alone sucks." I jerk my thumb to my butler. "And Harrison here is straight edge."

I push my wheelchair forward and gesture to the couch. "Sit down. Harrison, get the good bottle of brandy, please—top shelf in the liquor cabinet, on the left."

"Your medication . . ." he warns, but I wave him off.

"One drink will be fine."

Kennedy sits on the brown leather sofa, close enough that our knees almost touch. Harrison hands us each a rounded, bottom-heavy glass half filled with amber liquid, then quietly leaves the room.

I look at her. Where to start? So many questions—and even more land mines.

"Where did you go after boarding school? I went to your house that summer, but—"

"I don't want to talk about that, Brent." She stares straight ahead, her voice dead-end final.

I back off. "Okay. Then . . . how did this happen? The hair, the clothes, the contact lenses—your mother and your sister Claire wanted to make you their Barbie doll for years. What finally made you let them?"

A smile curves her lips. "I didn't let them." She leans my way, her shoulders relaxing a little. "Eventually the rebellious stage got old; watching my mother shit bricks over the way I dressed was less satisfying. But the summer after my first year in law school, I had an internship with the appellate court—"

"Where did you go to school?" I interrupt, hungry for every morsel.

"Yale." She takes a sip of her brandy, then goes on. "So . . . I was working under Justice Bradshaw, who was not only a phenomenal judge but a stunning woman. About a month into my internship, she called me into her office and said she was impressed with my work, but if I didn't do something about my appearance I wouldn't be interning with her for long."

"She actually said that to you?" I choke out. "Shit—that would've made for an interesting sexual harassment suit."

Kennedy nods. "I told her I wanted to be judged on my work, not my looks. And she said, 'That's fine for La-La Land, honey, but this is the real world.'"

Her tone grows more easy as she goes on. The icy mask

melts away and her face turns softer, more open. And I can't take my eyes off her—because this is the girl I grew up with. The girl I know.

"She told me that banker or gangbanger, we're all judged on how we look. And if I looked sloppy, people would think everything I did was sloppy. But if I looked impeccable, they'd give me the benefit of the doubt that my work could be impeccable too.

"So I started making an effort to look more polished. Within a few weeks, I was dyed, plucked, and tailored within an inch of my life." Her hand skims down her front. "It was my *Devil Wears Prada* moment."

I nod, even though I have no fucking idea what she's talking about.

And she calls me on it. "You don't know what that means, do you?"

"Not a clue."

Kennedy smiles. "It means Justice Bradshaw was my fashion mentor. And that was the summer I turned pretty."

I stare at her—at the soft curve of the cheekbone, her smooth skin, the thick long lashes and full pink mouth she always had.

"No—it really wasn't."

Her eyes flash to mine for a long moment, then she looks away. Swallowing some brandy, she coughs.

"Goes down kind of rough, doesn't it?" I say.

"Yes. Not to be rude, but if this is your good stuff, I'm afraid to find out what your cheap liquor tastes like."

I smile. "It's not the good brandy because of the taste." I crook my finger, drawing her closer until our arms brush, and

I'm able to detect the scent of peaches on her skin. Then I hold up my glass, swirling it gently. "Do you see the light brown color—how soft it looks, like crushed velvet?"

Kennedy peers at the glass and nods.

"But there's a deeper brown in there too, giving it more complexity. A richness."

"Uh-huh."

"And then there's the golden hue over the whole thing that makes it almost ethereal. Like it's lit from the inside."

"Yes." She nods again.

I stop swirling the glass. And say softly, "That is the exact shade of Kennedy Randolph's eyes."

Her breath hitches—almost a gasp.

"That's what I thought the first time I drank it, and it's what I've thought every time I drank it since." I turn to face her, my voice dropping lower. "I've never forgotten you, sweetheart. Not even close."

She wasn't expecting that. She looks surprised; small and suddenly vulnerable. Then she shuts it down and her face goes blank. And hard.

"That pisses you off." I try to catch her eyes again. "Why does that piss you off?"

"You know why." She moves to stand.

I grasp her hand. "No, Kennedy, I don't. I never did."

She jerks away and sets her glass on the coffee table. Then she backs up a step—putting space between us. "I'm not doing this with you again, Brent. You're not sucking me back in."

My jaw tightens. "Okay. How about you explain what that means?"

"How about you go fuck yourself with a lacrosse stick?"

Hello, Square One—long time, no see.

I tilt my head, like I'm thinking it over. "Sports equipment is a hard limit for me. But if you want to play with toys, count me in."

She doesn't appreciate my humor. "I'm leaving."

"You're running."

Her lips pinch and her eyes glare—and goddamn if she isn't cute when she's fired up. I can't wait to see what full-out furious looks like, and something tells me I'm gonna have my chance pretty soon.

One hand braces on her hip, the other stabs the air in front of me. "Chair or no chair, your ass better be in court tomorrow or I'll make your life hell."

"As opposed to the delight you're making it right now."

She throws up her hands and moves to the doorway.

"See you tomorrow, angel," I call to her back.

A minute later, Harrison steps sedately into the room after seeing her to the front door.

"Angel?" he wonders.

"Sure." I raise my glass to my lips. "It was an angel who brought the plagues down on Egypt."

"Ah, I see." He nods. "But something tells me the frogs and locusts were easier to handle."

And I don't disagree.

6

The next morning, I get to the office early to make up for being sidelined yesterday. I get lost in motions and appeals and before I know it, the building comes alive around me—midmorning sunshine streaming through the windows, the sound of Mrs. Higgens's footsteps, the smell of coffee in the air . . . the resounding thump that comes through the wall, rattling my desktop dart game in its box.

What the hell?

Before I reach my door, the thump comes again, this time accompanied by a muffled yell—shocked, pained, and distinctly male.

What the fuck?

I jump up and run into the hallway, and realize the sound came from behind Sofia's office door. Jake and Stanton come out of their offices at the same time, their concerned expressions matching mine. When another thump sounds, Stanton's mouth presses into a hard line and his eyes look like two nukes about to detonate. He takes the lead as we burst through Sofia's office door.

Sofia's always had the Brazilian bombshell thing going on, but now she's sporting an extra curve—the seven-month baby bump across her middle. Which makes the fact that she's holding a guy facedown across her desk, his arm pulled unnaturally far behind his back, even more disturbing. And . . . kind of awesome.

"Aaaarrrgh, you're gonna break my arm!" the guy moans.

"Are you all right?" Stanton asks her.

"Dandy." She actually smiles.

He steps up just as Sofia steps back—then Stanton grabs the guy and pins him to the wall, his big hand wrapped around the guy's throat.

"What the fuck did you do?" Stanton growls.

The guy's eyes bulge "Me? She almost broke my goddamn arm!"

Stanton pulls him a few inches from the wall and slams him back against it. "What'd you do that made her almost break your arm?"

"I told him he was going to have to do jail time." Sofia pushes her long, dark hair back, fanning her sweaty neck. "That there wasn't a deal I could make that wouldn't include two to four years, minimum. He didn't appreciate that, and took a swing at me."

"You took a fucking swing at my *wife*?" Stanton's fingers clench around the guy's windpipe. "My *pregnant* wife!"

Sofia becomes the voice of reason. "I'm okay, Stanton. Really. Please just get him out of here." Then she gives the piece of shit a look that may kill him faster than Stanton's grip.

"I'm dropping your case and keeping your retainer. Whatever lawyer you end up with won't be good enough to get you even two to four, so have fun with that, asshole. Get out."

"Let me help you," Jake says, low and dangerous. Then he takes the bastard off Stanton's hands—literally—and drags him out the door.

Stanton's hands run over Sofia's stomach, her shoulders. "You sure you're okay?"

"Totally fine. He didn't even touch me."

Stanton nods and hugs her. But by the time Jake is back in the room, he's all fired up again. "This is it, Soph—you're done." His hand cuts through the air, his stubborn jaw like a block of granite.

"Don't start that again," Sofia shoots back.

You might want to grab some popcorn. Because a good lawyer could argue with himself. *Two* attorneys going head to head is like a verbal MMA cage match with no rules.

"I'm finishin' it, Sofia. Maternity leave starts now." Stanton folds his arms—never a good sign.

"No, it doesn't, Stanton. I'm not going to feed into your 'barefoot and pregnant in the kitchen' fantasy!"

Stanton leans forward. "You're more than welcome to wear shoes. I'm partial to heels."

Yeah, that's gonna go over real well.

Then Stanton—displaying none of his trademark charm—loses it. "You're my wife, this is our son! I'm not gonna stand by and let either of you get hurt—so you're done with the violent assholes and drug addicts. You want to sit behind your desk, put your feet up with a nice tax evader or money launderer, be my fucking guest!"

"That's not a decision you get to make!"

"I just did!"

Under my breath, I tell Jake, "I hate it when Mom and Dad fight."

He cracks a smile.

Sofia glares smugly at her husband. "Then it's a good thing this is an equal partnership, and we make those kinds of firm decisions *together*."

Stanton nods, unconcerned. "Good point. We should vote on it—since it is a firm decision."

Sofia's smug smile falters.

"Jake?" Stanton asks, gaze focused on his wife.

There's a pause for just one beat, and Jake says, "I agree with Stanton."

Sofia's face tightens, but before she can argue, he goes on. "Soldiers, firefighters, policewomen all go on restricted duty when they're pregnant."

"But I'm not any of those things!" She throws up her hands. "I don't have to carry people out of burning buildings or avoid mortar fire, goddamn it!"

Jake's voice is firm as steel. "Still not worth the risk of some asshole lashing out at you. And it's got nothing to do with you being a chick—if Stanton was the incubator, I'd say the exact same fucking thing to him. Thank God that's not the case."

Stanton's self-satisfaction fills the air and echoes in his voice. "Brent? What's your vote?"

Sofia's hazel eyes turn to me pleadingly.

I look her right in the face. "You're one of my best friends, so I can tell you that I think you're being an idiot."

"But—"

I hold up my hand. "It's a few weeks of limited clients—not the end of the world. And it'll give all of us peace of mind."

Then I channel my inner-Waldo.

"You don't have to prove anything to us, Sofia—though maybe you feel like you have to prove something to yourself. But it's not worth your health. Or the health of little Becker Mason Santos Shaw."

Stanton chuckles. "Thank you."

"Not so fast—I'm not finished." I take a breath. "Although I see your point, Sofia's a grown woman, not a child. I'm not going to take the decision away from her. So my vote is to do whatever Sofia wants to do."

Stanton grinds his teeth. "Are you shittin' me?"

"Nope."

Sofia folds her arms victoriously. "Thank you, Brent."

But Stanton's not done. Because even though we're the same age, the three of them have always looked at me like a kid brother or something. Like I need to be taught or lectured. I don't know where the fuck that comes from—I mean, there must be a ton of grown men who have a whole shelf in their office just for comic books.

Right?

Stanton gets that Big Daddy look on his face and tells me, "One of these days you're gonna care about someone more than you care about yourself. And then you'll know what this feels like—and why you just voted wrong."

"I'll keep that in mind, but my vote still stands." I check my watch. "And now I have to go get my ass handed to me in court."

As I turn and walk out the door, I hear Stanton threatening to call Sofia's mother.

Sofia's a badass, but she's also a bit of a drama queen.

"You bring my mother into this, I'll never forgive you!"

And I can hear the wink in her husband's voice. "Forever's a long time, darlin'. I'll take my chances."

• • •

A couple of hours later, Kennedy has one of Justin Longhorn's victims on the stand. She wrapped up the more technical part of her case yesterday, and while Sofia gave a strong cross-examination, damage was done.

But not nearly as much as the damage that's occurring right now.

Because Kennedy—looking as delicious as a vanilla cupcake in her form-fitting cream suit—is questioning Eloise Potter. A tiny, gray-haired, soft-voiced, totally fucking adorable little old lady.

She looks like my Gram-Gram. She looks like *everyone's* Gram-Gram.

By the time Kennedy's done walking her through how she painstakingly pinched pennies all her life, to plan for her and Mr. Potter's retirement—after she tearfully recounts the devastation and fear of seeing that life savings literally disappear—the jury is looking at my client like he's the long-lost Menendez brother. They're the monsters who blew both their parents away with shotguns just to get their hands on their inheritance, in case you weren't sure.

So, yeah—not good.

"That's all for now, Your Honor," Kennedy tells the judge.

She smiles deviously right at me as she walks back to her

seat behind the prosecution table. And when I inhale, that sweet, fruity scent gives me an instant semi.

Fucking great. Now I have to cross-examine Mrs. Clause at half-mast.

I take a deep breath and stand up, buttoning my suit. Then I smile warmly. "Good afternoon, Mrs. Potter, I'm Brent Mason."

She nods and smiles. "Hello, young man."

I step out from behind the table. "Mrs. Potter, did the detectives investigating this case tell you that your funds had been recovered?"

"Yes, they did, thank goodness. Harold and I were so relieved."

"I'm sure you were. And they also explained that your money would be returned to you?"

"Yes, that's right."

I gesture to Justin, sitting meekly but attentive, in his schoolboy blue blazer and tan slacks, hands folded docilely on the table. "How do you feel about my client, Mrs. Potter? Knowing he's just seventeen years old? Do you feel he should go to jail, that the rest of his life should be ruined because of one alleged adolescent mistake?"

Kennedy jumps to her feet—like I knew she would. "Objection! The witness's feelings about the defendant have no bearing on the facts of the case."

But this time, I'm ready for her.

"Ms. Randolph opened the door to the witness's feelings when *she* asked about them in relation to Mrs. Potter's discovery of the funds missing from her account, Your Honor."

Judge Phillips takes a moment to consider, then sides with me.

"Your objection is overruled, Ms. Randolph."

Satisfaction pumps so hard in my veins it escapes in a low *ha*.

Things go downhill pretty quickly after that.

"Did you just *ha* me?" Kennedy hisses, like a wet cat.

I turn, facing her full frontal. "No I didn't *ha* you. That would be unprofessional."

"I definitely heard a *ha*."

"Then you're hearing things, honey."

Her eyes flare, then narrow sharply. She speaks to the judge, but her gaze stays trained on me. "I request that Mr. Mason be disciplined by the court. For referring to opposing council in a derogatory fashion—"

I step closer to her. "There's nothing derogatory about *honey*. It's a term of endearment."

"It's demeaning!"

"It's admiring!"

"Which is neither appreciated or permitted." Kennedy sneers. "As clearly ruled in Billings v. Hobbs."

"You'd be right, if it weren't for Probst v. Clayton."

Our eyes clash. She steps toward me, breathing heavier. "Probst v. Clayton was overturned."

I move forward—pulse pounding—until we're practically nose to nose. "Dwyer v. Bocci, then." And I murmur so only she can hear, "Suck it."

Her eyes focus on my mouth. "Bite me," she whispers back. Then, louder, "I'll see your Dwyer v. Bocci and raise you an Evans v. Chase."

And fuck, I want to kiss her. She's right there; it would be so easy.

It would be so *good*.

Judge Phillips clears his throat, and we break apart. The room is dead silent—all eyes on us.

"Would you two like to be alone?" He frowns. "I could clear the courtroom."

My gaze drops to the floor and I can practically feel Kennedy withering with embarrassment. "No, Your Honor."

"Won't be necessary, Judge."

"Ah, you remember I'm the judge. That's encouraging." He picks up his gavel. "I, however, would like a moment alone—with the two of you." His voice projects as he addresses the court. "It's Friday, so we're closing up shop early. We'll reconvene at 9 a.m., Monday morning." He bangs the gavel. "Adjourned. Miss Randolph, Mr. Mason, my chambers."

Chatter and motion swamp the courtroom. Everyone stands as the judge vacates the bench, the spectators file out the door, and Mrs. Potter steps down from the witness stand— heading toward the hunched, gray-haired guy in suspenders who I assume is Harold Potter. She pauses as she passes me, with a twinkle in her eye.

"I thought for sure you were about to ravish her. I've read a lot of books, and that was just like a scene that ends with the hero ravishing the maiden."

"I was closer to strangling her."

The little old lady chuckles in a knowing kind of way. "That's a different kind of book, sonny."

I head to the judge's chambers with Kennedy behind me— practically stepping on my heels. The bailiff closes the door after we enter. Judge Phillips hangs his black robe in the small closet, adjusts the cuffs of his shirt, then sits behind his massive dark-wood desk.

"Mr. Mason, Miss Randolph, we have a problem." He sighs like a fed-up parent.

Kennedy jumps right in. "May I speak freely, Your Honor?"

"This is not the military, Miss Randolph. Say what you need to say."

She points at me. "He's an ass."

"I'm an ass?" I choke. "What about you? You've been busting my balls since day one!"

Her mouth drops open in horror. "I have no interest in your balls!"

"Protesting a little too much, aren't you?"

And we're back to the nose-to-nose thing. Except even in heels, Kennedy's really short—so I have to dip my head.

"I'm getting the feeling you two know each other," Judge Phillips interrupts.

Kennedy and I answer at the same time.

"Not really."

"That's right."

I give her an exasperated look, then inform the judge, "We grew up next door to each other."

Kennedy snorts and folds her arms. "In houses that were twenty acres apart—it's not like we were roomies."

"We made out once when we were teenagers," I volunteer. "Then she broke my heart. It was brutal."

Kennedy's mouth drops open again. It's actually a nice look for her.

If it weren't for the murderous expression that goes along with it.

"I broke *your* heart! Ha! That's a lie!"

I gesture with my hands and raise my voice. "You went out with William Penderghast before the saliva was dry on my lips!"

And before the come was dry on my stomach. But I keep that particular detail to myself, because I'm a gentleman.

Kennedy gets right in my face. "Because you were already back together with your raging bitch girlfriend!"

And the judge clears his throat. Again.

Oops.

"Yeah, you two definitely know each other." He leans back in his chair, eyes going between the two of us.

Kennedy steps forward to his desk, so I can't see her expression. But her voice is softer, and deliberately even. "We haven't seen each other in almost fifteen years, Judge. So the truth is, we don't know each other at all." She shakes her head, just a bit. "Not anymore."

Maybe it's the way she says it—monotone—without a hint of anger or annoyance or even sadness. Or maybe it's just that the words are true. But my stomach drops. It falls in that sharp, unexpected, yearning sort of way—that feels exactly like regret.

Judge Phillips looks at us for a moment longer. Then he spins in his chair, plucks a framed photograph from the shelf behind him, and shows it to us. "I have five boys. Even after the first three, my Alice was determined to get her daughter. After Timothy came along, she finally accepted that she'd have to be content with daughters-in-law."

In the picture, Judge Phillips and his aging-pretty-damn-well-looking wife stand in front of a lighthouse, flanked by five dark-haired, twenty-something-year-old guys in light blue button-downs and jeans.

"You have a beautiful family, Judge," I tell him.

"They seem like fine, upstanding young men," Kennedy adds.

"They are. *Now*. When they were teenagers, they were destructive, hot-tempered bastards who loved to piss each other off."

I grin, because he sounds just like Jake and his wild brood of McQuaids.

"When two of them would really get into it," the judge continues, "I'd lock them together in a bedroom and let them duke it out. Sometimes I'd hear a crash or a thump against the wall, but for the most part they'd work out their issues. And more importantly—I didn't have to listen to them while they did it."

He takes his wallet out of his pocket and tosses a couple of twenties down on the desk. He looks at the pile, joggles his head back and forth, and throws out a few more twenties.

"That strategy worked out so well I'm going to use it with the two of you." He gestures to the money. "Go out, sit down, get some dinner and maybe a few beverages, and work out whatever issues you have that are turning my courtroom into a circus."

The judge's plan scores me court-mandated alone time with Kennedy—so I like it.

She doesn't.

"Your Honor, this is highly irregular—"

"Yes, it is, Miss Randolph, but I'm ordering it anyway. Watching you two swipe and spit at each other has gotten on my last nerve."

"Judge Phillips, I can assure you—"

"I don't want your assurances, little lady, I want a smooth-running trial." He points again to the money on the desk. "This will get me that—so don't even think of walking back in here on Monday until your and Mr. Mason's issues have been hashed out."

She stamps her foot. "We don't have issues! You can't—"

"Oh, for Christ's sake." I take the money and grab Kennedy's hand in an iron grip. "We'll work it out. Have a good weekend, Judge."

Then I walk out of the room, pulling her behind me like a stubborn wagon.

In the hall outside the judge's chambers, she yanks at her hand. "Don't drag me!"

"Then fucking walk," I growl back.

When I feel her resistance lessen, I give her back her hand and she keeps in step beside me.

"He can't do this! He can't order us to have dinner! What the hell kind of medieval—"

"He's the judge, genius—he can order anything he damn well pleases. And we've already ticked him off. Riling him up further won't play out well for either one of us."

"But—"

I stop short and turn to face her. I drop my voice lower, tempting and persuasive. "It's one meal. One conversation. Then we put it all behind us and you can go back to pretending like I don't exist. Isn't that what you want?"

She searches my face.

I'm lying, of course. Because now that she's back, here

where I can see her and touch her, where I can talk to her and tease her, maybe even one day make her smile—there's no fucking way I'm letting her go ever again.

She doesn't blink. And she doesn't back down. She releases a long breath, then says, "Fine. One meal—one conversation. That's it."

My smile is appeasing. Charming. "See, was that so hard? I'll even be nice and let you pick the restaurant, Viper."

Her lips tighten as she turns to continue walking down the hall. "Don't call me Viper. It sounds like a stripper's name."

I walk next to her. "What's wrong with a stripper's name? Some of the best people I know are strippers. Besides, Viper was a badass character from the Captain America comics. She was my favorite villain—and she was hot. Most teenage boys had *Playboy* to inspire their fantasies. I had Marvel. You should take it as the highest compliment."

She snorts, shaking her head. But it almost sounds like a laugh.

And that, right there, is progress.

• • •

We sit at a round table in the back corner of an empty pub just a few blocks from the courthouse. The lights are dim and the music is low enough to talk with our indoor voices but still fill any silences.

"Two bacon cheeseburgers, medium rare," I tell the waitress. "She'll have onion rings instead of fries and barbecue sauce instead of ketchup. And two draft beers, please." I glance at Kennedy as I return the menus. "We should pace ourselves— save the hard stuff for later."

After the waitress goes on her merry way, the blond viper stares at me, her mouth an adorable—annoyed—bow.

"What?"

"Maybe I wanted the veggie burger. I could be vegetarian now."

I grimace. "Are you?"

"No."

"Then kindly cease the bitching." I lean back in my chair, legs open, getting comfortable—debating how to begin.

Kennedy takes the issue out of my hands. "I can't believe you told Judge Phillips I broke your heart." Then she kind of snorts, shaking her head, like the notion itself is ridiculous.

I look at her straight on. "You did. It's been fourteen years, but I can still remember how it felt—I was shattered when you went out with William."

"You don't know the meaning of the word *shattered*."

"Yeah—I do. It's when you give me the greatest orgasm of my seventeen-year-old life, let me hear you moan my name as you come spectacularly around my fingers—and then ten hours later, push me to the fucking curb for William goddamn Penderghast."

Did that sound bitter? Good.

Kennedy leans forward, eyes blazing. "You were already back together with Cashmere before I agreed to go out with William!"

I blink. "No, I wasn't."

"Yes, you were."

And the waitress brings our beers—perfect timing. We both take a healthy chug.

After my frosty mug is back on the table, I suggest, "Let's start at the beginning."

"Fine," she agrees. "Parents' weekend, junior year."

You up for a little time travel? 'Cause it's time to party like it's 1999 . . .

7

Saint Arthur's boarding school, junior year

"**K**itty!"

  "Mitzy!"

Our mothers hug like they haven't seen each other in years. A Welcome Parents sign hangs across the entrance to the main building, the sun is shining, and the air is warm with a hint of early spring crispness. Eagle-Eye Cherry plays from a radio somewhere across the quad, and clusters of families dot the lush green grass.

"I feel like it's been ages!" Mitzy says. "We should all have lunch together! There's that fabulous little place down by the lake . . ."

As my mother quietly agrees, I take advantage of my dark, *Risky Business*–era sunglasses to check Kennedy out. She looks especially cute today. Her brown hair's wrapped around the top of her head in a messy, kind of sexy bun. She's wearing snug blue jeans and an open, oversized navy checkered flannel shirt, but the white tank top beneath it shows off her flat waist and sweet-looking tits. She got her braces taken off last month too. *Bonus.*

And at the moment, she's doing that thing with her lip—clasping the plump bottom one between her teeth, sucking just a bit. That move gave me my very first boner when I was thirteen years old, and, damn, if it doesn't hit me the exact same way right now.

Kennedy and I have always been tight . . . up until this year. When I became captain on the lacrosse team and started seriously dating Cazz. Seriously, as in—fucking her. These days, Kennedy hangs with her roommate, Vicki Russo, and I hang with . . . other people.

She adjusts her glasses and smiles up at me. "Hey."

"Hey."

Like a disapproving blond wraith, Kennedy's sister appears at her side. "Would it have killed you to dress up a little bit? Honestly, Kennedy, Mother and Father drove all this way . . ."

I slip my hands into my pockets and rock back on my heels. "Hi, Claire. It's good to see you."

"Brent." She smiles tightly. "You're looking . . ." She takes note of my jeans, sneakers, and white-collared shirt under a navy blue sweater. ". . . typical."

I put my hand up. "Claire, please—I realize I'm an irresistible specimen of male perfection, but your obsession with me is getting embarrassing."

Kennedy snorts. The uncontrollable urge to laugh bubbles up from my chest and I don't even try to resist it—because the sour look on Claire Randolph's face feels so much more hilarious than it actually is. She turns away and follows our parents up the path, leaving Kennedy and me relatively alone.

"Are you high?" she asks me in a hushed voice.

I lean in close to her. "As fuck. It was the only way I could make it through this weekend."

I know some guys who are major stoners, and I'm not one of them. But an herbal refreshment before a long, stressful day is totally acceptable.

She shakes her head and her nose wrinkles with exasperation. This too is also really fucking cute.

We fall in step beside each other, trailing behind our chattering parents.

"I see your sister still hasn't elected to have that surgery yet."

She comes right back with, "You mean the one that will remove the stick from up her ass? Nope, not yet."

I laugh out loud. "Shit, Kennedy, it feels like we haven't hung out in forever. Where have you been?"

I've seen her around—campus isn't that big. But I haven't *seen her*, seen her. Can't remember the last time I really talked to her, and she's a cool girl to talk to.

She turns her head, looking at me for a few seconds, and her voice is almost a sigh. "I've been right here the whole time."

• • •

"Posture, Kennedy. Slouching is for girls with weak spines."

"Why won't you wear contact lenses, Kennedy? Your eyes are your best feature, yet you insist on hiding them."

"Another roll, Kennedy? Tsk-tsk, those carbs are a dancer's enemy."

It's been like this since we sat down. For the last hour,

Mitzy Randolph has criticized Kennedy right down to her goddamn fingernails.

My buzz is gone and my head feels like it's going to explode if I have to listen to one more bitchy comment from Mrs. Randolph.

So, of course she says, "Kennedy could have been a classic prima ballerina—if only she had managed to be taller."

And I say, "Well maybe the rack will come back into fashion and we can strap her on for a nice stretch."

All four parents stop. And look at me with blank faces.

Just as I'm about to tell them where to go, Kennedy starts to giggle beside me. It's that forced kind of giggle—a signal to everyone else that a joke was told and they should laugh to be polite. And as long as you're not her younger daughter, Mitzy Randolph is the epitome of politeness.

Same goes for my mother. "Brent, darling, take off those sunglasses. It's rude to wear them at the table."

I take them off and try to hide my eyes by looking down. My mother's gasp is horrified, so that plan obviously tanked.

"My goodness, why are your eyes so red? Do you have an infection?"

Claire Randolph finally cracks a smile. I bet she enjoys watching worms squirm under a magnifying glass on a sunny day too.

"No, Mom, they're not infected."

"But they look terrible!" Her hand rests on my father's forearm. "Donald, dear, perhaps we should have the doctor come look at Brent?"

"Allergies," Kennedy pipes up—sounding like she just thought of it herself. "His eyes are red from allergies."

"Brent doesn't have any allergies."

Kennedy smiles at my mother, and sounds so confident I'd believe her. "We all have allergies here. Something to do with the special species of trees in Connecticut. The pollen they . . . ejaculate."

Ejaculate?

Then she sneezes for added effect.

It's obvious Claire doesn't buy it, but the rest of them swallow it like hundred-year-old scotch.

Then it only takes a few minutes before:

"Do make a salon appointment, Kennedy. I can see your split ends from here."

I stand up so fast the glasses on the table rattle. "We're going for a walk."

My mother's eyes are wide like an owl's. "Why?"

Saying I'm on the verge of stuffing the tablecloth down her best friend's throat probably won't go over well. "I just spotted a . . . double-breasted blue robin down by the lake. They're super rare. Kennedy and I need to study it for horticulture—"

"Horticulture's plants," Kennedy whispers frantically.

"—and winged wildlife class."

I'm a lacrosse goalie—I'm all about the save.

And they go for it.

Five minutes later, Kennedy and I are walking on the bank of the lake outside. I pick up a rock and throw it hard into the water. "How do you stand it?"

"Stand what?"

"*Posture, Kennedy, split ends, Kennedy, fucking carbs, Kennedy* . . . I wanted to jam my fork into my ear just so I wouldn't have to listen to it anymore—and she wasn't even talking about me!"

Kennedy smiles. And it's not sad or fake or bitter at all. It's just pretty. "She doesn't mean those things the way they sound."

"Then how the hell does she mean them?"

Kennedy shrugs a shoulder and tosses a rock of her own.

"She wants me to be happy. What she thinks happiness is. If she didn't care, she wouldn't say anything at all. She'd just ignore me. And that would be worse."

Our eyes hold for a few seconds and I realize how much I've missed this girl. It's not manly to say—but it's really fucking true. The people I spend my time with, talk to every day—they're not real. They don't look at things the way she does.

They don't look at *me* the way she does. Even today, after all this time of not hanging out, we don't miss a beat. Because she knows me, beginning to end. All the pieces, good and bad, that make me who I am.

And no one else makes me feel the way I feel, right now, looking back at her. The ache in my chest, the clench of my stomach, the thrumming of my pulse.

"I'm surprised you're not having lunch with Cashmere's family," Kennedy says.

That makes my gut clench for a whole different reason.

Cashmere's the hottest girl in school, and things started out wild between us. Fun. But in the year we've been dating . . . she's changed. She's become clingy and bossy at the same time. Miserably jealous and insecure. That's another reason Kennedy and I haven't really hung out lately—Cashmere's not too keen on her.

"We broke up."

Kennedy's eyebrows rise. "Really? When? Why?"

And going by the happy spark in her eyes, it looks like the feeling is mutual.

"Yes. Yesterday. I'm not exactly sure why."

"You're not sure?"

"There was a lot of screaming; it was hard to make out the actual words. It's somewhere between I'm suffocating her and I'm not giving her the attention she deserves." Palms up, I shrug again.

Kennedy swallows as we walk along the water. "Wow. You, ah . . . you don't seem too broken up about it."

"I'm not."

A light breeze blows and she pushes a loose strand of hair from her cheek. "Do you think—"

"Kennedy!" Mitzy Randolph calls from up the hill to where we stand. "Kennedy!"

Her voice reminds me of Auntie Em calling for Dorothy as the twister was coming in.

She gestures for us to come up and reluctantly, we do.

Mitzy talks with her hands as she explains to us both. "We've all had the grandest idea! The Remington Hotel is just a few miles away—they have the most fabulous bar and casino—very exclusive. So we're all going to spend the night there and we'll take you back to school tomorrow. Doesn't that sound like fun?"

I smile at Mitzy and throw an arm around Kennedy's

shoulders. This means solo time with Kennedy. "It sounds like a lot of fun, Mrs. Randolph."

• • •

"Kennedy, are you awake?" I whisper.

I listen outside the door of the Randolphs' suite, but I don't hear any movement on the other side. Disappointment drops in my stomach. Because we spent the entire day with our parents, walking and talking and frigging talking some more. We had a late dinner in the "fabulous" restaurant downstairs, then our parents pretty much sent us to bed. While *they* hit the casino.

Ageism is a terrible thing.

But now it's just after midnight, and I have an awesome idea.

Which only works if Kennedy is still awake.

I knock again, louder this time. "Kennedy?"

The door opens halfway, and Kennedy peers up at me. Her glasses are off and her eyes—I never noticed before, but they're spectacular.

Thick, long lashes frame sparkling, golden-brown orbs. Soft and so . . . warm. The kind of eyes a guy would want to look down into while he's moving above her—the kind you'd hope she'll leave open while you kiss, deep and slow.

The rest of her? Well—I've always kind of noticed that.

Ever since she started wearing a training bra and I discovered the delicious sin of masturbation.

And I'd have to be blind not to notice her now. A thin-strapped silky pink tank top that's kind of draped across her chest. It doesn't show any cleavage, but if she moves just the right way, we're talking a prime view. The bottom half is matching pink shorts that are swishy around her thighs, showing off killer toned legs.

And I'm not the only one noticing things.

Kennedy's eyes slide across the chest of my sleeveless shirt and down the ridged muscles of my biceps. My skin is surfer-boy tan from outdoor workouts and afternoon practices. Then her eyes cut across to my waist, maybe picturing the six-pack beneath it, and then . . . lower. And I wonder if she notices how hard I'm reacting to watching her watch me.

The tinge of pink on her cheeks tells me she just might be.

Her gaze settles on my smiling face. She licks her lips and says, "Hey. What's up, Brent?"

I hold up the keys to my father's 1961 Ferrari 250 GT California. Also known as the *Ferris Bueller's Day Off* car.

Less than a hundred were made and, just like in the movie, it's my father's pride and joy. And it's parked downstairs right now.

I found out today that Kennedy doesn't have her driver's license. With her family's chauffeurs, her mother didn't see the point.

And I'm going to rectify that.

"Ready for your first driving lesson?"

• • •

". . . then you ease your foot back at the same time."

We're in the big empty parking lot of a darkened building a few miles from the hotel. Kennedy listens to my instructions intently, brow furrowed, adjusting her glasses. She seems excited, determined, and totally adorable.

"Got it?"

"Got it." She nods.

And she goes for it.

There's a grinding sound as she moves the stick shift, and I mentally thank the clutch for his brave sacrifice. We start to move forward, bucking, inch by inch and I tell her, "Now gun it. Hit the gas."

And then we're moving.

Kennedy's smile is huge and bright, like Christmas morning and the Fourth of July rolled into one.

The car gives a slight stutter as she shifts into second gear, but smooths back down after her foot is off the clutch. With one hand on the wheel, she grabs my arm with the other.

"I'm doing it, Brent!"

It's awesome, and I chuckle. "Yeah, you are."

• • •

"You need a nickname. Kennedy is kind of a mouthful to say."

We're parked at a picnic area high above the lights in the town below. It's still and quiet. The top of the car is open, but the sky feels like a dark canopy above us, dotted with countless bright stars.

We didn't crash into anything and the car is still running, so in my mind, Kennedy's driving lessons were a roaring success. She said she wasn't ready for the open road, but I'll get her there eventually. The look on her face when she really got the hang of shifting—it was pure elation and gratitude. Seeing that expression felt just like when I block an opposing team's goal—like something I was born to do again and again.

"My name is too long? Do you often have difficulty with big words?" she asks with a smartass smirk. "Maybe you should see someone about that." Then she asks, "What's *your* nickname?"

"BC."

She frowns, trying to figure it out. "Because your middle name is Charles?"

I shake my head and tell her with the straightest face, "Big Cock."

Kennedy laughs. "Did you think of that all by yourself?"

"The guys on the team gave it to me. It's a lot to live up to—don't want to disappoint the younger classmen. But in the immortal words of Spider-Man, *with great power comes great responsibility.*"

"Uncle Ben, actually."

"What?"

She tilts her head. "Uncle Ben said that, not Spider-Man. Remember?"

I do. But the fact that she remembers . . . is pure fucking awesome. It does things to me—deep, thoughtful, serious emotion type of things.

But I've never been the serious kind of guy, so I tease, "How about Randy? Randy Randolph. Can I call you that?"

Kennedy frowns. "Not if you expect me to answer."

We talk more, about everything and nothing in particular. And somehow, even though it wasn't what I planned—or expected—my arm ends up around her shoulders, her head resting against my collarbone.

Slowly, I slide her glasses off and carefully fold them before placing them on the dashboard. Like it's the most natural thing in the world, I dip my head and press my lips against hers. They're achingly soft and warm. I trace her lips with my tongue, but they stay tightly closed, and I laugh against her mouth.

She pulls back. "What?"

I look into the gorgeous eyes of the girl I've known my whole life, and my only thought is, what the hell took me so long to do this?

My thumb slides slowly across her jaw. "Have you ever kissed anyone before?"

The last time we talked about it, sophomore year, she hadn't.

But she doesn't blush or recoil at the question. Her voice is low and kind of panting. "Of course I have. Why? Are you saying I'm bad?"

I don't know who the hell she's been kissing, but whoever it was—they must've been piss poor at it. This pleases me.

"Nope. But you're about to get even better." I lean forward, brushing against her lips again. "Open your mouth for me, Kennedy."

Then there's only kissing—head-turning, lip-sucking, tongue-sliding kind of kisses. Her taste makes me feel a little drunk. And the whisper of my name from her lips makes me feel a little crazy.

Clothes find their way to the floor of the car. And every moment is easy and natural, and so fucking right.

Afterward, we're pressed against each other in the same seat, boneless and spent. And I get why they make so many cheesy movie scenes that end just like this—because it just doesn't get more perfect than right here, right now.

Kennedy smiles up at me and I kiss her forehead, and together we watch the sun rise.

• • •

The next morning, my parents make me get up early—drop me back at school early—because my father has some meeting to get to back home. They leave a message for the Randolphs at the front desk. It sucks that I don't get to see Kennedy before we go, but I'm consoled by the thought that I'll see her at school.

Everything is going to be different now.

When I get to my room, I hop in the shower. My thoughts helplessly drift to last night. The feel of Kennedy's hands on me. The sounds she made—little moans and greedy whimpers.

Let's just say it's convenient that I'm in the shower.

I step out of the bathroom with a towel around my hips and water still trickling down between the grooves of my abs.

"Hey, baby."

Cashmere is laid out on my bed—wearing my lacrosse jersey and nothing else. She's all hooded eyes, pouty lips, tan skin, and teased blond hair—ready for a *Playboy* photo shoot. There was a time my dick would've led me straight to her and I would've happily followed—all our problems solved.

But not anymore. I'm done letting my dick lead me around—it's time to start following my heart. And I know how corny that sounds, but I don't give a shit.

"What are you doing here?" I slip boxer briefs on under

the towel—it just doesn't feel right to let her see me bare-assed anymore.

"Do I need a reason to visit my boyfriend?"

"Not your boyfriend anymore."

Her eyes roll. "Of course you are."

"You broke up with me, remember?" I pull my practice jersey over my head.

Cashmere crawls toward the end of the bed. "It was a mistake." She purrs, "I'm sorry. Let me make it up to you."

I've been with this girl for a year. Screwed her every way I know how, and thought that was love—but at his moment, I feel nothing for her. It's almost scary. No guilt, no tender urge to protect her feelings. I'm not sure she has any. It's really fucked up.

"If you didn't, I would've broken up with you. We're done, Cazz."

Her eyes drop to the bulge in my boxers and she licks her lips. She rises to her knees and moves to wrap her arms around my neck. "You don't look done to me."

I catch her wrists and look at her hard.

"Trust me, I'm *done*."

Anger flashes in her hazel eyes, sharp and vindictive and oh-so familiar. "I heard you hung out with your little freaka-zoid friend this weekend."

My grip on her wrists tightens. "Don't call her that."

Her mouth twists into a nasty knot. "Did you fuck her? Is that what this is about?"

I drop her wrists and take a step back. "This has nothing to do with Kennedy."

"Oh, please. You would never turn me down unless you

already had someplace new to stick your dick into. I know you, Brent." She slides off the bed and trails the tip of her finger slowly up my arm. "And that's why I know when you're done with your little trip into Loserville—you're going to come right back to me. We're too good together."

Because she's the hottest girl in school, I used to get a charge out of hearing her talk like that—a rush of confidence. Now it just makes me think that Cashmere is total bunny-boiling material.

"Take my jersey off. We have a game tomorrow night; it's bad luck if you wear it. Leave it on the bed."

And before she even starts to take it off, I'm out the door.

• • •

Lacrosse practice runs overtime. One of our starting defenders busted his ankle last week, trying to parkour between two garbage dumpsters. He's kind of an idiot. The second string taking his place is a freshman—good but nervous—so Coach and I stayed after practice to work with him and to go over the opposing team's game tapes. It's dusk by the time I leave the gym.

Walking back to my dorm, my lacrosse bag over my shoulder, I'm in a great mood. I don't think I've stopped smiling all day. I may even whistle a merry tune. My mother had a thing for Gene Kelly when I was a kid, and in my head, I'm totally doing the "Singin' in the Rain" dance.

Three guys are standing on the dorm building's steps. And even though I'm not the type who listens to other people's conversations, two words zoom straight to my eardrums, like a nuclear missile: Kennedy Randolph.

And my mental Gene Kelly is struck by a bolt of lightning and bursts into flames.

"I told you she'd say yes, dumbass. I don't know why you waited three years to ask her."

That's Peter Elliot. He's a science kid—biology. He got a grant from the federal government last year to cross-breed poisonous caterpillars, I think. And he's talking to William Penderghast and Alfonso DiGaldi. They're on the brainier end of the spectrum too—quiet, kinda bland guys who spend most of the weekend in the library.

"You can't rush these things. The timing had to be just right. But now the stars have aligned and Kennedy Randolph is going to the movies with me this Friday. Maybe I should rent a limo."

William laughs for no reason. Smiles so big and bright it almost hurts to look at him—because he looks like how I felt just ten seconds ago.

I walk straight up to them, eyes on William. "Did you just say you're going out with Kennedy Randolph?"

William puffs himself up a little bit. "That's right."

No fucking way.

"When . . . when did you ask her?"

He looks at me. "Like, a couple hours ago. Why?"

No fucking way.

"I . . . just . . ."

There's only one explanation—there are two Kennedy Randolphs at this school.

I go with that.

"Kennedy?" I ask, using my hands to imitate her height. "Short, glasses, brown hair? My . . ." I swallow. "*That* Kennedy?"

And out of the blue, he starts to look pissed. Affronted. "That's right. She's smart, funny, and has the biggest heart of anyone I know. She's also got a beautiful smile and eyes that are the most fascinating—"

I walk away. I can't listen anymore. If I do—I'll fucking lay him out.

I head straight for the girls' upperclassmen dorm. I don't think, I don't stop to talk to anyone, and my jaw is so tight it's a miracle my teeth haven't cracked by the time I get there.

I pound on her door with the side of my fist—and I don't stop until it opens.

Her eyes look shiny behind the glasses, her nose a little red—like she's getting a cold. Her gaze traces over my face for a few seconds and then her back straightens. "What's up?"

"Are you going out with William Penderghast?"

She steps out into the hall with me, closing the door behind her.

And then she blows my soul to kingdom come.

"Yes, I am. Why do you ask?"

For a second I don't answer her. It takes me time to find any words.

"*Why do I ask*? Because what about last night?" I try to keep the devastation out of my voice, but I don't know if I manage it. "I thought . . . I wanted . . ."

Her voice cuts, like a razor blade to the wrists. "Last night was fun. But it didn't mean anything—I know that. I can handle fun just like everybody else. And now I'll do my thing with William and you do yours with—"

"You'll do your *thing* with William? Seriously? What the fuck was I—the warm-up act?" I yell, anger on full display.

Fury flashes in her eyes, turning them aflame. "What's the matter, Brent? Did I hurt your precious boy-feelings? Did you expect me to follow you around like every other girl in school? Take your crumbs when you're feeling charitable?"

I don't really understand everything she's saying—the haze of disappointment is too crushing. Because, yeah, it hurts. As lame as it sounds, last night meant something to me. *She* means something to me. And apparently I don't mean dick to her.

So I do what comes natural. Cover it up. "I'm just surprised, is all. If I knew you were so easy, I would've hooked up with you years ago."

Her cheeks go fire-flaming red—with embarrassment or anger, I can't tell.

"I'm not easy."

"You sure? You may not think you're easy, but actions speak louder than words. William and I will have to compare notes to see. Because I didn't even have to try last night. It felt pretty fucking easy to me."

It's a shitty thing to say. I wouldn't be surprised if she slapped me—that's what girls do when they're offended. That's why they call it a *bitch-slap*.

But, like I've always known, Kennedy Randolph isn't your average girl. She doesn't slap me.

She punches me. Right in the mouth.

My head snaps back and I taste blood.

"Damn it!"

But when I open my eyes, when I look back at her face, all the anger bleeds out, like a hemorrhaging artery. Because Kennedy doesn't look furious anymore, or even angry.

She looks . . . crushed. Holding back tears—but just barely.

"I hate you," she forces out, shaking her head. "I *hate* you."

Her words reverberate in my bones, echo in my head.

In history, we watched a documentary on the Vietnam War, with actual footage of a battle from a reporter's camera—of a soldier, a young guy who was shot.

Badly.

And when it happened, his face, more than anything, looked surprised—stark white with shock . . . because there was suddenly a hole in his chest where his heart had just been.

When Kennedy turns her back and slams the door in my face—I feel the exact same way.

8

The present, in the pub

"I went to your room that morning. She answered the door in your jersey—said you were in the shower. She offered to let me wait, but she warned me that you two were back together. That I'd look really desperate just showing up at your room like that." Kennedy swallows hard and breathes deep. Like the memory alone is causing her actual pain.

"She never told me—"

"No, she wouldn't have, would she?" Kennedy looks into my eyes, smiling bitterly. "I was going to wait. I thought I at least deserved to hear it from you." Her voice strangles at the end, her eyes shinier than they should be. "But then Cashmere asked me what I had really expected. She said you were a hero and I was a zero and nothing was going to change that. Did I really think you would leave someone like her for someone like me?" She licks her lips slowly.

"I was still reeling from the night before. From the excitement, the total fucking joy over what we'd done. But when she put it like that . . . I believed her. So I left. William stopped me in the quad on the way back to the dorm. He asked me out . . . and I said yes."

I can't speak; I'm too busy reliving those moments, seeing them now from her side. And realizing all the things I didn't do, all the things I never said.

"I liked you," I whisper to the table. Then I look at her. "I liked you so much."

I still do. Behind those contact lenses, under makeup and designer clothes, she's still her. I can still taste her, feel her on my fingertips, so smooth and slick. Fearless in the way she wanted me, clutched me close like she'd never wanted to let go.

Her forehead crinkles with confusion. "But you did get back together with Cashmere. You didn't speak to me that whole year until—"

Kennedy obviously still doesn't understand jack shit about men. Or boys—because back then, I was definitely a boy.

"You told me our hookup meant nothing to you. That I was nothing and you were dating William. When I got pissed about it, you told me you hated me." I wipe a hand down my face. "I got back together with Cashmere because you didn't want me and she did. She was a substitute. I didn't want to look like a loser. And I didn't speak to you because it was too fucking hard."

"We were friends—"

"Not to me." I shake my head, capturing her gaze and holding it tight. "Not after that night. I didn't want your friendship, Kennedy—I wanted *you*. And if I couldn't have you—I had to pretend you didn't exist. Because then I could tell myself I wasn't missing out on everything I knew I was."

But I'd still thought about her. I'd dreamed about her.

And I missed her—all the time.

She gazes at the table, lost in her thoughts. Then she looks up, wetting her lips—seeming like she's decided something.

"So that's why you did it," she says softly. "You wanted to get back at me, and hurt me. Congratulations—you succeeded."

Something in her tone puts me on alert, and I lean in closer. "What exactly do you think I did?"

Her mouth is hard. "You set me up. You humiliated me. You . . . broke me that night, Brent."

I double-check. "The night of the senior dance?"

"Yes."

This is it. *This* is what I've been waiting fourteen years to know.

I tell her, "Pretend that you're a witness on the stand. Start from the beginning and tell me about the dance. Make me understand."

Kennedy scrapes her lip with her teeth. "In April, I started getting instant messages when I was online. From you. They said 'I'm sorry' and 'I miss you.' You talked about how you wanted to be with me, but you couldn't break up with Cashmere right then. You said it was a family thing—something about a business deal between your fathers."

She takes a drink of her beer, then goes on.

"I didn't believe it was you, at first. I thought it was a prank. But the messages kept coming, and they sounded so much like you. So as a test, I asked you about our first kiss. Where it was."

She pauses and I hold my breath.

"You said the roof, on New Year's Eve, when we were nine.

And that's when I knew it was you. I was so excited. For so long, I'd wanted . . .

"Anyway, the week before the dance, you sent me an IM saying you wanted to see me. You wanted to dance just one dance with me. You asked me to meet you by the lake behind the auditorium. Vicki didn't like it, but I was too far gone to care. I called Claire and asked her to come help me with my makeup and a dress. She was so happy—like a fairy god-mother."

Her voice cracks on the last word, and I feel sick. Because I know how this story ends.

"My dress was white—it was lovely, and it made me feel lovely too. My hair was down, curled and shinier than I ever remember it being."

She looks at my face with the saddest smile.

"And I wore contact lenses, for the first time in my life."

My hands fist on the table; my throat so dry I can barely swallow.

"I waited by the lake—I could hear the music from the auditorium. I heard a sound, like a footstep, and I called your name. But no one answered."

She takes a deep, slow breath.

"And then, I got hit in the chest with mud. There was more than one person and they were laughing. It seemed like it came from all directions, all at once. It was cold and gritty. It hit my arms, my dress, my face. A stone cut me." She motions to a tiny scar on her cheek. "It only lasted a few seconds, but it felt like forever. I fell down and I begged them to stop. And I cried."

She's not crying now. Her eyes are dry and far away.

"I didn't even realize it had stopped at first. I stayed there on the ground for a long time. I couldn't believe you had done this to me—and I was so angry with myself for believing you. Eventually, I stood up, wiped myself off as best I could. I knew I'd have to walk past the auditorium. And of course, it was just my luck that the entire senior class was outside when I did."

I remember seeing her—her eyes wild and wounded. I didn't know what had happened, and she wouldn't talk to me.

"You looked so horrified, Brent. So devastated—and when you wrapped your jacket around me, I almost believed you really didn't have anything to do with it. But then Cashmere came up, offered me a tissue, and pretended to be so sympathetic. I could see in her eyes that she was laughing, but she sounded really convincing. So I knew you must have been a part of it too."

I can still hear her, her voice a raw whisper when she told me, *"You're sick. There's something wrong with you. Stay away from me. Just . . . stay away."*

"Then Vicki and Brian came and took me to the infirmary, then back to our room."

And there it is.

Rage makes my hands shake on the table. So fucked up.

Did I say sometimes kids are assholes? No—sometimes they're sociopaths. And apparently I was dating their queen.

"I should have followed you," my voice scrapes out. More than anything, I want to go back in time and kick the shit out of my seventeen-year-old self. "That night—I should have gone with you to the infirmary. I've always regretted it."

She says nothing.

"When I went to your dorm the next morning, you were gone."

"Claire came to get me," she answers quietly. "She tore into Headmaster Winston on the phone and convinced him to let me finish my classes online."

"I waited for you—all summer, I kept going to your house. You never came home." It's important that she knows I looked for her.

"Claire and I spent the summer in Europe. The whole thing actually made us closer."

"I didn't know."

Her head tilts to the side and she shakes it in doubt. "Brent, come on . . ."

I just barely keep myself from shouting. "Why would I lie? After all this time—all these years, what could I *possibly* have to gain from lying to you now? I wouldn't do that to you. *I didn't know.*"

But still Kennedy's not convinced. "The messages—they came from your school account."

"It had to be Cashmere. She was always in my room, and she knew all my passwords. She was the only one who . . . would want to hurt you like that."

There's never a good reason to lay your hands on a woman. But if my ex-girlfriend was here now, I'd have a hard time holding to that.

Kennedy's face is blank as she examines the evidence from all angles. "How did she know about the kiss on the roof? I didn't believe it was really you, until that moment."

I rub the back of my neck; the muscles are tight and knotted. "Maybe I told her about it at some point? Or during one of the stupid Truth or Dare drinking games we used to play. Somebody probably asked me about my first kiss."

Her eyes soften just a bit. "You considered me your first kiss?"

The corner of my mouth quirks. "You were a girl, your lips were on my face—so yeah. I've always remembered it that way."

She nods.

Slowly I reach out and cup her jaw, holding her. "Do you believe me? I need you to believe me, Kennedy."

She searches my eyes. "I don't know. All these years, I was so sure. Now . . . talking to you . . . what you say makes sense." Her jaw goes tight. "But I won't be anyone's fool ever again."

I drop my hand, drain the rest of my beer.

Kennedy's silent for a moment. Then she says, "I'm ready to call it a night. Can we get out of here?"

I hear her. Revelations are fucking exhausting. I feel like I've taken a sledgehammer to the chest. Bruised and drained.

"Sure." I throw the bills on the table, slide my chair back, and hold out my hand to her.

Out on the sidewalk, I offer to grab Kennedy a cab.

"My place is only a few blocks away. I'll walk."

"Okay, then I'll walk you home. Lead the way, Lassie."

She cracks a smile and pushes her hair behind her ear. "You don't have to—"

"Yeah, I really fucking do, okay? Just . . . let me do this. Please."

She looks at me, eyes crinkling, nose scrunching up, like I'm a puzzle she's trying to figure out. It makes her look younger—cuter.

"All right. I'm this way."

We walk side by side in easy silence, and about ten minutes

later, we arrive. The house looks like a Victorian dollhouse, with a rounded tower on one side, a wraparound second-floor balcony, arched windows, and a spiked wrought-iron fence framing the roof. The same fencing surrounds the big corner lot. The house needs a paint job, new shutters, new steps where the old ones are sunk and uneven—but there's so much potential. With a little love, it could be magnificent.

"I'm having it restored—which is about as miserable as it sounds when you're living here," Kennedy says. "But it'll be worth it. My Aunt Edna left it to me."

My head turns sharply. "Aunt Edna died? Shit, she was cool. Why didn't anyone tell me?"

Kennedy nods. "You were on a skiing trip—I overheard someone talking about it at the wake. Your mother probably forgot to mention it when you came home."

I look back toward the house. "I'm glad she left it to you." Then I grin, easily imagining her as a kid in that big old house with its cobwebs and secrets. "I bet you had a blast going through the attic."

Her eyes widen. "I did, yeah." Bull's-eye.

Because people really don't change when it comes to qualities like that. A love of adventure, of exploration, even if it's of the past. She hasn't changed.

"Maybe you can give me a tour sometime?"

She still looks a little wary, distrustful of my intentions. Old habits die hard, and this one's gonna go down screaming.

She unlocks the front door, then turns. "Good-bye, Brent."

I run my hand down her arm, 'cause I just can't help myself. "Good night, Kennedy. I'm . . . I'm glad we talked.

Cleared the air. And if I didn't say it before, I'm really fucking glad you're home."

Her smile is small—but it's there.

"Me too."

I give her arm a gentle squeeze, then walk down the front steps toward the gate. Halfway there she calls, "Brent?"

I turn around.

"This doesn't change anything. About the case, I mean. On Monday, I expect you to come at me with everything you have. If you go easy on me it'll mean you don't respect me—that you think I can't handle it. And I'd never forgive you for that."

I give her a quick nod and she goes inside, closing the door behind her.

My eleven-year-old self was right: girls are weird.

• • •

I wake up earlier than usual on Saturday, with the echo of Kennedy's words in my head. Curiosity rubs me raw, like two jagged sticks sparking a fire. So I skip my morning run and spend an hour in my home office doing online research.

It's amazing, and kind of fucking frightening, how much of our personal information is floating around out there, and how simple it is to access. After I get the info I wanted—an address just an hour outside of DC—I tap the address into Google Maps, then I head out.

When I knock on the door, I hear muffled voices inside, then the sound of walking feet.

And then the door opens.

And Victoria Russo, Kennedy's old boarding school room-mate, stares at me. "Brent Mason?"

I nod. "Hey, Vicki."

She looks good, almost exactly the same. Her laugh lines are a little more pronounced, but her shoulder-length hair is still jet black with a streak of bright blue, her nose is still pierced with a diamond stud, and she still has that sharp, no-bullshit-taking shine in her eyes. The last time I saw her she tried to kick me in the balls.

"Why are you here?" she asks.

I look her straight in the eyes. "I need your help."

9

Ten minutes later, Vicki sets a coffee cup down in front of me at her kitchen table. She has a nice house—a family house—in a development with green lawns and brick-paved driveways and swimming pools in yards lined with arborvitaes to have some privacy from the neighbors. Her kitchen's huge, with mauve-colored walls and cream cabinets. There are framed pictures all around—some of dark-haired little girls, some of Vicki and Brian Gunderson.

Brian was a student at Saint Arthur's too. A tall, lanky kid who sagged his pants, listened to Snoop Dogg, and attended on scholarship. I remember seeing them together around campus—he was her date the night of the senior dance . . . and it looks like they're married now.

In the den off the kitchen, there's a cluster of book covers with shirtless men in various stages of embracing equally hot, half-naked women. And the author is V. Russo.

"You're a writer?" I ask, sipping my coffee.

"Yeah. I write romance."

I glance at the pictures again. "Brian's a lucky guy."

She chuckles. "Yes, he is." Then her expression turns thoughtful. "A romantic hero with a prosthetic leg would make for an interesting story."

"Well, if you need a technical advisor, give me a call." Then I ask, "Do you still talk with Kennedy?"

She lifts one perfectly penciled brow. Then calls down the hallway, "Louise! Come here please."

A tiny little thing, maybe about five years old, with long black messy hair walks into the kitchen and stands next to Vicki. "Yes, Momma?"

Vicki crouches down next to her. "Louise, this is an old classmate of Mommy's—Mr. Mason. Can you say hello?"

The little girl smiles, not at all shyly. "Hello, Mr. Mason."

"Hi, Louise."

"Can you tell Mr. Mason your full name, honey?"

"Louise Kennedy Gunderson."

I nod in understanding. "That's a beautiful name."

Vicki pats her daughter's shoulder. "You can go back and play now, baby."

As Louise leaves the room, Vicki raises her coffee cup to her lips. "Kennedy's the godmother to all our girls. And she gets full custody if we kick the bucket, even though I have two married brothers and Brian has a sister."

That's going to make this conversation slightly more complicated, but it shouldn't be a problem.

"I assume Kennedy's told you about our court case?" I ask.

"The case where she's wiping the floor with you? Yeah—heard all about it." She smiles a little too broadly for my liking, but I let it go.

"She also told me about your chat last night. How you proclaimed your innocence." There's a bite to her words at the end.

"I didn't have anything to do with what happened to her at the dance."

"You had *everything* to do with it. Your girlfriend and her friends made life hell for Kennedy because of you—and you did nothing."

"I didn't know it was that bad."

"You knew enough."

And I've got no comeback. Because she's right. It's easy to look back, with the knowledge and confidence of an adult, and see everything that we should have done differently.

My words are strong and demanding. "That's why I'm here. I need you to tell me what else I don't know."

She tosses back, "Why?"

My hand runs through my hair. "Because I don't think she will—not all of it. Because I want to make it up to her. Because, I feel like a black-out drunk who just sobered up, and I need to hear about the chunks of time I'm missing. Because . . . she was always the one."

Vicki rolls her eyes. "The one? Seriously? I'm a romance writer and even I'm about to gag."

I shake my head, trying to be clearer. "Didn't you ever have someone that you compare every other person against? This one's nice, but not as nice . . . that one's smart, but not as smart . . .

"She's always been in my thoughts, even when I didn't realize it. The one every other woman has gotten compared to, and fallen short. And I . . . I've missed her, Vicki. I want to know her again."

She stares me down, biting the inside of her cheek. And then she nods.

"Okay."

· · ·

For the next hour, Vicki Russo recounts two years of psychological and emotional torture. Some of it was schoolyard stuff—dirty looks and shoulder bumps. Some of it was more sinister—notes slipped under dorm doors telling her to kill herself, calling her ugly, freak show, worthless. It was calculated, organized, and relentless.

"Why the hell didn't she complain? Report Cashmere to the headmaster?" I ask, frustration in every word.

Vicki shrugs. "Lots of reasons. Call it the Pretty in Pink Syndrome—Kennedy didn't want Cashmere to think she'd won, that she'd broken her. Plus the bitch had her pack of mean girls behind her—if it came down to their word against mine and Kennedy's, who do you think the headmaster would've believed? And if she had reported it and the school sided with Cashmere, it would've gotten so much worse. Things like that always do."

Jesus fucking Christ

Somebody needs to burn Saint Arthur's to the ground. Scorch the earth and never rebuild.

My fists clench on the table. "Why didn't she tell *me*?"

"Because your head was so far up your girlfriend's snatch, Kennedy didn't know if you would've cared."

I pin her with my eyes. "I would have."

"She was embarrassed. You have to understand . . . you were everything to her, Brent. When you started to drift away . . . even if she couldn't have your friendship anymore, she never wanted your pity.

"It messed with her head for a long time," Vicki says. "I mean, Kennedy knows who she is, but it knocked down her self-confidence. How could it not? And her ability to trust— after what happened to her in college—that was obliterated."

I look at Vicki warily. "What happened in college?"

She flinches, not meaning to have said it.

Every statistic I know flickers through my head, and I go taut with preemptive rage. "Was she . . . was she raped?"

"I shouldn't—"

My voice rises. "If she was raped, Vicki, I swear to God I'm gonna fucking *kill* someone."

"She wasn't raped," Vicki assures me quickly. "She had a boyfriend in college—her first 'real' boyfriend if you know what I mean. A frat guy. They dated for a few months, and she thought they were in love. And then one day he told her that he'd started dating her because of a bet."

"A bet?"

She nods. "A competition at the frat. Who could bag the most girls—extra points if she was a virgin."

I rub my eyes. I don't know how women do it. I don't know how they even like any of us—a significant portion of the male population deserves to have their dicks cut off. And don't think I say that lightly.

"The sad thing is," Vicki continues, "the bastard genuinely ended up having feelings for her. That's why he told her—he didn't want to base their relationship on a lie. But after Kennedy knew, she broke up with him. And now, no one gets in. Me, Brian, and her sister—we're the only ones she trusts."

• • •

Later, at her front door, I thank Vicki for filling in the gaps of information. She's still unsure about me, reserving judgment, but I can live with that.

I say, "You're going to tell her I was here, aren't you?"

Vicki smiles. "In the spirit of full disclosure—I'm going to be on the phone with her before you get to your car."

• • •

On the drive back to DC, one thought sticks in my head like the blade of a knife: I never said I was sorry. All the shit Kennedy and I talked about last night, all the things we got straightened out . . . but I never said I was sorry. And I should have.

Because I am. And she deserves to hear it.

I didn't defend her when it mattered. I didn't stick my neck out for her. I didn't shield her. I didn't even try.

And it's the biggest regret of my life.

I think about the things Vicki told me. The shit Kennedy dealt with and, on some level, still has to live with. Kind of like my leg: it is what it is, and it doesn't stand in my way. But it's something I have to deal with every day. Part of what makes me who I am. A part I'll never get back.

And I think there's a part of Kennedy—a piece of her

childhood, her self-confidence—that's forever altered because of Saint Arthur's.

I need to tell her I'm sorry. It can't wait another day.

That's how I end up in the ballroom of one of DC's poshest, most look-how-much-money-I-have-because-I-can-stay-here hotels. It's a fund-raiser for David Prince, ten thousand bucks a plate. I had to call a few cousins who know a few people to get the last-minute ticket, but I got one.

Wearing my tuxedo—and looking pretty fucking James Bond, if I do say so myself—I weave through the tables, scanning the crowd, looking, looking. Prince stands at the front of the room, giving a speech. And I spot Kennedy in the back, near the bar. She's wearing a snug, strapless white gown that ends at her calves, accentuating sexy, strappy silver high heels. Her hair is down, a shiny curtain of gold.

She's talking to someone, smiling, just on the verge of laughing. And she literally takes my breath away.

As I walk toward her, she sees me approach. And she doesn't look anywhere else. When I reach her, the other person has stepped away, so it's just her and me, standing a few inches apart.

"What are you doing here?"

"I had to see you."

"I don't think—"

"I'm sorry, Kennedy."

Whatever she was going to say is lost in a breath. And there's a softening in her features, the slight curve of her mouth, the relaxing of her jaw that tells me she's relieved. That even if she didn't realize it, she's been waiting for this. Wanting the words.

"I should have stuck up for you. And I will always be

sorry that I didn't. I was selfish and stupid, and you deserved better."

She looks away, like it's all too much. But when her eyes turn back to me, there's a peace in them that I haven't seen for a very long time.

"Thank you."

And it's only then that I notice what's different about her. Why every cell in my body is content to just stand here and watch her.

It's her eyes.

The turquoise contact lenses are gone—her gaze washes over me in pure, breath-stealing brandy-colored beauty.

And even though she didn't know I'd be here tonight— I want to believe it's for me. Some kind of sign. Because those eyes are mine—the girl behind them, once, was mine.

And maybe she's willing to be mine again.

While I happily drown in the eyes I haven't glimpsed in so long, all the other eyes in the audience are focused on Prince. Microphone in hand, he works the room, his white teeth gleaming beneath the lights.

"And I can think of no other announcement more precious to me than to proclaim that the beautiful Kennedy Randolph is going to be my wife."

My head snaps up. "What did he just say?"

Kennedy's head snapped even faster. "*What* did he just say?"

The room explodes into thunderous applause.

I lean in so she can hear me above the noise. "You're *engaged*?"

Her head tilts. "No?"

"Sure about that?"

She doesn't sound very sure, and it seems like the kind of thing she should have the inside track on.

"David flew out to speak with my father last week. He said they had to discuss something important," Kennedy explains, her eyes squinting like she's trying to decode ancient hieroglyphics in her head.

"But he didn't actually ask you?"

"No. I guess he skipped that part."

The crowd comes at us like a tsunami, and Kennedy's swallowed up in a sea of well-wishers and carried away toward the front of the room.

I scowl so hard my face hurts.

The ever-elegant Mrs. Randolph appears beside me, in the spot her daughter just vacated, watching the hubbub with a smile.

"It seems congratulations are in order," I tell her.

"It appears so."

My gaze never wavers from Kennedy as she's ushered forward. And there's a pulling sensation in my chest, like my lungs have been snagged by a hook and they're being yanked out of my rib cage.

The feeling turns my voice scratchy. "Does she love him?"

Mrs. Randolph thinks for a moment, then she answers smoothly, "David is a fine young man. I believe he'll be president one day. He's an excellent match for my daughter."

"That's not what I asked."

She sighs. "Claire and I have always been close; we understand each other. But Kennedy . . . I fear she will forever be an enigma to me. What do you think, Brent? Is that the look of a young woman in love?"

Kennedy's standing next to Prince now. Black microphones are thrust at her, and bright lights illuminate her pale face and wide eyes.

In love? No.

Scared out of her mind? Absolutely.

She looks like a mouse caught in a trap, ready to chew its own leg off to escape.

I was a shitty friend to Kennedy in boarding school, I see that now. But you know something?

This isn't fucking boarding school.

I march forward, pushing and elbowing my way through the crowd. "Pardon me. Excuse me. Coming through."

Finally, I reach the unhappy couple. I nod to Prince. "How's it going, Dave?"

He looks a little confused. "Uh . . . fine, thanks."

"Good."

Then I scoop Kennedy up into my arms—and I run.

The element of surprise is on our side, several moments pass before anyone behind us thinks to react.

"What are you doing?" Kennedy squeaks.

"Saving you."

For a horrible second, I think maybe she didn't want to be saved. Until her arms tighten around my neck and her body presses closer. "Hurry. They're coming."

I pick up the pace and smile. "Relax. I've got you."

10

We burst out the side doors onto the sidewalk and haul ass down the block. Without breaking stride, I fish out my phone. "Harrison, meet me in the back of the building. Code *Fast and Furious.*"

Kennedy leans back to look at my face. "*Fast and Furious?*"

I shrug. "He's twenty-two; they all love those movies. I don't pretend to understand it."

Moments later, my Rolls comes screeching around the corner and stops at my feet. Shouting voices follow us as Harrison jumps out and opens the door. I toss Kennedy inside before diving in behind her. My trusty manservant floors it, as I'm sure he has done in his nitrous-oxide-booster-filled dreams, and we make our escape.

Kennedy faces me on the bench seat, breathing hard and flustered. "Oh my god! Oh my fucking god, Brent!"

I hold up my hand.

"If any situation calls for alcohol, it's this one." I press a button on the teak center console between the seats across from us, revealing the mirrored minibar with a crystal decanter. I pour two glasses of scotch, then hand her one.

And she chugs it like a frat boy during pledge week.

Impressive.

Kennedy exhales harshly, then opens her mouth to speak.

"Not yet." I refill her glass.

Which she summarily drains, flinching as the eighty-year-old liquor scorches down her throat. "Wooh."

I sip from my own glass and point at her. "Now go."

She exhales again. "Did that really just happen?"

"I think it did."

"David and I aren't even serious! We've been seeing each other for two months and we've lived in different states for half that time. He brought up possibly moving in together once, which was crazy enough—but never marriage. Who *does* that? Who announces to a room full of people—and *television cameras*—that I'm going to be his wife, without even discussing it with me?"

It's possible Davie-boy thought he was being romantic, but she won't be hearing that from me.

I shake my head. "What a prick."

"Right?"

I refill her glass again.

And she sips.

"Plus, I'm pretty sure he's screwing around. With an intern!"

I snort. "Who does this clown think he is—Bill Clinton? Next thing you know, he'll be playing the saxophone and not inhaling."

"Exactly!" Then she stares at her hands and her voice goes

softer. "The worst part is, it didn't bother me. Not even a little. That means something, right?"

"Shit, yeah. It means you should've kicked that asshole to the curb a long time ago."

As she finishes off drink number three, I can tell she's starting to get a little fuzzy around the edges. Just the slightest thickening of her voice. "But still—I can't believe I did that. When a man proposes, he deserves not to have you run away, doesn't he?"

I keep nursing my own drink. "Technically you were carried away, but, tomato/tomahto."

"My parents . . ." She smacks her palm to her forehead. "My mother loves David. She's going to be so disappointed in me."

"My father's been disappointed in me for years—it's not as bad as you think." I finish off my drink.

Time to move on to happier topics. "We should go out and blow off some steam. You've earned it. Call Vicki and Brian—we'll pick them up."

Kennedy gets Vicki on the phone and gives her the Cliffs-Notes version of our epic escape. From this end, it sounds like Vicki wasn't a huge fan of Prince either. And when Kennedy asks her if they want to come out with us, I hear Vicki's voice from across the car.

"Brian! Call your mother!"

And it looks like we're a quartet.

• • •

We end up at a college bar not far from Brian and Vicki's house. It doesn't look like any of the press followed us. After a few rounds, Brian Gunderson tries his hand at karaoke. He sings "I Can't Feel My Face When I'm with You" and his wife claps and dances the whole time.

A couple of rounds later, Kennedy goes for it. She sings "Fight Song," and while her voice isn't anything she should quit her day job over, her smoking little body wrapped in that white dress, swiveling and gyrating, gets her a standing ovation from every frat boy in the place—and there's a lot of them.

An hour before closing, I'm enjoying a good buzz and my three companions are totally hammered. Vicki begs Kennedy to do another song, but when she tries to climb on the stage, she ends up on her ass, laughing like a nutcase.

A college kid moves to help her, but I'm already there. I chase him away with a dark look, then I tell her, "Okaaay. Time to go, peanut."

"Go? But I like it here! It's fun."

I sweep her into my arms. Even at dead weight, she feels like nothing. "It's all fun and games until someone gets a concussion."

• • •

Brian climbs out of the car in front of their house. He rests his forearm on the roof and offers me his other hand. "Dude, we should do this again sometime—I'm so happy you're not the asshole you were in high school anymore."

I guess it's a compliment. At least that's how I choose to see it.

"Thanks, man. That means a lot."

Vicki gives Kennedy a bear hug in the backseat.

"I love you, Vicki!" Kennedy slurs.

"I love you, Ken-ken!" Vicki returns.

Then Vicki pokes my shoulder. "And you! You take good care of my Kenny! Don't make me hafta kick (*poke*) yer (*poke*) ass (*double poke*)!"

I give her a nod. "The ass-kicking days are behind us now."

"Good! Then there's somethin' you should know." Vicki's expression sobers, and she gestures me closer before ruining the effect by whispering loudly, "Kennedy hasn't had an orgamsum . . . orgamsam . . . Kennedy hasn't come in a loooong time. Like, years. At least, not with a guy."

"Shhhhhhh!" Kennedy swats her best friend like a fly. "Tha's a secret!"

"Maybe Brent can help you wif it?"

I give Vicki the thumbs-up—and it's not the only thing that's up, that's for sure.

"Don't worry, Vick, I'm on the case. And I believe in retroactive pay, so she'll be compensated for all the fun she missed out on."

With that, Brian helps his wife out of the car and into the house.

They were fun. Kinda nuts, in a way that makes me think they'd fit right in at one of my family functions—but still fun.

• • •

"Do you remember when we were fourteen and we talked about masturbating?"

This, however, is *not* fun.

"I asked you if you really did *that*, and you said, 'They cut my leg off, Kennedy, not my hand—I do it all the fucking time.'" She presses her face against my neck, dissolving in a fit of adorable giggles.

It started in the car. A slip of her hand, an innocent touch that didn't feel innocent at all. And the talking—*Christ*— Wasted Kennedy likes to talk.

"Then you asked me if I did it. And I said, 'Absolutely not.'"

About sex. All kinds of sex. Oral sex—she loves giving and getting it. Anal sex—never tried it, but she really, really wants to.

"I lied. I used to do it in my dorm room—quietly so Vicki wouldn't hear."

I carried her into the house. Harrison held the door open and closed it behind us—then he couldn't leave the room fast enough, his cheeks as red as Bozo's nose. I brought her to my place because if she gets sick, I want to be here to take care of her. Hold her hair back for her.

But Kennedy's not feeling sick at all. She's feeling very, very good.

She lifts her head and licks her lips, staring hungrily at my jawline. "And I always thought of you."

This is what hell is. Right here, right now.

She shifts, moves her legs so she can slide down my front to her feet—pressing her chest against me, rubbing her hips.

"I'd lay there in my bed, spread my legs so wide, and—"

I cover her mouth with mine so she'll stop talking. I keep it there, because she tastes really goddamn good.

We kiss for a few moments, and then I pull away, before I'm not able to.

"I want you so much, Brent."

She doesn't mean it, not really. She's drunk—I know that. My cock, on the other hand—he's not so sure.

"Make love to me."

Her voice is deeper and every word, every syllable, chips away at my tenuous control. Kennedy takes a step back, holding my gaze as her fingers slide over her glistening collarbone, down to her breasts, circling where her nipples wait beneath the white, silken fabric.

"*Please* make love to me."

Finally, I find my strangled voice. "We can't, baby." I grab her hand and kiss her forehead, smelling her sweet-scented hair. "You're drunk."

Her gorgeous, wounded eyes completely wreck me.

"You don't want to make love to me?"

Deflect! Deflect! It's a trick question—there is no right answer! Not now.

I cup her cheek. "You're drunk. We can't make love now."

She wraps her arms around my neck. And she sighs against me.

"Okay. You can just fuck me, then."

I whimper.

And I am not ashamed. Because if anything is gonna bring a guy to his knees, it's those six words, when—no, he *can't* in fact fuck you. 'Cause it would be wrong.

Awesome and earth-shattering. But wrong.

The fulfillment of fourteen years of erotic fantasies. But wrong.

Trumpets-sounding, angels-singing, fireworks-bursting-in-the-sky kind of pleasurable. But wrong.

I repeat the mantra in my head to make sure I don't forget. But it's hard.

So. *Hard.*

And the hits just keep on coming.

Kennedy reaches around behind her back, tugging on the zipper of her dress. A heartbeat later, the fabric slips to the floor, revealing perfect peaches-and-cream skin. Her breasts are bare and more beautiful than any dream I ever had.

Tight, dark pink nipples beg for my lips, my teeth, my tongue.

Then she turns, graceful hips swaying as she walks down the hallway. She pushes at the gauzy fabric of her beige panties and they fall down her legs to the floor.

Just like magic.

Revealing a luscious heart-shaped ass that deserves to be worshipped and glorified. I think I whimper again, but I can't be sure.

As she walks up the stairs, she doesn't look over her shoulder at me, doesn't call my name. She doesn't have to.

Because I'm already moving forward.

I follow her up the stairs to the bedroom.

And close the door behind us.

11

I wait patiently on the chaise longue in the corner, legs stretched out, watching her. Enjoying the pretty picture she makes lying in the middle of my big bed.

Without warning, Kennedy bolts straight up, so fast that her long honey-colored hair covers her face. She blows at it with a puff of breath, eyes darting around the room. She glances down at her body, covered in my black Spider-Man T-shirt—the one I had to practically put her in a headlock to get on her.

"Morning, cupcake." I smile.

She glares.

"Did you have sex with me?"

I tap my lips with a finger, contemplating her question.

"I can't decide if I'm more offended that you think we'd have sex while you were shitfaced—or that you actually think you wouldn't remember it if we had."

"You didn't answer my question."

I roll my eyes. "Of course we didn't have sex. Not from

any lack of trying on *your* part, by the way. I felt so objecti-fied. Does all alcohol turn you into a cat in heat, or just scotch specifically?"

If it's the latter, I'm buying stock in it. Maybe a whole company.

She covers her face and lies back on the bed. "Fuck my life. Fuck it hard."

"Let's be careful with the imagery—not sure I can handle a hard-on right now."

Or harder-on, if I'm being completely honest.

I check my watch. "We haven't even gotten to the best part yet. Three, two, one—"

My phone rings on the table beside me.

I bring it to my ear. "Hi, Mom."

News travels fast—and news of your children potentially hooking up with the person you picked out for them when they were three years old? That's fucking warp-speed fast.

My mother dives headfirst into the interrogation.

"Yes, she's right here." I smile at Kennedy, who peeks out at me from behind her hands of shame, looking miserable.

"No, Mom, we didn't elope. Sorry to disappoint."

I cover the phone with my palm and give Kennedy the bad news. "Your mother's looking for you."

She fully covers her eyes.

But she groans when she hears my answer to my mother's next question.

"No, Kennedy's not pregnant with my child. At least—not that I know of."

A pillow comes flying at my head.

And I respond to my mother's next question. "She didn't

officially say no to Prince's proposal—but the odds look pretty good it'll go down that way the next time she sees him." I laugh. "A picture, huh? I'll check it out. Yeah, I think we make a handsome couple too."

"Where's my phone?" Kennedy moan-hisses.

"Listen, Mom, I have to go, okay? Yes, I'll call you back later. No, we can't put this in the family newsletter. I love you too. Bye."

I tap the end button and watch as Kennedy drags herself to the edge of the bed. I tilt my head, trying to get another look at the paradise I glimpsed last night.

I've been a good, chivalrous guy. I think that deserves a reward.

"My mother says hi, by the way. Your phone is in your purse next to the bed, but it's dead—your mother killed it last night with call after unanswered call."

Kennedy's feet hit the floor. She takes a deep breath, then slowly stands. "They're going to disown me."

"Would that really be so bad?"

She limps toward the chair where her clothes are neatly folded.

"Father always wanted a boy. Mother never liked me. This is the moment they've been waiting for. They're going to disinherit me."

I stand, walking toward her. "I'll cover you with a loan. At very attractive interest rates—that's what friends are for."

Finally her eyes meet mine, and she looks so despondent my heart twists.

"My life is a mess, Brent."

I brush her hair back. "If you want to make an omelet, you

gotta break some eggs. And you, my Little Lush, deserve only gourmet. Your parents will get over it. Everything's gonna be okay—I promise."

. . .

Before I drive Kennedy home, I change out of last night's clothes into running shorts and a T-shirt. She climbs out of my car wearing my sweatpants. And even folded at the ankle and cuffed to death at her waist, they're about twelve sizes too large.

She looks fucking adorable.

As we get to her front porch, the rear door of a black SUV with tinted windows parked at the curb opens. And out steps David Prince—dark sunglasses on his face, his brown hair perfectly sideswept and visibly hair sprayed.

Though I'm annoyed that the bastard hasn't even given Kennedy the morning to process, I'm delighted that I'll be around for this little exchange. 'Cause I *really* want to watch her tell him to screw off. And if she's not feeling up to it, I'll do it for her.

I follow Kennedy through her door and Prince slips in behind me. He closes the door and they square off a few feet apart in the middle of a tastefully decorated living room. I position myself next to the beige couch, far enough away to let their confrontation play out but close enough to step between them if needed.

Prince looks predictably unhappy, but far from broken-hearted. The grin that graces his campaign posters is replaced with an ugly scowl. He throws his arms up from his sides, "What the hell, Kennedy?"

Kennedy's shoulders are back, her chin high—the same stance she takes in court, fearless and brash, ready to throw down.

"I could ask you the same thing, David."

"You humiliated me last night!"

"You humiliated yourself. The sympathy you'll garner will only help your polls—and we both know that's what you're *really* worried about. If you had bothered to ask me what I wanted—"

"I thought we were on the same page." He takes a step toward her.

But she holds her ground. "No, you didn't—otherwise you wouldn't have ambushed me."

"It was a surprise! A gesture of my affection."

"It was a sound bite!" Kennedy shoots back. "We both knew what this relationship was about. I was a pretty, professional face to smile next to you in your photo ops, and you—"

"Yes," he interrupts, stepping even closer. "What was I?"

"You were convenient. Someone I enjoyed spending time with, but didn't care enough about to be upset about your screwing the intern."

He pales just slightly and his eyes narrow. Then he moves to grab her arm, but I move faster. I wrap my hand around his wrist. And squeeze.

"If having a functioning wrist is important to you, you're going to want to step back. And calm down."

Dave drops his hand and I let him go.

He glares at me from head to toe, then he turns back to Kennedy and spits, "This is what I've been replaced by? A cripple?"

As Kennedy opens her mouth to tear into him, I throw my head back and laugh.

"Cripple, Dave? That's the best you've got? Not even gimp or stumpy or quarter-man? If you're going to insult someone, have the decency to make it a clever insult. Otherwise, you don't just look like an asshole—you look like a dumb asshole. Also, go fuck yourself, you entitled, parasitic, two-faced, bloodsucking prick."

David does his best to ignore me and looks at Kennedy with an expression that tries for persuasive, but falls short.

"We're good together, Kennedy."

She shakes her head. "Not good enough."

"We could've gone all the way to the White House. We still could."

How romantic. Does this douche want a girlfriend or a running mate?

"I like this house just fine. We're done, David. Good-bye."

And just like that, he gives up. If putting your fingers up in front of your forehead in the shape of a capital L was still a thing, I'd do it right now—'cause this guy is a *loser*.

He turns toward the door, but he only takes two steps before he turns back around. "I know you didn't sign an NDA, but if you even think of speaking to the press—"

"Are you serious?" Her tone is biting. "I'm not going to be speaking to anyone. I have important matters to deal with—airing your dirty laundry isn't one of them." She raises her arm, pointing at the door. "Now get the hell out."

To help him along, I open the door wide. "Bye-bye, Dave."

I let it swing closed with a bang after he walks out.

I move toward Kennedy, stretching my arms above my

head. "Well, I certainly feel better now that *that's* out of the way."

I thought she'd giggle; at least smile. But she just kind of collapses onto the couch—elbows on her knees, head in her hands.

I kneel down in front of her, rubbing my palms up her legs. "You okay, Sparkles?"

Weary eyes meet mine. "Sparkles?"

With two fingers I trace her collarbone, then show her the residual glitter from last night's festivities. That gets me a small smile as she says, "I'm exhausted."

I stand. "I'm sure you are. So . . . relax, take a bubble bath, take a nap, recharge—then be at my place tonight at six. I'm making you dinner."

Kennedy's eyes drag closed. "Brent . . ."

"I'm not as talented in the kitchen as Harrison, but I can hold my own." Lifting her chin gently, I tilt her head up. And my voice goes soft. "I want to feed you, Kennedy. I want to talk to you—and I want to kiss you again for a long time, knowing you'll actually remember it in the morning."

That bring s the fire back into those stunning brown eyes. "We *did* kiss last night!" Her finger jabs my thigh. "I knew it!"

"Technically, you kissed me. Attacked me, actually—and I'm not complaining." I lean down and press my lips to her forehead. "I just really, really want to return the favor."

Before she can say no, I walk to the door. Her voice stops me as I reach for the knob.

"What are we doing? I mean, what is this, Brent?" And she sounds genuinely curious.

"We're starting over. This is a new beginning."

"But the case—"

"We won't talk about the case," I reassure her. "We'll be grown-ups. Compartmentalize—there'll be no conflict of interest."

"Maybe I don't want to start over." She sighs. "There's so much between us, I don't know if a new beginning is possible."

"Then we'll talk about that tonight too. Six o'clock, doll-face. Don't be late."

• • •

I head over to the National Mall to run my favorite route. High-octane energy sparks along every nerve ending like I've never felt before. The adrenaline rush before a lacrosse game was similar, but this is *more*. Because I'm so psyched for tonight.

Two hours later, I walk through my front door to find Harrison dusting in the living room. I toss my keys onto the table. "Harrison, my good man."

He turns, a mixture of curiosity and mild surprise in his eyes. "Yes, Brent?"

I throw an arm around his young shoulders. "You know the Swedish au pair down the street who you've been crushing on the last six months?"

He gulps. "Jane?"

"That's the one. I know for a fact that tonight's her night off." I slap three hundred-dollar bills into his palm. "It's time to carpe diem, buddy. Take the car, take her out, show her a good time, and if you get lucky—go to a hotel. If you don't get lucky—spend the night at your father's. Whatever you do, don't come home."

He looks at the money in his hand, brows touching. "I don't understand."

"I'm having company tonight." This is the first time I've ever asked him to make himself scarce; usually I'm encouraging him to watch. So I spell it out.

"Kennedy's coming over. I'm making her dinner. Though you're always impeccably discreet, I want her to be completely comfortable, so we're free to talk about our feelings."

Talk.

Strip.

Break the furniture, dent the walls, and defile every surface in the house. Could be wishful thinking on my part, but like the Boy Scouts say, it's good to be prepared.

Understanding brightens Harrison's eyes. "Ah, now I see." He puts his feather duster down. "I should go change into something more appropriate for a visit with Jane."

I smack his back. "Go get her, tiger."

Doubt falls like a gray specter across his face. "Do you . . . do you think she'll say yes?"

I rub his head, messing with his hair the way an older brother would. "She'd be batshit crazy not to. You're a total catch."

Harrison smiles, looking more relaxed.

We walk toward the stairs near the kitchen.

"Would you like me to prepare dinner for you and Miss Randolph before I go?" Harrison asks.

I step into the kitchen and wave him off. "No. I want to do it myself."

"Very good, then."

As Harrison continues toward the stairs, I call, "There's just one small thing. How do I turn this stove on?"

• • •

By five fifteen, I have a simple lemon and chicken recipe in an "oven-safe dish" like the online instructions said, ready to go. I slide it into the oven and go take a shower.

By five thirty, I'm dressed in jeans and a long-sleeved dark blue button-down.

By five forty-five, the table is set—linen napkins, crystal glasses, china plates, silver utensils—Harrison would be proud. I turn the lights down low and put a bottle of white wine in the ice bucket to chill.

By five to six, I have the cooked chicken warming on top of the stove, hoping it tastes better than it looks. I light the candles on the table, sit on the couch, and wait for Kennedy to get here.

By six fifteen, I'm still waiting—but I've never met a woman who was actually on time, so it's all good.

By six thirty, I turn on the TV and use my handgrips as I walk around the room. Watching and waiting.

By six forty-five, I pour myself a glass of wine.

By seven, I risk looking completely pathetic and dial Kennedy's number. It goes to voice mail and I don't leave a message.

By seven thirty, I'm on glass number two. And I blow out the candles.

At eight, I thought I heard someone on the front step, but when I went to check, there was no one there.

By nine, it starts to rain hard, thunder and lightning galore. I lie on the couch, arm bent under my head, legs stretched out, shirt open.

But it's not until ten that I actually believe Kennedy's not going to show.

12

When I first open my eyes, I'm disoriented. I don't know what time it is, or how long I've been asleep. Then I realize I'm on the couch, it's still dark and raining outside—and as the recollection of Kennedy not showing for dinner hits me like a sharp jab below the ribs, the knowledge of what woke me up breaks through my foggy brain.

It was a knock on the door.

I walk to the door and open it, just in time to catch a petite blonde going down the steps.

"Kennedy?"

She stops on the sidewalk and slowly turns to face me. She's soaked through—her jeans molded to the curves of her legs, the sleeves of her white and navy striped sweater dripping, her hair flat, lips slightly tinged with blue.

"I wasn't going to come," she says.

My voice is drowsy and deep. "Yeah, I kind of figured that when you didn't show up." I open the door wider. "Come inside."

Instead, Miss Vinegar to my Mr. Water takes a step back.

"I don't know why I'm here." And she sounds genuinely bewildered—even a little panicked.

"Obviously because I'm irresistible." The wind blows, spraying ice cold drops across my bare skin where my shirt hangs open. "You're shivering, honey, come inside."

She stares at me, so many emotions swirling in her expression. She's like a skittish kitten who can't decide if she should let the stranger pat her head or haul ass up the nearest tree.

And it breaks my heart.

"I don't think I can."

So I go to her.

The rain is cold and hard, soaking my shirt. Her eyes dart from the sidewalk, to my chest, up to my eyes and back again, like she's ready to bolt—but her feet stay planted.

I lean in so she can hear me above the deluge. "Do you remember when I first learned to ride a bike again?"

The corners of her mouth tug up a little. "Yeah, I remember."

"And we only had your girly bike, so you sat on the handle-bars and I pedaled?"

She nods.

"And one day, I was going way too fast and we hit a rock, and both of us went flying. I didn't want to ride like that any-more, because I was afraid you'd get hurt. Do you remember what you told me?"

Her eyes meet mine. "I said . . . I said we had to keep rid-ing . . . because the ride was the only thing that made falling worth it."

I nod tenderly.

And she adds, "Then you called me a fortune cookie."

And we both laugh.

When our chuckles settle, I hold out my hand. "I'm not going to let us fall this time, Kennedy."

Her eyes are back on my chest. "I'm not sure—"

"All you have to do is take my hand."

It's like I was saying before—you never really know who someone is inside. That someone as magnificently ferocious in court as Kennedy could be hiding such a fragile, delicate soul. And don't think for a second it's because she's weak. The fact that she's even fucking standing here shows how strong she is. It's just . . . instinct.

We shy away from the things that hurt us—that have hurt us in the past.

That's what scars are for. They protect the wounds. Cover them with thick, numb tissue so we'll never have to feel that same pain again. The bottom of my stump is one big, hard callus.

But the scars Kennedy has inside? They're even tougher.

When she continues to stare at my hand, I plead, "Please, just come inside."

Slowly, tentatively, her small hand slides into mine.

And we go in out of the rain.

• • •

Her teeth chatter as she sits on the edge of my bed. I throw a blanket over her shoulders, rubbing her arms, sliding down to cup her hands.

"Jesus, you're freezing. How long were you out there?"

"Awhile. I was walking . . . thinking."

"Your family has more money than most small governments. Next time you go a-wandering, stop and buy an umbrella."

Kennedy shivers as she laughs. I pull the blanket closer around her and rub her back.

Her voice comes out soft and wavering in the dark room. "None of this is going like I imagined."

"Me neither. I figured I'd be busy getting you *out* of your clothes, not wrapping you up like a burrito."

That gets me another chuckle. "I meant coming home, seeing you again . . . I thought it'd be so different."

I hold her hands between mine, rubbing the chill from them. "Different how?"

"I knew we'd run into each other eventually. But when I saw your name on the Longhorn case, I thought it was fate. My opportunity for payback. I thought you'd be bowled over by my new look. Infatuated with me."

She can check that one off the list.

"I pictured flirting with you, toying with you—and then totally crushing you. You were going to be devastated. And I was going to laugh over the remains of your broken heart."

"You're a vengeful little thing, aren't you?"

Her eyes drift to the ceiling and she shakes her head at herself. "Sometimes. When it comes to my cases, the victims, I want to punish the people who've wronged them. But you . . . you're still you. And when I saw you . . . it all felt exactly the same. Like how it was before the dance, before I went to your dorm room that morning. Like I was seventeen again, just hoping you'd . . ."

Her words trail off and my chest clenches with that sublime mix of excitement and trepidation. Of wanting something so much it's like every cell in your body is stretching, reaching for it, yet there's a gray shadow of worry that you might never get to touch it. And keep it. That all you'll be left with is the memory of how great it could have been.

"Does that make sense, Brent?"

I swallow. "Yeah. Perfect sense."

I cup my hands around hers and blow into them. Another shiver vibrates through her.

"You have to get out of these wet clothes," I say gently, with no teasing suggestion.

Because we're right on the precipice. I can feel it. And I have to tread so carefully, because one wrong move could send Kennedy away, truly lost to me.

The room is quiet. I peel my soaked shirt off and let it drop to the floor. Only her eyes move, trailing over my shoulders, down the bronzed peaks and valleys of my torso. I stand and slowly unbutton my jeans, then push the heavy, wet fabric down my hips, sliding one leg out before bracing my hand on the bed to pull them over my prosthetic, leaving me in black boxer briefs.

Free of the cold, damp clothes, my skin feels hot. Like the surface of a furnace, warmed from the fire burning within.

Her wide brown eyes follow my every move, looking up at me. Waiting.

I push the blanket off her shoulders and let it drop to the floor. My tongue wets my bottom lip as I grasp her sopping sweater at the bottom and lift slowly, taking note of every inch of creamy skin as it's revealed.

Kennedy raises her arms. I pull the sweater over her head and it lands with a plop on the floor. I saw her naked last night, but that was different. I couldn't enjoy the view; I was trying too hard not to look.

But I look now.

And, oh, do I enjoy it.

Firm, round breasts encased in white lace. Her nipples, dark mauve and taut, tease beneath their sheer covering. Her collarbone is delicate, her shoulders and arms toned. Her stomach is flat, with a hint of muscle, and I bite the inside of my mouth—because I want to suck on that skin, slide my tongue across it, press my teeth against it until I hear her moan.

My chest rises and falls as rapidly as hers. I sink to my knees in front of Kennedy and reach for the button of her pants.

And I feel those gentle amber brown eyes beckoning, like a candle in the window that shows the way home.

She lifts her hips and my fingertips graze her smooth skin as I slide her pants down her thighs, leaving the tiny scrap of white silk panties in place. Her legs are beautifully sculpted and the perfect length to wrap around my waist, my shoulders . . . my neck.

Then I stand up and take it all in, gazing at the sweet image of her beautiful form perched at the end of my bed.

"Get under the covers," I whisper.

As Kennedy settles in the center, her head on the pillow, I sit on the edge of the bed and remove my prosthetic. Then I turn and slide under the covers beside her. Without a word, she molds against me. The cool feel of her flesh is a shock at first, but in just a few moments, my heat chases away her chill.

Except for her feet. I practically hit the ceiling when she runs one up my calf.

"You're like a fucking ice cube!"

She laughs kind of evilly.

We face each other, almost nose to nose. Her hair still drips at the ends and a drop trickles over her collarbone, down her chest, and I have to take a deep breath—because I want to lick it off her so badly.

"Talk to me," she says softly. "Do you . . . do you still talk to anyone from school?"

"No."

"Tell me about your friends. Your partners at the firm. What are they like?"

It's true that you can tell a lot about a person by the company they keep. Assholes tend to gravitate toward each other, making themselves look better or worse, depending on the circumstance.

"Stanton's a really good guy. Solid, you know? He tries to do the right thing—it's important to him—but sometimes he can't get out of his own way. But still, he's the kind of guy you could call if you've got a flat tire at 2 a.m. in the middle of a blizzard—he wouldn't hesitate to throw on his boots and come get you."

I see Kennedy's responding smile in the dim light.

"Sofia has three older brothers, so she's tough, but it hides a very soft center. She's passionate and funny . . . she's like the big sister I never had."

Kennedy's palm runs over my bicep—tentative at first—then with a surer touch.

"And Jake . . . you'll like Jake. He's really mean."

Her muffled laugh fills the air. "He's mean?"

There's a grin in my voice when I answer. "Totally. He puts

up this hard-ass front—and he *is* tough—but it's only because he doesn't want people to see how deeply he cares. He notices everything—every detail. And he'd happily commit murder for the people he loves."

"They sound like really good friends."

"Yeah, they're the best. I'm lucky."

We're silent for a few minutes. The thrum of my heartbeat jacks up as her hand continues to stroke my arm. *Up and down*, smooth and warm.

"Brent?" Her voice is the barest whisper, like she's checking to see if I'm asleep.

"Mmm?"

"I . . . I missed you so much."

And I'm done.

The need to kiss her, to touch her, has been pulling at me like a raging current ever since I saw her on my front step, and with those few words, I let the current take me.

I close the miniscule distance between us and press my lips against hers. She sinks into me with a sigh. Her mouth molds to mine—I cup her jaw with one hand, and she opens for my tongue to slide against hers. It feels unreal—sweet and amazingly familiar. I groan with the taste of her.

And it's like I'm seventeen again, back in that Ferrari. Hot excitement courses through my bloodstream with every pound of my heart. Need and desire; wanting to touch her everywhere, yet wanting to savor every second.

And suddenly I realize why what I felt back then was so powerful. It wasn't because I was a horny kid who couldn't wait to blow his load.

It was her.

This beautiful, sweet, strong girl in my arms. She got to me forever ago—under my skin, into my heart—and she's been there, waiting, ever since. And now she's here—in my bed—her skin flushed with excitement, her fingers gripping my shoulders, her teeth nibbling at my lips in a way that makes me almost lose my fucking mind.

Without breaking contact with her mouth, I raise up on one elbow so I'm hovering above her. Her stomach contracts under my palm as my other hand slides over it and comes to rest on one perfect breast. She fits beautifully in my hand, and when I squeeze its softness, Kennedy moans and sucks hard on my tongue, showing me how much she likes it.

I rub my hand in a slow circle, squeezing with my fingers, feeling the fevered point of her hard nipple against the center of my palm. And she whimpers in my mouth, arches up into my touch. I spread kisses from her lips, down her jaw, covering the spot on her neck where her pulse jumps with pleasure. I suction that skin, tasting the remnants of rain and sweat and that special flavor that is hers alone

She breathes hard, and her hands are everywhere—running through my hair, sliding down my back, kneading the muscles in my shoulders and arms. I lick my way up to her ear, scraping her lobe between my teeth, and my hand reverses course. Sliding back down with teasing slowness to where her pelvis is rising, looking for friction but only finding air.

And I'm going to take care of that for her.

When my hand settles between her legs, over her panties,

my fingers resting against her pussy, I rasp into her ear, "Is this okay?"

And she gives me the sweetest of all three-letter words.

"Yes."

My hand contracts, my fingers press against her opening—letting her feel the pressure, letting her imagine how fucking fantastic it's going to be when they plunge inside. A frenzied sound comes from her throat and her hips gyrate against me, begging for more.

"What do you want me to do, Kennedy?"

I slide my hand back and forth, teasing, taunting, stoking her fire.

She yanks on my hair. "Touch me."

She pulls my mouth back to hers, wild now, her tongue swirling and licking, wet and desperate. And my hand never stops its sliding motion. I can feel her clit now beneath the silk, swollen and reaching for release.

"More," she pants, her eyes squeezed closed. "Please, touch me more."

I move my hand up to her stomach, covering her belly button, and then I slip beneath that silk. And something about my hand being under her panties makes it even hotter.

A moment later I'm the one moaning, my eyes squeezed tight against the overwhelming sensation of Kennedy's smooth, bare skin sliding against my hand.

Oh fuck, she's so wet. And her heat is scorching and perfect. I want to drive my tongue deep into that heat—feel it wrapped tight around my cock.

Resisting that need, wanting to please her more, I slide two fingers between her swollen lips, but don't yet plunge inside. I spread her wetness on her clit, around her opening, rubbing tight circles that make Kennedy's legs spread wider.

"Like this?" I tease against her neck.

Her mouth opens on a moan.

But then she turns the tables on me. Her hand dips into my boxers, wrapping around my dick and squeezing with the perfect amount of pressure, stopping just short of pain.

And then she strokes up—twisting her wrist at the tip. And I feel light-headed, drunk on her touch, and thirsty for more.

Kennedy presses her head back against the pillow, away from my lips, until I open my eyes and look into hers.

And then she smirks. "Like this?" she asks in a teasing tone.

Her thumb traces the tip of my cock, sliding back and forth, moving the precum to her palm for lubrication—but not yet stroking again. Because she's waiting for my answer.

I grin down at her. "Faster."

She doesn't hesitate. Her slick hand pumps me in smooth, firm jerks—and my eyes want to roll back in my head, it feels so goddamn good. But I keep them focused on Kennedy.

Waiting for her answer.

And she orders, "Deeper."

My two fingers instantly slide into her pussy. And I groan, because she's wet, fucking heaven. Her muscles squeeze my fingers as they drive in and out, in perfect time with her stroking hand.

My thumb finds her clit and she keens, arching her neck—pressing into my touch.

And then I'm kissing her again. Because when she comes—and by the feel of it, she's close—I want to taste her moan.

My hips thrust into her tight hand. My tongue delves into her warm mouth. My fingers rub and plunge. And I feel the tightening in my balls, the tingling in my spine, the carnal pressure low in my gut.

Fuck, I'm going to come so hard. And I want her with me when I do. I want us to shatter together, 'til there's nothing left of her or me. There'll only be *us*.

And then Kennedy's pussy clenches tight around my fingers in silky, rhythmic contractions, again and again. She comes with a scream against my lips—and I let out a long, serrated groan against her. Wave after wave of intense pleasure streams through me as I pulse in her hand and come on her stomach.

For several long moments, we gasp and pant, holding on to each other. Spots float before my eyes—because it was just that fucking intense. With a contented sigh, Kennedy rests her face against my arm. I lean down and kiss her lips sweetly.

When it's time to clean up, I'd love to just rub my come into her skin and call it a night. But I'm guessing it's too soon for that.

I use the crutches leaning against the wall to head into the bathroom, and return with a warm, wet cloth. Kneeling beside her, I wipe her stomach. She follows my intimate movements with glazed, drowsy eyes and a small satisfied smile. She giggles when my fingers tease her rib cage.

Then I toss the rag and collapse in the bed next to her. She eagerly comes into my arms, and we both fall asleep.

• • •

A few hours later, gray morning light is just peeking through the shades when my eyes crack open to see Kennedy standing in the middle of my room. Jiggling her ass into her wet jeans.

It takes a few seconds for my mouth to get the message from my brain.

"What are you doing?"

She turns sharply, like she wasn't expecting me to wake up. "I have to get home. I have to shower and get ready for court."

With a yawn, I say, "Okay, I'll drive you."

"Don't bother. A cab will be faster."

Ahhhhhh. Sweet, cuddly, open Kennedy has left the building.

Defensive, jumpy, prickly-like-a-cactus Kennedy is in the house.

Goddamn it.

When she grabs her soaked sweater from the floor, I offer, "Do you want some dry clothes? You don't have to—"

"No thanks." She yanks the sweater over her head and smiles tightly. "Wet clothes aren't going to kill me."

I sit up—wide awake now. My voice rings clear and sharp. "Kennedy."

She freezes like a doe caught in the crosshairs of a rifle's sight—and looks at me like I'm the hunter.

"We need to talk about last night," I tell her.

"Let's not, and say we did."

Then she walks the fuck out.

I cup my hands around my mouth. "I'm so glad we agreed to be grown-ups about this. That's working out great."

Her only answer is the closing front door.

I throw myself back, pick up a pillow, and hold it over my face, trying to smother the frustration that is Kennedy Randolph from my mind.

It doesn't work.

Looks like this is gonna be One Step Forward, Two Steps Back.

Screw you, Paula Abdul. I never liked you.

13

I think about Kennedy the rest of the early morning. Occasionally, like during my long XXX-rated shower, I think about her in those teeny lace panties and matching bra.

Though out of them would be more accurate.

But mostly I just think about her. By the time I arrive at the courthouse, I come to the obvious conclusion that Kennedy has issues. Deeply rooted, steel-reinforced, gonna-be-a-mother-to-frigging-conquer issues.

But it's okay. I've been in and out of therapy for twenty years; if anybody knows about issues, it's me. Actually, this demonstrates another way that we're perfect for each other. We're soul mates. Destined to be together, written in the stars, Bogie-and-Bacall perfect.

Kennedy doesn't see it yet—but that's all right. Because I'm patient. And relentless. When I set my mind on something, there's nothing I can't do.

And my mind's on her.

I want to figure her out, to learn every part of her—the soft curves, the sharp edges, the dark, shadowy corners she tries so hard to hide. I want to break down her doors, climb her ivory tower. I want to slay all her fucking dragons.

She probably won't appreciate it at first—but eventually she'll come around. It'll be great.

• • •

Kennedy's not in court when I arrive. I sit at the defense table, my hand on Justin's shoulder, filling him in on today's strategy and reassuring him that I've got his back, that it's all going to be okay. It seems like I'm the only adult in his life who gives a shit; his parents aren't here yet.

Five minutes before court is scheduled to begin, I feel her. I know it sounds corny and absurd—but it's true. The air becomes charged and drags my gaze toward the door. When she appears in the doorway, a barricade goes up in my lungs, caging my breath. Her suit jacket is dark burgundy, the color of a deep, red wine—high collared and short waisted—perfectly tailored for her petite form. The matching skirt molds to her hips and thighs, falling just above her knee. Sheer black silk stockings and sky-high heels finish the outfit. To the casual observer it's a polished, professional look. But because I know the smooth skin and sweet curves encased within, it's a teasingly erotic delight to me. Sexier than any Playboy bunny ensemble.

Are her panties black? Red? Lace or silk?

My dick thickens when I consider she might not be wearing any at all. *Even better.*

Kennedy walks into the courtroom like a queen walking

toward her throne. Her long hair is pulled back into a low bun, with one rebel strand brushing the delicate skin below her ear. And I remember how succulent that exact spot tasted last night, like sweet, ripened fruit.

Just before she turns toward her table, she spares me a glance. Her face shows only professionalism, but in her eyes, need and indifference, affection and trepidation, all swirl in their depths. She looks lost. And my chest clenches with the fierce desire to protect her, to encourage her—to promise her that everything is going to be all right.

I'm going to make sure of it.

I give her an easy, reassuring smile, and something like relief passes over her features. Her returning nod is formal, then she gets settled at the prosecution table.

After the judge calls us to order and runs through the pre-liminaries, dear old Mrs. Potter resumes her place in the witness box. I stand up to continue my cross-examination, buttoning my charcoal-gray suit jacket, and I wonder if things will be different between Kennedy and me in court from now on.

If *she's* going to be different.

Kinder. Gentler. More . . . friendly.

Halfway through my second question to Mrs. Potter, Kennedy hops to her feet.

"Objection!"

Okay—guess that answers that.

• • •

The moment the judge smacks his gavel to adjourn us for the day, Kennedy's high heels click briskly as she grabs her briefcase and dashes past me out the door. My eyes follow her, but the rest of me sticks around to offer Justin a ride home, because neither of his parents showed today. An hour and a half later, Harrison drops me in front of the U.S. Attorney's building. I take the stone steps two at a time and make my way to Kennedy's closed office door.

Her secretary says she's in a meeting. A stealthy glance through the window tells me it's an important meeting, considering there's four serious-faced, lawyerish-looking men in suits hunched over in deep discussion around her desk.

"I'll wait." I tell the secretary.

I hate waiting, especially when I have an ass spanking to deliver. And in this case, I mean that every way it can be taken.

I sit in the empty chair outside Kennedy's door, my right knee bouncing and my head tilted back against the wall.

After forever, her door opens and the parade of men exits. The last one out, a burly, gray-haired guy, nods to her. "We'll speak soon, Kennedy."

"Yes. Keep me informed." She nods back, her face set like a seventeenth-century plaster bust. That was a very unhappy era for ceramics.

I wait until the last man turns the corner, then I step into Kennedy's office, closing the door behind me. She sits at her desk, staring down at a file like she wants to set it on fire with her eyes.

I reach behind my back and lock her door. Then I pull down the blinds, concealing us from the outside world. If Kennedy picks up on my actions, she doesn't show it.

I stroll toward her desk, doing my best Heath Ledger–Joker impersonation. "Why so serious?"

Kennedy sighs, still glaring down at the file. "My mob case from Vegas just got kicked back on appeal. Moriotti got himself a new trial."

I lean against the corner of her desk. "Are you going to retry him?"

"Absolutely. The son of a bitch deserves to spend the rest of his life in a cold, dark hole, and I'm going to be the one to put him there."

My whistle is long and impressed. "In case I haven't mentioned it before, that vengeful streak is damn sexy."

She doesn't laugh. She doesn't smile. "I really don't have time to talk right now."

"Yeah . . . I don't particularly feel like talking either. But—"

Surprising her, I yank her chair out, spin it around, and brace my hands on the arms, leaning down. Caging her in.

For a hot second I'm distracted by the way her chest heaves, the way her eyes round, and her lips part—just wide enough to slip my tongue in. My cock would require her to open wider— and that thought's pretty damn distracting too.

"*But*—whether we want to talk or not, it looks like I need to lay some ground rules." My gaze burns into hers and my voice is almost as hard as my dick. "Rule number one—you don't set one pretty toe out of my bed without waking me up first. Ever."

I lean in and skim my nose up the delicate line of her neck, then I drag my tongue down the same path to her pulse point—wrapping my lips around it and sucking—hard enough to leave one bitch of a mark.

But . . . that's the price she pays.

"I jerked off twice in the shower," I hiss against her skin.

"And I was still hard as a goddamn rock watching you in court."

That little tidbit gets me a nice whimper. But I'm not done. "And I swear to Christ, I could still smell you on my fingers. It drove me crazy all fucking day."

I tilt back until I'm looking into her eyes. They're lit up with heat and sublimely stimulated.

"Stop looking at me like that," I bark.

"Like what?"

"Like you want me to kiss you. I'm not going to kiss you, Kennedy—I'm pissed off at you."

She squirms in her seat, her eyes flickering between my lips and my Adam's apple, rubbing her thighs together ever so slightly. And a groan catches in my chest—because she apparently likes me being pissed off at her.

Jesus, the fun I could have with that.

But I stay focused. "Ground rule two—we talk. Not about the case, but everything else is on the table. No more running away."

Her throats constrict as she swallows—and I can almost hear her heart pounding. Or maybe it's mine.

"Three—we take this one day at a time. You're freaked, there's shit between us—I get it. I won't ask for more than you can give me."

Her brow crinkles. "Brent, I don't think—"

"You say that a lot. You seem confused, so I'm going to make it real easy for you. Four—I'm coming to your house tonight. I'm bringing food. We'll hang out. If we happen to spend a good portion of that time without any clothes on—we'll roll with that too. Say yes."

She's silent for several heartbeats, making me hold my breath.

Then she relents. "Yes."

"Good girl."

Her eyes narrow at me. But because I'm so pleased—because I've wanted to all damn day—I eat my own words, lean in, and kiss the fuck out of her. It's hard, demanding—and infused with every ounce of possessiveness I feel for her. A teeth-clashing, tongue-lashing kiss that leaves her trembling.

I'm a big believer in a well-timed exit. During final summations, the last image you give to the jury, the final words you leave ringing in their ears, are the most powerful. They can make a difference between an acquittal or a life sentence.

And that kiss was one hell of a closing.

So I stand up, turn, and stroll out of Kennedy's office.

• • •

Just before sunset, I stand on the rickety porch of her Victorian house and knock on her front door. It swings open almost immediately, like she was waiting for me. Kennedy stands in the glow of the fading sunlight wearing worn, light blue jeans that hug her hips and show off her sweet ass in a fantastic fucking way. Her top is loose and thin strapped, a layer of white lace over a layer of chiffon, the neckline dipping to a low V that puts her pert, braless tits on perfect display.

With my mouth watering, and my imagination raging, I mutter, "I'm sending Justice Bradshaw a thank-you note."

She giggles and I feel her eyes trail up my own faded jeans, over my black T-shirt, pausing right where the short sleeves wrap tight around my biceps. "You look very nice too."

Meow.

Peeking out from behind Kennedy's calf are two big black eyes attached to a puffball of gray fur. Cats aren't my favorite animals—they come in behind dogs, pot-bellied pigs, and the cutest creature God ever created: the hedgehog. But, unlike my possible-future-serial-killer freshman-year college roommate—who tried to run over every stray cat that crossed his path—I don't hate them either.

"Who's this?"

"That's Jasper."

Meow.

I crouch down and reach out my hand. "Hey, Jasper . . ."

"Brent, wait—"

But before I can heed her warning, Jasper's eyes transform into sharp slits and his paw slashes at my hand like Wolverine on a bad day. One claw nicks my middle finger.

"Bastard!"

"So sorry," Kennedy coos.

I shake my hand, then stick the tip in my mouth, tasting blood.

"I hate to be the one to break it to you, but your cat's a dick."

She takes my hand, inspecting my injury. "He's just wary of people he doesn't know. Like a guard cat." She glances behind her. "Jacob and Edward are a lot friendlier."

"How many do you have?"

She shrugs. "Just the three."

I nod slowly. "I came back into your life just in time. Old

house, multiple feline companions, an inappropriate interest in vampire books that were meant to be enjoyed by teenage virgin girls." I pinch my thumb and forefinger together. "You realize you're this close to becoming a full-fledged Cat Lady."

Kennedy sticks her tongue out at me.

I smirk. "Do that again later; I'll demonstrate much better uses for that tongue."

She laughs, shaking her head as if she thinks I'm kidding.

"All right, let's get going," I tell her. "We've got a walk ahead of us."

Her brows crinkle. "I thought you said you were bringing food?"

"I did. But I didn't say we were eating it here."

I hold out my hand, and she puts hers in mine. It's warm and soft and a perfect fit.

"Where are we going?"

I lean down and whisper in her ear, raising goose bumps along her collarbone. "It's a surprise."

• • •

We walk through the city beneath the pink-orange dusk sky, hands entwined. We pass the World War II Memorial and the Reflecting Pool across from the glowing warmth of the Lincoln Memorial, weaving between the picture-snapping, map-studying tourists that are a permanent fixture. And then we reach the Tidal Basin, its calm, still waters reflecting the soft orbs of the lampposts that illuminate the circling path around it. In the spring, the trees here are laden with cherry blossoms, making a thick light-pink wreath around the water, but by this time of year, the blossoms have all fallen, leaving only healthy greenery on their branches—the promise of next year's bloom.

I lead Kennedy off the path closer to the water's edge, where a flannel blanket awaits us on the grass, lit lanterns stationed at each of the four corners. In the center are a bottle of white wine and two picnic baskets—one with cutlery, plates, and napkins, the other insulated to keep the containers of Chinese takeout inside it warm. I wasn't sure what kind of Chinese food she liked, so I ordered a variety. The surrounding shrubbery sequesters the spot from the path—it feels like from the entire city—creating our own personal oasis. Our own little world for just her and me.

Kennedy stops, taking it all in. The light from the lanterns shines in her sparkling eyes and her smile takes my fucking breath away.

"This is . . . it's beautiful, Brent. Thank you."

My thumb traces her bottom lip. "That smile is all the thanks I need."

Then I rethink that statement.

"Well, maybe not *all* the thanks." I wink. "Let's see how the night goes."

And then we eat and drink, talk and laugh. Kennedy tells me about her scuba-diving trip to Belize this past spring and I tell her about my kayaking excursion in Alaska last year. I talk to her about the men's lacrosse league I play with on the weekends and her face lights up as she tells me about her Sunday garage-sale antique hunts. We catch up on each other's relatives and the latest gossip about distant family acquaintances. We tell each other stories—funny, horrifying, raunchy stories about college and law school.

Basically, it's a really fantastic date. The kind that would play in a montage with some terrible pop song in the background if this was a cheesy romantic comedy. The kind a guy would tell his friends about the next day—even if he didn't get laid.

The hours go by without either of us realizing it, and by the time we walk back up Kennedy's front porch steps, it's after midnight. We're both relaxed and smiling—and her cheeks bloom with the loveliest flush of good wine and great conversation.

She unlocks the door and asks, "Do you want to come inside?"

Inside, back, stomach, mouth—I want to come everywhere she'll let me.

"For 'coffee'?" I tease, making air quotes with my fingers.

Her eyes darken to simmering chocolate brown. "No, but I could give you a tour. Show you how the restoration is going. We were able to keep all the original moldings."

I grin. "I know how that goes. First it's 'come see my moldings' . . . then it's 'tear down my Sheetrock and take a look at my brickwork, big boy.' And if I'm lucky, you'll let me peek under your carpet for some floor action that'll make us both lose our minds."

She chuckles. "Don't forget the fireplace—do you want me to show you my mantel, Brent?"

"You bet your sweet soffits I do."

• • •

The house is an awe-inspiring combination of top-of-the-line modern convenience and gleaming old-world charm. We talk about the wood beams she's keeping exposed in the den, and the hidden Bluetooth-capable speakers that will be installed in every room. She shows me a tiny drawing room with original wallpaper, which if you look at very closely contains hidden images of naked women and men.

That's the Victorians for you. Repressed perverts.

Then we go upstairs, to her bedroom.

The lighting is low, but welcoming—one lone crystal lamp on a mahogany bedside table. The walls are beige with a warm, deep red accent wall behind the bed. Kennedy's actual bed is humongous, a four-poster with a thousand big puffy pillows that make me think of cumulous clouds. It's the kind of bed you'd want to stay in for days—and with the way Kennedy is looking at me, that might just be the plan.

I stop in front of the fireplace, running my hand along the impressive marble mantel. "This is nice."

Kennedy watches me from just inside the closed door. "Yes . . . it is."

When our eyes meet and hold, it's like we both just know. No words are needed. Good or bad, right or wrong, everything that's happened in our entwined lives has led us here—to this moment.

My voice is deep, rough. "Come here, Kennedy."

She steps forward straight into my arms. I lift her right off her feet, holding her against me. Her hands bury in my hair, tugging a bit, then holding on tight.

And we kiss like it's the end of the world.

The air goes thick around us and time stops as our mouths slant, our tongues fuck, our throats moan and hum with a desperate urgency. Kennedy arches in my arms, her head tilting toward the ceiling when my lips traverse the pristine expanse of her throat.

"Brent . . ." She gasps, fingers running through my hair. "This is real. Tell me this is real."

My eyes jerk up to hers and I cup her jaw in one hand. "It's real. This is so real I can't stop shaking."

She searches my face . . . and then she smiles. Because she believes me.

And the emotions that swell in my chest, my feelings for her—they're indescribable. It's like . . . piss off Jack Dawson . . . I'm the king of the world now.

I slip one strap of Kennedy's top down her arm, far enough to expose one pale, flawless breast. I bend my knees, pepper the soft mound with kisses, and close my lips over the hard, tight bud of her nipple. Her moan is deep and long with approval as I suck on that hard point. Worshiping it with my tongue, tracing, caressing, and flicking.

Without breaking contact, I wrap my arms around her hips and lift, carrying her to the bed. I lay her down, sucking and laving her with my mouth. She grips the back of my shirt and I release her nipple with a pop, lifting my arms so she can pull my shirt off. Her hands scorch their way across my torso, fingernails digging. One strap of her shirt gives way as I yank it down her body in a fast tug, leaving her bare from the waist up. My eyes roam and consume—so much pale, perfect flesh.

I kiss her stomach, licking and grazing with my teeth—working my way up. Kennedy arches and moans, her hands driving into my hair. The heat of our skin, our bare chests rubbing—it's almost too much—and yet not even close to enough. Back at her mouth, I nip her plump bottom lip with

my teeth, then cover both her lips with my own. Relishing
the taste of her wet, sweet mouth, her soft, slick tongue . . .
her whimpers and moans. Feeling my way blindly, the button
on her jeans is released and with her help, I strip them off her
legs—panties and all—leaving her bare.

The desperate need to look at her gives me the strength
to rise up on my knees beside her on the bed, but my fingers
never lose contact with her flesh. They trail up her rib cage,
cupping her breasts, teasing those beautiful nipples, tracing her
collarbone, skimming down her arms. My eyes are everywhere,
memorizing each detail—the pink flush of flawless skin, the
hint of rib bone, the soft indent of her pelvis, the smooth,
immaculate canvas below—and best of all, the bare, plump
lips of her glistening pussy.

My eyes threaten to close with a groan as the image is
scored into my brain, but I force them open. I grasp Kennedy's
ankles and pull her around, spreading her legs for a better view.
I groan again—long and low and guttural—as my hands rub,
and my fingers dip inside her, making way for my mouth. I lie
down on my stomach, my breath against her skin, my fingers
opening the pink flesh.

"Christ, Kennedy, your pussy is so fucking pretty."

She moans at my words.

"This is made to be kissed and licked and fucked all damn
day—and night."

I press my open mouth against her skin and she screams.
My tongue searches, pierces—and now my eyes do roll closed.
Because her taste is sweet and wet and hot. I could lose myself
in her cunt. This could ruin me—because I don't know how
I'm going to function without thinking about these ripe,

smooth lips. So soft, so fucking delicious. My mouth moves rough over her—inside her. My beard is scratching the tender skin on her thighs, probably leaving bright pink abrasions, and the thought turns me on even more.

My nose rubs her clit as I suck and flick my tongue in the paradise between her legs. And when I move up, when my tongue rubs against that swollen nub, Kennedy's hips jerk, and she comes against my mouth—legs trembling—crying my name.

I barely pause to let her recover. I turn my head and suck on the skin of her thighs—definitely leaving a mark this time. I lick my way to the sensitive indentation just below her pelvic bone. She takes big, gulping breaths and pulls at my shoulders.

"Come up here." She pants. "Kiss me, Brent."

And I happily oblige.

Her hands caress my face with tender, loving touches. Then she pushes on my chest with surprising strength until I'm up on my knees. When I'm where she wants me, she yanks frantically at the button on my jeans. A frustrated grunt escapes her, making me grin.

But when she gets them open, my grin turns into an open-mouthed groan. Because she doesn't mess around—she pulls my pants down just low enough to free my hard, straining dick, and then she's all over it. She lathers the shaft with her tongue and lips, wetting the delicate skin, sliding up to the tip and slipping the fucker all the way into her hot, wet mouth.

My hips jerk, and I have to brace my hand on her back to keep from falling over.

"Shit . . . fuuuuck . . ."

The curses fall from me as Kennedy goes to town on my

cock. Swirling her tongue fantastically around the tip, bobbing her head, sucking on me so hard it may bring on cardiac arrest.

Wouldn't that be the fucking way to go?

The back of her hand scrapes against the open zipper of my jeans when she cups my balls, massaging them, then adding a playful tug that sends electric pleasure shooting up my spine. She's really good at this—too good. Because when my hand burrows into her soft hair to do some nice tugging of my own, she hums around my cock—and the vibrations bring me right to the edge.

And as glorious as it feels, as much as I want to go through life with her mouth permanently wrapped around my dick . . . no . . . *no* . . . I'm not going to come in her mouth.

Not the first time.

If Kennedy and I had actually "done it" all those years ago in my father's Ferrari, it would've been the slow, gentle, sweet kind of lovemaking they write about in books.

There's nothing slow or gentle about us now.

We're devouring each other—kind of crazed—beautifully fucking wild.

But there's still a tenderness, because we want to be closer, kiss deeper, make each other feel so much better than good. My fist tightens in her hair, pulling her off my cock, until we're chest to chest, face-to-face.

And she practically growls at me.

I kiss the hell out of her and laugh against her lips. "Hoover seems like a pretty fitting nickname at the moment."

Kennedy gazes into my eyes and laughs back, and, Christ, she's so beautiful it hurts.

Then she lies back with the delicate grace of a butterfly

landing on a leaf, leaning up on her elbows. Her eyes rake me up and down and her voice goes husky. "Take your pants off. And come here."

That would be the command dreams are made of.

"Yes, ma'am."

I turn my back to her, sit on the edge of the bed, and pull my pants off. I take the three condoms out of my wallet. Then I pop the pin on my leg and slip it and the liner off, because it's easier to move around the bed without it catching on the sheets. And I plan on moving a whole lot.

Kennedy's impatient, because instead of lying back and waiting for me to come worship her, she peppers a hot trail of kisses up my spine. She moves to my neck and her breasts press against my back, making me groan. I turn and slide my hand behind her neck, holding her still as I plunder her warm, eager mouth. My other arm slips around her waist, hoisting her against me as I rise to my knees.

Needy little moans and whimpers echo from her mouth to mine. Then she surprises me—pushing on my shoulders and taking us down to the bed so she lands on my hard chest with a soft *oomph*. She plants a kiss on one pec, then grins sexily as she rises up.

"I want to look at you."

And look she does—with hungry eyes and exploring hands.

But then—something fucking weird happens. I swallow hard, and it tastes like self-consciousness. Vulnerability. I imagine this is what women must feel like—if they have stretch marks or cellulite or a spare tire around the midsection. Something about their body they would change if they could.

Here's the thing—I got past any issues with my leg and

women a long time ago. It doesn't bother me, and the girls I've
been with have been more interested in my long, thick third
leg, if you know what I mean.

But—if I'm being honest—my lack of a lower limb is . . .
odd. It's . . . missing. Your brain tells you there's supposed to
be more. You naturally expect to see two full legs, but the one
just . . . ends.

My chest rises and falls rapidly under Kennedy's roaming
gaze. And I don't know if it's the expression on my face, or
some small unconscious movement—but she reads my fucking mind.

"Do you know what I think of when I look at you, Brent?"

My response comes out scratchy—rough. "What?"

She caresses my abs, my arms, up both legs. "I don't think,
'Oh, Brent is so strong,' even though you are. I don't think,
'He's survived so much,' even though you have." She looks into
my eyes. "I just think—*perfect*. You're . . . perfect."

And I didn't realize how badly I wanted to hear those words
from her—until she gave them to me. I grab her arms and pull
her down, putting every wild, sweet, insane emotion I have for
her into a kiss.

Enough talking. No more gazing or caressing. We need to
fuck—now.

I roll her over so I'm above her—pressing and grinding
her into the mattress. Kennedy's movements are as unbridled
as my own—fingers scratching and pulling, hips gyrating, legs
wrapping, thighs squeezing so hard I can barely breathe. I
reach for a condom wrapper on the bed, tear it with my teeth,
and expertly roll it on one-handed. Bracing on my elbow, I

slide my cock through her bare nether lips, groaning at the wet heat I can feel even through the latex. Kennedy's hips cradle me, her legs spread wider, beckoning me—and then I slide smoothly into her.

For a long moment, I don't move. I'm inside *Kennedy*. She's so beautifully fucking snug. I let her body stretch around me, get accustomed to my size while I relish the tight clench of her muscles—the feel of her slick cunt wrapped around my full length.

Then I look down into her heartbreakingly beautiful brown eyes—and I move. Withdrawing and pumping, flexing my hips in a slow, steady rhythm. Her lips are parted, sweet breath escaping with every thrust. Our noses rub, and then I give into the pure sensation—closing my eyes, capturing her mouth—riding her faster.

Kennedy's tongue dances against mine and she moans against my lips.

"I knew . . . I knew it'd be like this. Yes . . . oh yes, Brent."

Her hands grip my ass, pushing me deeper. My mouth scours her neck and my hips quicken—driving harder—circling between her thighs each time I'm buried fully. I'd be embarrassed by how fast I feel the surging blissful pleasure of my orgasm coming on if I didn't know she was right there with me. Because it's so fucking good.

Perfect—like she said.

Kennedy's pussy clenches around me with her own building pleasure. I circle my hips harder, faster, rubbing my pelvis against her clit. And then thought becomes impossible. With a high-pitched moan, she contracts so hard around me it's almost painful. I push in deep with one final thrust, coming so hard that the blood rushing through my ears drowns out the sound of my groans.

Slowly, my ability to hear returns. Kennedy's hands slide up my back, soft and almost . . . grateful. I lift my face from her neck and open my eyes. She blinks up at me.

I feel like I should say something, something meaningful and profound. But she's screwed me stupid—robbed me of words. So I kiss her lips—softer now, reverently. And I feel her joy as she holds me close against her and doesn't let go.

14

We don't sleep.

We start to, but then light kisses turn deeper, gentle touches morph into greedy grasps, and despite the exhaustion that pulls at us both, we fuck all through the night.

Kennedy spends a lot of time on her stomach in the prelude to round two, because I've become obsessed with her ass. The round firm feel beneath my hands, the smooth, supple sensation as I trace the globes with my tongue, the gorgeous way it jiggles as I pound into her from behind. I dig my fingers into it, leaving a dusting of light bruises on the heart-shaped flesh. I scrape and nip it with my teeth, I kiss and worship it with my lips. If Kennedy's ass were bronzed, I would prostrate myself before it and pray.

During our third trip around the bases, she rides me. She took a few equestrian lessons back in the day, and boy, were they worth their weight in gold. She gets herself off and I find the view of that position particularly delightful. The way her breasts bounce when she drives down onto my cock, the way her elegant back arches as her hips swivel, and the sublime, stunning look that sweeps over her face when my orgasm triggers hers, and she comes for the second time with my name on her lips. *Gorgeous.*

Kennedy doesn't stock condoms, so after round three we're all out. But that doesn't stop us from going for it one last time. Though it takes a little persuasion at first, she straddles my face and I make her come with my tongue buried deep inside. Then she lies back, totally spent, as I slide my cock between her breasts and fuck them slowly. She garners just enough energy to lift her head and suck on the tip, and she moans when I come hard all over her.

I can't recall much after that—but I'm fairly sure I collapsed on top of her, and we both passed the hell out.

• • •

I'm pulled from well-earned slumber by the feel of a wet, rough tongue lapping just behind my ear. It tickles, and there's a smile on my face before I even open my eyes. I roll to my back, expecting to find warm brown eyes gazing adoringly at me— and see almond-shaped, midnight-black eyes staring back at me from a long-whiskered, fluffy white face.

Meow.

I feel another wet tongue on my leg, and glance down to see a brown-and-black calico practically making love to my knee. My throat feels dry and a little sore—probably from all the breathy groaning. I force down a swallow and look back at the snow-white fluff ball curled beside my head.

"You must be Edward." I assume because of his pale coat,

as opposed to the feline farther down—who's probably Jacob, because his fur is more wolf colored.

And yes, I'm fucking horrified that I know that.

I scratch the cat's head and sit up, rubbing my beard, looking for Kennedy.

And I see a note on the bedside table, propped against the lamp.

Had to go into the office. See you in court this afternoon.

A *note*? Is she fucking kidding? After last night—the kissing, the grinding, the plethora of goddamn orgasms—I get a *note*?

I don't think so. Not. At. All.

• • •

I stomp through my front door and take a shower in record time. Harrison offers breakfast, looking at me the same way the Avengers regard Bruce Banner right before he goes full-out Hulk. I shove an omelet down my throat, grab my briefcase, and march out the door with my shirt only half buttoned and my tie hanging from my neck.

Ten minutes later I slam into Kennedy's office—locking the door behind me and snapping the blinds down.

She smiles brightly from behind her desk, hands folded. "Hey."

My scowl weighs on my face. "Do you not understand the concept of ground rules?"

Kennedy's smile goes from bright to bewildered. "What?"

I stalk her slowly, purposefully. "You're a Yale graduate, so you must understand the concept. The only conclusion I can come to is that you purposely broke those rules this morning." I lean over her, and the pulse at her neck thrums faster. "And broken rules have consequences, little rebel."

She fidgets nervously under my gaze, but there's excitement in her eyes.

Anticipation.

Lust.

"I wasn't running, Brent. I got an email. There've been developments in the Moriotti case and I had to come in early . . . to work . . ."

Her words trail off as she stares at the hard line of my mouth.

I nod. And slowly slide my tie from around my neck.

Then in one quick move, I hoist her out of her chair and plant her ass in the middle of her desk.

"Brent—"

She doesn't say anything else. She can't, because I slip my tie between her teeth and knot it behind her head. Not too tight, of course—just secure enough to keep it in place.

And muffle her sounds.

Can't have anyone hearing us. Professional image and all that.

"Apparently I didn't make myself clear enough yesterday." I reach under Kennedy's skirt and yank her panties off, shoving them into my pocket. "I'll remedy that now."

I push her legs apart, drag her forward, and drop to my knees.

My tongue touches her first, tracing her already slick slit.

My lips quickly follow, kissing and sucking that pretty, pretty pussy. Kennedy leans back, moaning low and long, one hand braced on the desk behind her, the other burrowing through my dark hair.

I make love to her cunt with my mouth, the way I wanted to when we woke up this morning. And I fuck her with my tongue—'cause I'd wanted to do that too. With time of the essence, I pay hard, hot homage to her clit, pressing and rubbing—scraping just a bit with my teeth. It stiffens against my tongue, enjoying the attention. Within five minutes she's writhing against my face, hissing around the gag and right on the razor edge of a massive orgasm.

That's when I stop. And calmly sit back on my heels.

I stand, unzip my pants, and take my cock out, stroking my erection with a tight fist. Kennedy watches me with wide eyes.

"Did you want to come?" I ask with raised eyebrows.

"Humph."

I nod, still jerking myself off. "Only women who follow the rules get to come."

And now she looks pissed. *Really* pissed.

"But if you say you're sorry—I'll let it slide this time."

"Thrry," she mumbles, looking anything but.

I tilt my ear toward her. "I couldn't make that out. Try again?"

"*Thrry*," she growls.

My brow furrows, then smooths in exaggerated realization. "Oh—you can't say sorry, can you? Cause there's a gag in your mouth." I tsk my tongue. "Sucks to be you."

She takes a swing at me, closed-fisted and fast.

I catch her wrist and hold it at her lower back, standing between her knees—my dick wedged against the soft fabric of her blue silk blouse. She comes at me with her other hand, but I catch that one too—locking them both behind her back with one hand.

Her eyes slice over my face. "Uck ooh."

I give her a great big smile. "Now, *that* I understand. And I don't mind if I do."

I grip my dick at the base, lean forward half on top of Kennedy, and thrust inside her to the hilt. She feels fucking beautiful around me. I pump into her without mercy and her eyes slide closed. She rests her forehead against my jaw. I release her hands to hold her hips, pulling her closer.

You'd think she'd take off the gag, but instead her arms wrap around me, holding on for the ride of her life. It only takes a few minutes to build her back up—till I feel the telltale pulse of her muscles, hear the high-pitched keen of her breath that says she's about to get off.

And my hips grind to a halt. She tries to do the job herself—jerks up against me—but in her position, that's not going to get it done.

"If I wake up and you're not next to me, I'll tie you to the goddamn bed." The needy, desperate thread in my voice diminishes the effect of my threat. "And I'll do this for hours. I won't leave you hanging, because I'm not that mean. But I'll make you beg, and I'll make you scream before I let you come. And that's a fucking promise."

I tongue her ear, swirling the shell, ending with a kiss. Then I untie the gag behind her head. "Now say please."

She bites my ear. Hard.

I jerk away and laugh. "Easy there, Mike Tyson."

I pull out just an inch and nudge my hips forward, teasing her. "Just say please, Kennedy. For both of us. It's gonna be so fucking good."

I feel her lips on my cheek. Against my neck. "Please, Brent. Oh . . . please."

And that's all it takes.

I pound into her, hurling us toward the edge and plunging straight over. We come together, groaning and grasping, like two wild, mindless things.

It's frigging awesome.

Breathing hard, I don't move for a few minutes—not until my heart slows back to normal. Then I stand upright and straighten her clothes. After tucking my dick away, I wag my finger at her. "I hope you've learned your lesson. I'm going to keep your panties for the rest of the day as a reminder."

She doesn't look happy with me. And after the monumentally hot experience we just shared, that's unacceptable.

So I hold her face in both my hands and kiss her gently. My thumb strokes her cheek. "Last night was the best night of my life. I would've told you that this morning, if you'd bothered to wake me up before you left."

Her anger melts away, changing into something that looks more like cautious glee.

I kiss her forehead and step back, licking my lips—still tasting her. "I'll see you in court, Counselor."

I give her a wink and walk out the door, a much happier camper than when I entered it.

• • •

In court that afternoon, Kennedy's distracted. Off her game. Maybe it's because she's not used to getting laid in the workplace. Maybe it's the fact that I took custody of her panties—and finger them in my pocket throughout the session, just for my own perverse pleasure. Whatever the reason—she has a bad day.

And she holds me responsible for it.

I know this when she shows up at my place that evening, walking right in unannounced. Harrison makes her a stiff drink, which she downs in two gulps—glaring at me the whole time.

She returns the empty glass to my butler, and with the practiced tone of a woman who was raised in a house full of servants, tells him, "Thank you, Harrison. We won't be needing you for the rest of the night."

Then she turns those blazing eyes on me. "Brent—I'd like a word. In private."

I gesture with my hand. "Lead the way, firecracker. Where you go, I'll follow."

She leads us to my bedroom. And the second the door is shut, she slams me up against the wall. And tears my clothes off.

Which gives me all the motivation I'll ever need to best her in court every day. 'Cause if this is how she handles it? There is no stronger incentive than that.

• • •

A few days later, at lunch with Jake, Stanton, and Sofia, I fill them in on Kennedy.

The three of them stare at me. Blankly.

Then Jake shakes his head a little, like he's trying to clear his thoughts. "Let me make sure I have this right. You're banging the prosecutor on your case?"

I swallow a mouthful of turkey club. "Yep. Well, sometimes we bang—sometimes we just hang out."

Like yesterday—at Kennedy's house, we curled up on her couch and watched a movie. She picked it out: *Mad Max: Fury Road*. And if I didn't know she was a fuck-awesome woman before, after that choice I was completely sure of it. We cuddled and made out—she let me touch her boobs—which was hot. But that was it.

"Sometimes we talk . . ."

Like the night—after a thoroughly satisfying angry-screw—when Kennedy told me about those developments in the Moriotti case. They were big ones. The FBI caught some chatter of a threat against the prosecutor on the case. Kennedy. Moriotti put out feelers—a lucrative payment—to any lowlife scum who'll take her out. This is pretty common in Mafia cases, to try and intimidate prosecutors from going forward. The agents don't have any concrete evidence of a plan, but they've assigned her a federal marshal security detail just the same. Just in case.

"And sometimes we make sweet, sweet love."

Stanton clarifies, "And it doesn't affect how you're trying the case?"

"Nope. We go at each other hard all day in court, then we go at it harder all night in bed. And nothing about it isn't awesome."

"And the prosecutor is your childhood friend, who you

pretty much fell in love with when you were seventeen but didn't see again for fourteen years?" Sofia asks as she runs her hand up and down her husband's arm.

They're getting along better these days, since the Great Compromise. Stanton agreed not to give Sofia shit about her unrestricted access to all our clients, as long as Sherman, their giant Rottweiler, was right next to her when she did. Needless to say, not a single client has even raised their voice above a whisper since then.

"That's right." I pop a french fry into my mouth. I've been burning a shitload of calories lately—gotta replenish.

Jake leans forward, still looking like he doesn't quite understand. "And you want to have a relationship with her? A real one?"

I shrug. "We're not exactly picking out kids' names yet—but that's where it's headed, yeah."

I've already got my list made out—and *Waldo* is at the very top.

"And Kennedy feels the same way?" Sofia questions.

I take a gulp of soda. "More or less. She has issues. I'm working on it. She'll come around."

Stanton rests his elbows on the table. "Are you sure it's not just the thrill of the battle that's making you so hot for her?"

I frown. "Definitely not—why would you ask that?"

Sofia carefully answers, "Because besides your parents and your therapist, we're the longest relationship you've ever had."

Huh. So they are.

Stanton nods. "Exactly. And you said she's got 'issues.' So my question is—if you win, how is she going to handle not just losing her first DC case . . . but losing it to *you*?"

I haven't thought about that too much; I've been preoccupied with all the awesome screwing. But I probably should.

Suddenly, I'm not so hungry anymore.

• • •

Later that day, I'm in Waldo's office. It's not our usual day, but he squeezed me in.

"You're very quiet." He regards me patiently from behind his glasses. "Quiet and . . . still."

Like I said before, I usually think better on my feet. But there's so much action going on in my fucking head at the moment, all I can handle is sitting on the couch.

I lean forward, bracing my elbows on my knees. "Do you really think I have intimacy issues?"

A light goes on in his eyes; the proud gleam of realizing that weeks, months, years of work is about to pay off—that I'm on the verge of an epiphany. "I wouldn't have suggested it if I didn't think it was true."

I rub my beard, really thinking about it for the first time.

"But why do you think that? I have great relationships with my friends, my family—I'm a good boyfriend, a thoughtful, generous lover . . ."

He explains, "When it comes to your romantic endeavors, Brent, you make a concentrated—if unconscious—effort to maintain emotional distance. In your words, you keep it 'light' and 'fun' because you consider life too serious. You don't seek out true partners, just women with whom you can pass the time. Imagine a frozen pond. You skate across on the surface, never even thinking to delve below to see if the foundation beneath the ice is solid. It doesn't concern you, because you don't plan on staying in one place long enough to let yourself fall through."

He's right, and it's worked really well for me . . . until now.

"Do you know why I do that?"

He nods. "Yes."

Then nothing.

Fucking therapists. All about the head games.

I lift an eyebrow. "Care to share with the class?"

He clears his throat. "You experienced a severe trauma at a young age. Unlike most teenagers, you never underwent the 'invincibility phase'—the time in an adolescent's life when they hold the unreasonable belief that nothing bad will happen to them, regardless of any unhealthy behavior. Because you knew all too well that bad things do happen. That safety is an illusion, and awful events strike at random, through no fault of our own.

"The loss of your leg left you with two impressions that you carry with you to this very day. The first is that life is unpredictable and cruelly short. So you seize it, squeezing in as many experiences as you can, accomplishing goals with almost frenetic energy—because you never know when your time will run out.

"The second, which is emotionally counterproductive to the first, is you guard your feelings—for women in particular. You keep a tight rein on your affections because you never know when *their* time will run out. And the pain of possibly losing someone you love—that is your greatest fear."

His words bounce around in my head. And they sound spot-on.

Which doesn't mean I have to believe them.

"I've met someone." I take a sip of water from the glass on the table in front of me. "Well . . . I've become reacquainted with someone would be more accurate, I guess."

Now it's Waldo's turn to sit forward. Because he's never heard me talk about any woman in the tone I'm using right now.

Serious. Desperate.

I tell him all about Kennedy. About our childhood, boarding school, the Longhorn case, and everything that's happened between us since I saw her again at that party. I tell him how much I want to make things work with her, how I want to protect her and fulfill her every dream. And mostly, I talk about how badly I don't want to screw it all up. Including the Longhorn case.

After I've caught him up to speed, I ask, "Do you believe in soul mates, Waldo?"

He does the eyeglass-cleaning thing. After he slides them on his face he replies, "I think the more appropriate question is—do *you* believe in soul mates, Brent?"

"I do now." I try to put my surging thoughts into words. "All these years, Kennedy's never let anyone else in. She has her reasons, but the bottom line is, there hasn't been any guy who's gotten past her fire-breathing dragon. And what if . . . what if the reason I've never let myself fall in love with a woman is because I didn't have anything to give? Because I'd already given my heart to *her* when we were seventeen years old? And all these years . . . I've just been waiting for her to come back to me with it."

We're silent for several long moments; the only sound is the ticking of the antique grandfather clock.

"What do you think about that, Waldo?"

Slowly, he smiles at me with pride. And confidence.

"Well, Brent—I think of our two theories, I prefer yours."

15

"**G**od . . . yessss."

Kennedy's hips jerk as she rides me—the smooth strokes turning rough and desperate. I palm one tit, pinching the pointed nipple, while I suckle the other enthusiastically.

"Oh . . . *oh!*"

Her chin falls to the top of my head as she comes, her muscles milking my cock mercilessly—and I explode inside her with an unrestrained shout.

A few minutes later we lie tangled up—her head on my chest, our slick limbs and sweaty torsos clinging to each other in a soothing way. My fingers slide up and down her arm.

And I think.

Kennedy rested her case against Justin Longhorn a few days ago. I put my new computer expert on the stand the following day, to at least suggest some form of reasonable doubt. Now, all that's left is Justin. He'll testify in his own defense . . . and then it'll be done.

And I wonder if this is how Serena Williams or Peyton

Manning feel when they compete against their siblings. So fucking conflicted. I want to win the case—for Justin, for my own throbbing sense of competition. Yet I don't want Kennedy to lose.

I blow out a breath and start with, "So listen . . . I know you think you're winning the case . . ."

Kennedy's voice is velvet to my ears, the way she always sounds after I give her three orgasms. "I don't *think*. I *know* I am."

I squeeze her arm gently. "Right. But, the thing is, tomorrow—your case is gonna implode. I'm going to put Justin on the stand, and there's no way a jury will send him away for twenty years after they hear him testify. You haven't given them the option of a lesser charge, so it's going to be twenty years, or an acquittal. You need to make a plea deal with me, Kennedy."

She sits up and stares at me like she doesn't recognize me. "You rotten bastard!"

And you know how the *rest* of that conversation went. She takes a swing at me, I toss her clothes out the window, etc., etc.

· · ·

"Now listen up, buttercup."

I look down at her beautiful, infuriated face, locking my eyes with hers.

"I'm falling in love with you."

Kennedy goes completely still beneath me.

And I shake my head. "No, I *am* in love with you. When I look at you, think about you, I can't decide if I want to fuck you, strangle you, or just hold you in my arms. Usually all three. And if that's not love, I don't know what is."

She opens her mouth to argue, but I don't give her the chance. "You're everything I've been searching for, before I even knew I was looking. I pushed the plea deal because it's the right thing to do for the case—and because I'm terrified if I win you'll hold it against me. And I already have so much to make up for."

Her chest heaves, like she's sprinting—and in her head, she probably is.

"Let me up, Brent. Let me up right now."

I release her wrists and climb off, sitting next to her, my leg hanging over the bed. Kennedy sits up, but doesn't move from the space beside me. I can practically see the wheels spinning in her head.

I tuck her hair behind her ear. "You don't have to say anything back."

It'd be fucking nice if she did—but she doesn't have to yet.

When she speaks, she focuses on her folded hands in her lap. "This is all happening so fast."

"I know. It's fast, but it's real, Kennedy." I take her hand. "*We* are real."

She stares at our hands, but doesn't hold mine back. It lies like a weight in my palm.

"I care about you, Brent—you must already know that. I don't . . . I don't know if I have it in me to love you. I'm not sure I'm capable of it. I dreamed about being with you for so long . . . and then, after school, I let that dream die. Cremated it. Buried it. Sunk it to the bottom—"

"Yeah, thanks—I get the picture."

Her eyes tighten. "I think . . . I like it buried, Brent. It makes everything easier. My relationship with David and the relationships I had before were easy. I could enjoy them and then move on when they were over, because they didn't affect me. They didn't alter my life or who I am."

I think about Waldo and frozen ponds.

"You like skating the surface."

Her forehead wrinkles, not understanding. So I clarify.

"If you never dive in the deep end, you never have to worry about drowning."

She nods slowly. "Yeah. It's like that."

Kennedy withdraws her hand and stands up. She rubs her eyes and sighs. "I'm going to go home and think, okay?"

Am I disappointed? As fuck.

Beaten? Not a chance in hell.

I know where she's coming from—more than she'll probably ever understand. And like I said before, I'm patient. I'm relentless.

I don't believe for a second that she's incapable of loving me. There's too much passion between us—so much feeling. I think she might even love me already.

I just have to help her see it.

Kennedy faces me, her posture taking on a more professional air—even though she's still gorgeously bare.

"And there's not going to be a plea deal. I'm sticking to the plan I have. If I change that now, I'll always wonder if it was because it was the best choice for the case, or because I let my feelings for you sway me."

I nod, resigned but not really surprised.

"Okay."

She picks up my shirt from the bed, starts to slide her arms in, but I hold up my finger, stopping her. Then I open my bedroom door and there, in a neatly folded pile outside of it, are Kennedy's clothes. Like I knew they would be.

Kennedy chuckles a little when I pick them up and hand them to her. Then she calls out into the hallway, "Thank you, Harrison."

I should really pay him more.

We're both quiet as she gets dressed—minus her bra. Just can't bring myself to feel bad about that.

Then she approaches me, reaches up on tiptoes, and kisses me softly. "I'll see you tomorrow."

She will. It's our final matchup. Our Battle Royale. And when it's done, only one of us will be left standing.

• • •

"I call Justin Longhorn to the stand, Your Honor."

Justin adjusts his navy tie, smooths his hands nervously down his tan slacks, and takes the stand. After he's sworn in, he looks at me and I give him an encouraging nod.

"How are you doing, Justin?"

He swallows hard. "Not so good."

I gesture around the courtroom. "It's kind of crazy, isn't it? How quickly the legal system can move . . . swallow you up in its cold, hard machinery?"

Kennedy rises. "Does Mr. Mason have a relevant question for the witness, Your Honor?"

I glance back at her—eyeing her sweet legs beneath her dark blue skirt. "I have several."

"Let's get to them, then," the judge nudges.

"Yes, sir." I look back to Justin. "How old are you, Justin?"

His voice is small and squeaky with youth. "Seventeen."

"Do you have any interests? Hobbies?"

"Pretty much just computers."

I walk him through his childhood. How his interest began with Xbox games and Game Boys, then escalated into online gaming and coding. How he became friends with anonymous posters on message boards, which led him to secret chat rooms where hackers gather. And there he developed his hacking skills. How they would brag about their accomplishments, always trying to impress and outdo each other.

"Tell me about First Security Bank," I say.

He's more comfortable now. More animated.

"First Security's firewall was like legendary. The gold medal. Everyone wanted to crack it, but anyone who tried crashed and burned. Peeps started saying it really was impenetrable."

"So you gave it a shot? You attempted to hack into their online banking system."

His eyes jump to the jury, but then he admits, "Well . . . yeah. It was a challenge. Like the final boss level in a game."

He explains how he went at it for three sleepless days, fueled by Monster drinks and Hostess Twinkies.

"And then?" I ask.

And he can't keep the smile off his young face. "I was in. I couldn't believe it at first, but it was right in front of me. The accounts were all there."

"What did you do then? Hop on the message boards to tell the boys the big news?"

Justin's brows draw together. "No. I didn't tell anybody.

For a while I just wandered around, checked things out. I kept expecting to get booted out when they realized I was there." His voice goes soft. Almost sad. "But no one . . . no one saw me."

"What happened next?"

"I set up my own account. A dummy account."

I lean back against the defense table. "Why?"

"To see if anyone would notice."

"And did they, Justin? Did anyone notice you?"

His head shakes infinitesimally. "No."

Softly, I ask, "What did you do next?"

And here's the gamble. The risk. Justin's and mine, because he's essentially confessing his guilt.

"It was a mistake. I didn't mean to . . ."

"What didn't you mean to do, Justin?"

He takes a deep breath. "I took a penny from an account."

The corner of my mouth quirks. "A penny?"

He nods. "Yes. And then I waited twenty-four hours. To see . . ."

"To see if anyone would notice you?"

"Yes."

"Did they?"

He answers so quietly, the court reporter has him repeat his response.

"No."

"Then what happened, Justin?"

He stares at the microphone in front of him. "I took a hundred pennies. One each from a hundred different accounts."

I peek at the jury. Eight women, all mothers; six men, four fathers, two uncles. Twelve of them will decide Justin's fate, the remaining two are alternates. And every single one of them has their full attention focused on Justin. Watching his every move, hearing his every word. Noticing every nuance, just like I hoped they would. Not one of them looks pissed; their expressions range from curiosity to interest . . . to sympathy.

Perfect.

I choose my words deliberately. "And did anyone see you *then*, Justin?"

"No."

"So what did you do?"

He pauses, looks at me for guidance. And I nod.

"It's fuzzy . . . I don't remember the order exactly, but . . . I went back in. And I took more money from the accounts."

"Did you have plans to spend the money? A weekend in Aspen? A party at a swanky hotel?"

He flinches. "No. I wasn't going to do anything with the money."

"Then why did you take it?"

He shakes his head, looking truly bewildered. Lost—like the young boy he still is.

"I . . . I don't know. It was just . . . an accident. I didn't want any of this to happen."

I let the words hang for several moments. A meaningful pause. Then I walk back behind the defense table. "No more questions for the moment, Your Honor." I look to Kennedy. "He's all yours, Miss Randolph."

She doesn't spare me a glance; her razor-sharp gaze is fully centered on Justin. Like a predator with a wounded gazelle just steps away.

"Miss Randolph," the judge directs. "Proceed."

And Kennedy can't charge forward fast enough. Her voice is almost unrecognizable. Sharp and clipped—slicing the air.

"It was an *accident*? Did I hear that correctly? You stole $2.3 million from the retirement accounts of a dozen innocent, hardworking victims, by *accident*?"

Kennedy's choosing her words carefully too. Both of us trying to paint the picture for the jury we want them to see.

Justin blinks. "Yes."

Kennedy paces in front of him, looking aggressive, dangerous. If this wasn't such a pivotal moment, I'd definitely have a boner.

"How long did this 'accident' take you?" She asks.

"I . . . I don't remember."

"Longer than five minutes?"

"Yes."

"Longer than ten?"

"Uh . . . yeah."

"An hour?"

Justin fidgets. "An hour sounds right. It probably took that long."

She nods. "An accident, Mr. Longhorn, is an unfortunate, unforeseen event. Like when someone trips and falls on the sidewalk. Do you know the difference between your actions and falling on the sidewalk?"

Justin's panicked eyes dart to me. "What?"

"It doesn't take an hour to fall. That amount of time requires thought—deliberate, purposeful action."

She crosses her arms and changes tactics, like a boxer switching from a left hook to an uppercut. "Two point three million dollars is a lot of money, Mr. Longhorn."

His head nods hesitantly. "I guess."

"What could one do with $2.3 million?"

"I . . . I don't know. Almost anything, I guess."

Kennedy's finger jabs at Justin. "That's right. Almost anything. That kind of money buys freedom. Power. And you wanted that power, didn't you?"

"No. That's not why—"

"You thought you were better than your victims, didn't you? You didn't have to work for that money. Or save it. You could just go in and take it, anytime you wanted, isn't that correct?"

"I . . ."

She's badgering him. I could object, but I don't. I just sit back and let her do exactly what I knew she would.

"How did it feel when you breached First Security's firewall, Mr. Longhorn?"

Justin's brow wrinkles. "I don't know."

"Sure you do. Did it make you feel good?"

"I guess."

"I guess isn't an answer. Yes or no?"

"Yes. It felt good."

"And how did it feel to take all that money? To know your plan was successful?"

"It wasn't . . . I didn't—"

"Did you think about the people you were stealing from?"

"Not really."

"Of course you did. No one's buying your stuttering charade, Mr. Longhorn. Because we know the truth. Cracking First Security's system made you feel smarter than the other hackers, didn't it?"

"Yeah, in a way . . ."

"And taking that money made you feel powerful. Those weren't just accounts—they were people. People who you knew would be terrified to see their life savings drained away. And that made you feel good too, didn't it?"

"No, I never meant—"

"You wanted to show them you were better. Smarter. You wanted to scare them. To hurt them. Innocent, helpless people like Mrs. Potter." She points to the little old lady, who's frowning in the front row. "And you succeeded. Because when it's all said and done, you're a bully with a computer. A cyberterrorist."

Justin's cheeks go bright pink, his eyes shiny with threatening tears.

"I'm sorry!"

"Yes, Mr. Longhorn, you certainly are. They never—"

"I just wanted someone to see me!" Justin yells. Kennedy's mouth snaps closed. "I just wanted someone to know I was *there!*"

And he bursts into tears.

He sobs into one hand, his words muffled but heartbreakingly clear.

"No one *sees* me! I don't have any friends. I walk down the halls at school, and I'm like a ghost. Like I don't even exist."

He gestures to the empty seats behind me, where his parents should be. "My own parents aren't even here! They don't care. *No* one cares." Another sob breaks through and the entire courtroom watches with stunned eyes.

Including Kennedy.

"I . . . that's . . ." she stutters, trying to regain her composure, but Justin's words roll right over her.

"I could go to jail for twenty years, or die tomorrow, and it wouldn't make any difference to anyone." He looks at Mrs. Potter. "I'm so sorry. I didn't mean to scare you. I just wanted someone, *anyone*, to know I'm here."

The courtroom is silent except for the sound of Justin crying.

Kennedy stares at him, a thousand emotions playing out behind her eyes. And probably a thousand memories.

I hold up my hand. "Recess, Judge?"

"Granted." He bangs his gavel and the jury is ushered from the room.

I walk past Kennedy, who's standing stock-still, and meet Justin just outside the jury box. He wipes at his eyes and I tap his back.

"It's all right, buddy."

As we head back toward the defense table, Mrs. Potter glares at Kennedy. "You should be ashamed of yourself! Berating this poor sweet boy like that!"

"I . . . I didn't . . ."

Mrs. Potter pushes forward to hug Justin, patting his back gently. "There, there. Come on now, I have some cookies in my pocketbook. Harold, get this boy a cookie!"

Since Justin looks like he's in good hands, I take Kennedy's unresisting arm and pull her out the door.

"Conference?"

I walk her down the hall to one of the small, empty conference rooms. There I gently guide her onto the folding chair at the table.

"Oh my god," she says, still stunned.

"Breathe, Kennedy."

"I . . . holy shit . . ."

"Kennedy." I say it stronger, gaining her attention. "Breathe."

Her eyes go to my face. "He completely fell apart in there."

"Yeah."

"He's . . . he's not a criminal . . . he's just a lonely little boy."

"I know."

She rubs her forehead. "Oh my god—and I broke him down."

I nod. "Yep. You sure did."

"Because it felt good, Brent." She pats her chest. "It made me feel good. Strong."

"Yeah . . . I got that."

Her breath comes out quick and shocked. "I didn't want to ever feel weak again. So I went out of my way to rip into him. Because it made me feel powerful to make him feel bad."

"I know," I tell her softly.

And her voice rises, with horrible realization. "Brent—*I'm* the bully!"

Tears are imminent, and I put my hand on her shoulder. "Kennedy, it's okay."

Her forehead drops to the table, banging it.

"Hey!" I put my hand on the table so she can't do it again. "Easy there. I happen to like what's in that head of yours, so let's not damage it, okay?"

Guilty, wet eyes gaze up at me.

I sit down across from her. "Okay—look—Justin's a good kid. A lonely kid, yes, but you didn't break him. He'll recover, believe me." I hesitate, gauging just how freaked out she is. "I realize epiphanies are fucking exhausting—I've been there myself. But since we're kind of under the gun, time-wise, how do you feel about discussing a plea deal now?"

It only takes a moment for Kennedy's back to straighten and her chin to lift. And Federal Prosecutor K. S. Randolph stares back at me.

"What are you offering?"

"A guilty plea that stays on his juvenile record and won't follow him to adulthood. And a sentence of two years of probation, to be served under the computer tech division of the FBI or Homeland Security. With an agent who recognizes Justin's talents and wants him to use them for good."

She leans back. "That's a . . . unique arrangement."

I shrug. "A friend of mine had a similar setup when he was a young delinquent. It worked out really well for him. This way, Justin won't grow up into an evil cybergenius who hacks the nuclear codes because Mommy didn't love him. He'll have someone keeping an eye on him. He'll *matter*, Kennedy—and I think that's what all this was about in the first place."

She taps her fingernail on the table, thinking it over. "Four years. I want him supervised until he's twenty-one. And no more banking 'accidents.' He pulls anything like this again, he goes to prison."

I grin. "That vengeful streak is definitely sexy."

She smirks at me, then holds out her hand.

And I shake it. "You've got yourself a deal, Counselor."

Kennedy moves to stand, but I hold on to her hand— 'cause I'm not done yet.

"I had something delivered to your house today. It'll be

there when you get home. I want you to wear it tonight, when you come to my place at seven sharp."

I squeeze her hand. "Please say yes."

She does me one better. She leans over the table and kisses me.

Then she says yes.

• • •

After all the formalities are taken care of, I walk Justin out of the courthouse into the warm, sunny day. He's got Mrs. Potter's number in his pocket and a bocce date at the park with Harold this weekend. Since he needs a ride home, we head down the steps toward the corner where Harrison will pick us up.

Halfway down, Kennedy walks out of the courthouse to head back to her office for the afternoon. Two federal marshals in civilian clothes trail a few feet behind her when she's approached by a reporter in a yellow pantsuit with a notepad in her hand.

"Miss Randolph, what are your thoughts on the upcoming retrial of Gino Moriotti?"

Kennedy's tone is confident. Cocky.

It's pretty hot.

"Our case is every bit as solid as it was the first time around. I see no reason why the outcome won't be identical. Conviction on all counts."

"And how do you feel about the rumored contract that Mr. Moriotti has put on you? Are you concerned about your safety as the case moves forward?"

"Gino Moriotti has made a lifelong career of intimidating people, of getting his way through violence and fear. In this case, he should prepare for disappointment."

And as I watch the tiny blond badass practically strut away, I think proudly, *that's my girlfriend.*

16

This time, Kennedy shows up: at seven sharp there's a knock on the door. I wait in the backyard while Harrison goes to open it. The whole afternoon, my energy level was buzzing even higher than usual. I tried to get some work done, but I kept wondering when Kennedy would get home.

And what her expression would be when she opened the box I'd had delivered to her—a big white box with a red bow. Large enough for the dress, shoes, and purse that were inside it.

My mother has a personal shopper she's worked with for years. With the amount of time my hands have spent on Kennedy's body, I know her dimensions pretty frigging well. Well enough to describe the perfect dress that'll fit her like a custom-tailored glove.

And I'm every bit as good as I thought I was.

Because when Kennedy steps onto the back patio, she knocks the breath out of me. Her flawless neck and dainty arms are bare in the white strapless dress—practically glistening in the moonlight. The soft, shiny fabric hugs her breasts, pushing them up and together, creating a tasty cleavage line that I want to dip my tongue into. The dress cinches at her tiny waist, then flares just a bit, the gauzy chiffon fluttering slightly with the light breeze, just above her knees.

The dress is lovely. Sexy but elegant. Something a woman would wear on a special night out . . . or a girl would wear to her prom.

Her hair falls loose and curled around her delicate shoulders, her lips are shiny with a touch of gloss. And her smile— it's all hope and wonder and amazement. My heart pounds in my chest—because I was able to give that to her.

Kennedy looks around the yard, at the twinkling lights strewn through the trees and bushes, at the candles glowing softly on the table set for two. "Kiss Me" by Sixpence None the Richer plays out of the speakers—they were a big hit in the nineties. When those stunning eyes fall on me, I know she gets it. She understands what I'm trying to do.

I shrug. "You didn't get to go to the senior dance . . . I figured it's time to rectify that."

"Brent . . ." She sighs. "This is . . . wow."

I bite my bottom lip with a nod. "Oh, there's more." I open the small box on the table and step up to her.

"You got me a corsage?" There's laughter in her voice.

"Yep." I start to pin on the small red rosebuds. "When I was seventeen, I probably would've gotten you a wristlet— because I would've been too intimidated to pin this here." My fingers graze her soft skin beneath the top of her dress. "But I'm all man now, so this corsage is no match for me." Once it's on, my hand skims down her arm, making her shiver. "And I got to touch your boob, so—bonus."

The sound of her laughter echoes across the yard and warms my blood. Then her head tilts as the song changes. To Ed Sheeran's "Photograph." And Kennedy's smile glows even brighter.

"I love this song."

I lift one shoulder. "I didn't at first. The radio stations overplay it, make it annoying." And I look into her eyes. "But lately, I like it a lot more. It reminds me of you. Of us."

She nods slowly and takes my hand. "Dance with me, Brent."

"I thought you'd never ask."

My arms wrap around her, pulling her flush against me. I follow her small steps, but mostly we just sway. Kennedy's cheek rests against the lapel of my tuxedo and I kiss the crown of her head.

"You look beautiful," I tell her—although the tent in my pants, pressing against her, probably already gave that away.

"Thank you." She lifts her head and looks up at me. "Thank you for doing this. It's like . . . a dream come true."

Before I lean down to kiss her, my thumb strokes her cheek. "Yeah, it really is."

• • •

A week later, Kennedy calls me midmorning at the office. "Hey, you're coming over tonight, right?"

She's never seen the original *Escape from New York*—a cult

classic and favorite movie of mine. But she agreed to let me pop her Snake Plissken cherry tonight.

I lean back in my chair. "Wild dogs couldn't keep me away."

"Okay, good. I need your lacrosse stick. I need it really bad."

It takes me a second before I know how to answer.

"Is that, like, a code word for my dick?"

Her laugh tickles my ear through the phone.

"No—it's code for there's a bat in my attic and I need your lacrosse stick to catch it."

I sit up so I can fully process such a ridiculous statement. "There's a bat in your attic?"

"Yes."

"And you think you're going to catch it with a lacrosse stick?"

"That's what I said."

"Okay. Kennedy, let me lay it out for you. You are beautiful and brilliant and you're fucking mind-blowingly talented in the sack. But you suck at lacrosse. I've seen you play. You couldn't catch a basketball with a lacrosse stick if it was anchored to the ground."

I practically hear the eye roll.

"Well, I'm going to have to. I called two exterminators and both of them want to kill it. Bats are harmless creatures, and they eat their weight in bugs every night. I don't want it dead, I just don't want it living in my attic."

"Then it's lucky for you I have two lacrosse sticks. We'll catch it together."

That's code for she'll swing at the air and I'll actually do the catching.

I hear her smile. "I was hoping you'd say that."

• • •

With my sticks in hand, I roll up to Kennedy's house before dusk so we'll be in position when the flying rat shows itself. I nod to the marshal stationed in his unmarked car at the curb and walk in her door without knocking.

We're past that now.

I find her on the couch, stretched out on her stomach—giving me a sumptuous view of her tight ass cheeks peeking out beneath tiny running shorts—petting and talking to her cat Jasper. I'm beginning to suspect he's the demon spawn of Mephisto, evil ruler of hell in the Marvel universe.

"Who's a sweet kitty?" she purrs. "Such a pretty pussycat."

"His owner's prettier." I smirk.

Kennedy rolls to her side to look at me. "Ha-ha."

"Not even kidding." I lift the sticks. "You ready to do this?"

She pops off the couch. "Yep." Then she grabs a Yale football helmet from the table and slips it on her head. "Ready."

And she looks so fucking cute my cock lifts for a better view.

"Nice helmet. Did you date a football player you forgot to tell me about?"

She smiles. "No. This was a Halloween costume—junior year of college."

"Mmm . . ." And I start thinking of outfits. Specifically,

Kennedy in all types of outfits—and out of them. "Do you have a cheerleader costume?"

She shakes her head. "But I was Supergirl the year after."

And my mind explodes.

I bite my fist at the image of her tight, perfect little body wrapped in royal blue spandex and teeny—hopefully crotchless—red bottoms, with a satiny red cape swirling behind her.

Can't forget the cape.

"Why the hell am I just hearing about this now?" I complain. "Do you still have it?"

Her smile is slow and sultry. "I do. It's in the attic."

After I catch that bat—I'm going to fucking kiss him.

An hour later, after Kennedy swings a near-miss at my head that would've knocked me unconscious, we have the ugly little squatter in a closed cardboard box. We take him to the Tidal Basin after dark and release him into the wild.

Then we go back to Kennedy's and I screw Supergirl bent over the arm of the living room couch. Twice.

• • •

The following week, Kennedy is elbow deep in preparations for the Moriotti mobster retrial. We steal hours together—she slips into my bed after midnight, and I bring dinner, and my cock, to her office. So that Saturday, she agrees to shelve work and drive up to my parents' place on the Potomac River for the night. They're spending the weekend at the lake house in Saratoga, so we'll have the whole estate to ourselves.

I'm particularly looking forward to having her back in my

childhood home to act out every illicit fantasy I had in each of its rooms. And there's a lot of rooms in that house.

We drive up in my convertible with the top down, the sun shining, my hand resting on her thigh, and Tom Petty blaring from the radio.

Henderson, my parents' butler, greets us both with the warmth of a dear uncle. He takes care of our bags, and we take the boat out onto the river. After cruising for a while we anchor the boat, then swim and fish the afternoon away. The water's cold as a witch's tit, but the sun is warm when we climb out on shore. We spread out a blanket on the beach and then, because it's totally secluded, we warm up . . . in other ways.

Her skin smells like coconut—beachy suntan oil. The bare flesh around her pussy is smooth and tastes faintly of salt on my tongue. When I spread her with my fingers and dip inside, her knees dig into the sand on either side of my head. Kennedy lies on top of me, her blond head in my crotch, her mouth rising up and down over my dick with perfect suction. I press down on her ass, bringing her closer, giving my roving mouth fuller contact with her cunt. My blood zings through my eardrums like rushing water and I feel slightly drunk. I go to town on her—sucking and kissing, rubbing my face and tongue against her clit. She hums around me and my hips jerk up.

She's close. I know it by the way her hips roll wildly—losing all inhibitions—going mindless. Seeking, needing, only caring about that building sensation that's about to burst free. I squeeze her ass and trace the line between them with one finger—gliding, teasing.

Someday, one day—she'll take me there. And it'll be fucking magnificent. But if it's going to be good, anal requires a little more forethought than I had for this day trip. So instead, I slip one finger into her ass while at the same time I rub flat, tight circles on her clit with my tongue.

And she goes off like a fucking cherry bomb, with a long, endless moan that reverberates deep in my gut.

Then she goes slack and weighted on me. And as fantastic as her mouth feels, I don't come yet. I have other plans.

I roll us to the side and flip around so my chest is pressed up against her slick back. Pulling her hips against my pelvis, I lift her leg and slide effortlessly inside. Kennedy's head rests on the blanket as I pump into her—giving my mouth unfettered access to her neck, her shoulder. I suck and kiss and lick that soft skin. I scratch her with my chin and press my teeth against her, stopping just short of biting. And sounds like growls crawl up my throat. With my cock deep inside her, my free hand roams—rubbing her sensitive clit, sliding up her stomach, squeezing her velvet breasts.

My climax climbs, peaks, and ripples through me. The pleasure so heightened—so intense—I lose control of my movements. And my mouth.

"*So* good. Love this . . . Christ, fucking love you . . ."

When I regain command of my faculties, my forehead rests on Kennedy's shoulder blade and her weight leans easy against me. But as my heart rate slows, she stiffens. Tightens.

And pulls away.

Shit.

I lift up on an elbow and roll her so she's on her back, with nowhere to look but up at me. "Hey."

She smiles—but it's forced. "Hey."

My voice sounds deeper. Rough. "Are you good?"

"Yeah."

But I don't believe her.

She doesn't say anything for several moments. Then her brows inch closer to one another. "Is it because of how I look now?"

"What?" I honestly don't have any idea what the hell she's talking about.

"Is that why you want me? Is that why I'm here?"

A scowl pulls at my face. "No. Of course not." My eyes wander over her familiar features, remembering her at nine, and thirteen, and every year I've known her until now. "You were my best friend—I always thought you were fun. Awesome. And then, when we were older, I thought you were really fucking cute. Even behind your glasses and beneath your bulky sweaters, I thought you were pretty. Once the boners became a regular thing, the idea of your braces scared me a little—but they were never a turnoff."

She looks . . . thoughtful. Not happy at my revelation or relieved, like I thought she would be. She sits up and I shift over—leaning my elbows on my bent knees—as my dick lies exhausted against my thigh.

Kennedy's eyes peer out over the water. "Do you remember the last week of summer, just before junior year—when you had a few of the lacrosse team guys here for the weekend? They were in Cashmere's crowd of friends."

It takes me a minute to vaguely recall. "Yeah?"

"I didn't know they were here, so I came over to see if you wanted to do something. You were all in the pool. I was standing on the back patio, but none of you saw. You were talking about girls . . . about me."

My stomach knots itself and my eyes drag closed. Because I remember now.

"They said I was weird. That I smelled weird . . ."

My head snaps to her. "You didn't."

Her voice is softer than a whisper.

"And they said I was ugly. That they'd have to put a bag over my head if they wanted to—"

"Kennedy . . ." I beg.

Because I want to kill something. Pulverize something. I want to reach into her mind and wrench those memories away so she'll never have to think about them ever again.

"I left after that."

I grasp her shoulder. "They were assholes, okay? Stupid and cruel little dicks to say those things. *I* never said them."

"No, I know that." Then some iron comes into her voice. "You never said *anything*. After they were gone, you came to my house and we hung out . . . just like normal. Because I was good enough to be your friend—as long as no one else was around to see it."

All I can do is stare at her, pull the words from deep inside, and give them to her. "I'm sorry. I'm so sorry I hurt you. I was a jerk and a pussy for caring what they thought. But I *liked* you. Blond or brunette, designer clothes or a trash bag—I wanted to be close to you. Even then."

When her eyes dip, I lift her chin. "If I could go back and change all of that, I would. But this is where we are now. We have to move forward. I'm in love with you. And if it takes awhile for you to wrap your head around that—to wrap your heart around it—then I'll wait. Because you're worth waiting for. You always were."

• • •

Things are upbeat again between us by the time we walk into my parents' house, holding hands and heading up to my room for a shower.

Until we come to a screeching halt in the foyer.

Because standing there, staring at our entwined hands like it's a living, breathing miracle—is my mother.

"Hello, darling!" If she smiles any bigger, her face will break in half. "Kennedy, dearest, I can't tell you what a joy it is to see you again. Here. With Brent."

"Hi, Mrs. Mason—it's great to see you too."

There's hugs and cheek kisses all around.

I try my damnedest not to sound as disappointed as I feel. "What are you doing here, Mom? I thought you guys were in Saratoga."

"Your father's back was acting up, so we had to come home."

That's when my father walks past the open doorway of the library, on the phone and pacing, and his back seems just dandy to me.

My eyes narrow on Henderson. And I smell a traitor.

"Did you two have a nice day?" my mother asks.

"Yeah, it was great," I tell her. "We took the boat out. We were just going to head up and grab a shower."

So much for christening the ballroom with a blow job.

"That's nice," she coos softly. "In case you had planned on other arrangements, I think it's best that you both spend the night in Brent's room. And use his bathroom as well—the other rooms in the house, unfortunately, aren't prepared for guests."

Poor Henderson looks down right insulted. "Beg your pardon."

My mother waves her hand, shushing him. "They're not prepared, Henderson. And that is that."

Now she's just creeping me out. It's one thing if I want to screw Kennedy ten different ways. But to think of my mother cheering us on—sitting on the sidelines with a flag in one hand and a foam cock in the other—is just wrong.

"Okay. Thanks, Mom."

I lead Kennedy up the stairs. But we're not in my room for more than two minutes when her phone pings with an incoming message.

She sits on the end of my bed, reading it. From my swiveling desk chair I tap my forehead like a mind reader. "Wait—don't tell me. Because my mother couldn't stop herself from telling your mother we're here—it's a message from her. And we've been summoned to your house for dinner tonight."

Kennedy sighs and shows me her phone. "You should take your act to Vegas—you'll be a hit."

Then she throws herself back onto my bed and blows a frustrated raspberry at the ceiling.

• • •

Dinner at the Randolphs' is a formal affair. The men wear suits, the ladies cocktail dresses. I had appropriate attire at my parents', and my mother loaned Kennedy a little black dress she picked up years ago in Paris. I'll forever be grateful that it still had the tags on—that my mother never wore it. Otherwise, the massive erection it caused when Kennedy walked out of the dressing room could've been weird.

The dining room table is long enough to seat thirty and fully appointed. Without the classical music playing in the background, the room would've been awkwardly silent through the first three courses.

Because our parents aren't talking—they're all just kind of watching us. Expectantly.

Finally, Kennedy's father attempts normal conversation.

"How's your Nevada case coming along, princess?"

I frown at her and whisper, "He has a nickname for you? Why does he get to have a nickname and I don't?"

"Not now, Brent."

Begrudgingly, I let it go. But she can bet her sweet ass we'll be talking later—even if I have to tie her to the bed until the discussion reaches its full culmination. It's possible I'm just looking for an excuse to tie her to a bed.

"It's going well. I'm confident I'll be able to secure a second conviction."

Mitzy clears her throat, signaling that the observation portion of the evening is complete—and the examination segment will now commence.

"Yes, that's all very nice, Kennedy. But is there anything you would like to tell us? An announcement, perhaps, that it would behoove you to share?"

Kennedy blinks like a blond Kewpie doll. "Nothing comes to mind, no."

Mitzy throws down her linen napkin and narrows her eyes at her daughter, like a sharp-clawed hawk. "I was at the Prince benefit, young lady. I saw Brent whisk you away after David's tawdry proposal. So, what I'd like to know—what I believe all of us here are entitled to know—is what exactly is going on between the two of you?"

The cross-examination force is strong in Kennedy's family. Mitzy Randolph would've made a kick-ass attorney.

"Brent and I are . . . friends."

And fuck me, the benefits are fantastic.

Mitzy huffs. "Don't be coy, Kennedy—you're not good at it."

And I get why Kennedy's reluctant to share with her mother. It's like that scene from the original cartoon movie *Cinderella.* When Cinderella makes her own pink dress from scratch, and her bitchy stepsisters tear it to pieces. For as long as I've known her, there's not a single aspect of Kennedy's life that Mitzy wasn't waiting to rip to shreds.

But this'll be different. Kennedy has me now.

I throw my own napkin down, reach over the table, and take Kennedy's hand. "The truth, Mrs. Randolph, is Kennedy and I are dating. We're seeing how things go . . . enjoying each other's company. Beyond that, it is really none of your business."

Kennedy is looking at me like I'm the prince that just woke her with a kiss, found her glass slipper, took her on a flying carpet ride, and defeated the evil witch.

And we get lost for a moment—just looking at each other.

Until my mother squeals loud enough to shatter the crystal glasses on the table. She claps her hands together. "You were right, Mitzy! You were so very right!"

"I told you, Kitty. Just like we planned!"

Kennedy frowns. "What do you mean, like you planned?"

And like the villain from a Batman comic, Mitzy reveals her devious scheme.

"You're thirty-two years old, Kennedy; you obviously weren't going to get yourself married. Kitty and I knew that, once we orchestrated your and Brent's reunion, things would progress. And look how perfect it's all turned out."

"You didn't orchestrate anything, Mother. Brent and I saw each other again at the party. We were assigned to try the same case."

Mitzy lifts her penciled eyebrows. "And who brought you home—making it possible for you to be at the party and try your little case?"

Kennedy's jaw hits the floor.

"You said Father was sick! You said he needed tests!"

"A means to an end, darling."

Her indignant brown eyes zoom to her father. "You had an oxygen tank when I visited! And the"—her hand flutters in front of her face—"the nose thing!"

"That was your Aunt Edna's oxygen," her mother volunteers unhelpfully.

Her father has the decency to look ashamed—but only a little. "I just want you to be happy, princess."

That's when my mother reenters the conversation. "You know what I can't decide, Mitzy?"

"What's that, Kitty?"

"Summer or fall? June is classic, but the threat of thunderstorms will hang over the entire affair. And pish-posh to that 'rain is good luck on a wedding day' silliness. There's nothing lucky about mud and soggy gowns."

"It will depend on the location," Mitzi says. "Location is everything. We won't have it in the city. Perhaps Palm Beach?"

"Mother . . ." Kennedy growls.

"Though the humidity in Palm Beach is atrocious. But definitely outdoors. White tents, green hills, sunset . . ."

Kennedy stands up. "Mother—"

"And white flowers!" Mitzy says. "But no lilies—they remind me of a funeral."

Kennedy stamps her foot. "Mother!"

Mitzy makes a sound like a disgruntled hen. "Kennedy, really! What's gotten into you? Is this any way for a bride to behave?"

"You're not doing this! You don't get to be in charge!"

"Lower your voice. All that yelling will make you break a blood vessel—and your complexion really can't afford that."

"We will make our own decisions, and you will have no say in the matter, Mother! If we want to get married in Tahiti, we will!"

Mitzy gives Kennedy an indifferent wave. "Yes, yes, that's fine dear." Then she turns toward my mother and asks her who designed Ivanka Trump's wedding gown.

"In fact," Kennedy hisses to no one, "that's just what we'll do. We'll get married in Tahiti!" She bangs the table. "In a bar!"

"Is that a proposal? This is so sudden." I squint as if I'm thinking it over, then nod. "I accept."

"Naked!" Kennedy yells at her mother, wagging her finger. "And we won't take any pictures!"

"If we're going to be naked, we really should take a few pictures." I insist. "Or a video."

But our mothers just keep on chirping. Kennedy and I

might as well not even be here anymore—which is the best fucking idea I've heard all night.

I stand up and grab her hand. "Come on."

She doesn't come willingly at first, so I tug her along.

"Doesn't that bother you?" she complains, gesturing back toward the parents, who don't even notice we've left the room. They're having too serious a discussion.

About us.

"No, it doesn't bother me."

"How can it not? How can they—"

I cut her off with a deep kiss—one hand holding the base of her neck, the other at the small of her back—pressing her against me. Then I tell her, "Let them have their fun. Let them talk and plan their hearts out. When the time comes, we'll do whatever the hell we want anyway."

I pull her toward the back door. "Now, let's go for a walk. You can let me into your boathouse."

"Is that a euphemism?"

I'm surprised she has to ask.

"Yep."

17

My parents are on the boards of several charitable organizations, institutions, and societies whose goals are close to their hearts—feeding children in third-world countries, bestowing iPads to inner-city schools, protecting endangered plant life in the rain forest. Fund-raisers—high-end parties that drum up donations for those endowments—are par for the course. And sometimes my parents hit me up to stand in for them, to represent the Mason Foundation.

That's how Kennedy and I end up walking through the arched doors of the Smithsonian Institute the following Thursday night, for a gala supporting the creation of sustained clean drinking water in Africa. The room is lit with cool, strategically placed orange beams of light and bright, festive swaths of cloth draped across the ceiling. There's a steady roar of chatter and laughter and the tinkling of champagne glasses as tuxedo-clad gentlemen and jewel-dripping ladies enjoy themselves thoroughly.

Kennedy looks outstanding in a short, body-hugging ice-blue number with an off-the-shoulder neckline that gives the impression the dress could just slip off her at any moment. I'm going to test that theory later on. We have a drink and make small talk with the main organizer and emcee of the evening, Calvin Van Der Woodsen, an old acquaintance of my father's.

After a few minutes, Calvin's called away because the kitchen has run out of purple kale for the garnish. And that's when my wretched cousin walks up to us.

"Hey again, cuz. Didn't expect to see you tonight."

"Louis." I nod.

And he leers. At Kennedy. "Who do we have here?"

"Kennedy Randolph, you remember my cousin Louis, don't you?"

Her lips draw together like she'd sucked an unripe lemon. I take that as a yes.

"Randolph, huh? I used to hook up with your sister, back in the day. Claire . . ." Louis stresses the consonants in a sleazy kind of way. "You look like her. How's she doing?"

Kennedy stares him down. "She's married. Happily."

"Too bad." Then he points at me, spilling some of his scotch on the floor. "Speaking of marriage—from what I hear, I'm on my way to winning our bet."

Shit. I forgot about that.

Kennedy goes pale, and I can practically feel her heart stutter.

"A bet?" she whispers.

"Yep." Louis nods. "Thanks to you, Brent's gonna owe me a ten-thousand-dollar bottle of scotch." He winks at her. "I'll think of you every time I enjoy a glass."

After he walks away, Kennedy turns her back on me. I

lean in, hissing right against her ear. "Don't do this—don't you fucking dare. He was at the birthday party at my parents' house, and he bet me that my mother would have me married by the end of the year. That's *it*. So help me God, I'll cut my other fucking leg off if I'm lying to you."

I spin her around and her eyes are wide, uncertain. Looking for some reassurance that I'm not sure how to give.

"Do you believe me?"

She inhales slowly. "I want to. But . . . it's hard."

I curse under my breath. And wrap my hand around her arm.

"Let's go."

We pass Calvin on our way toward the door—I tell him Kennedy has a migraine and we won't be able to stay for the rest of the evening. Outside, I spot Harrison parked down the street and motion to him with my hand. Then I get Kennedy in the backseat and press the button to raise the divider that separates us from the driver's seat.

For a minute, the backseat is silent.

Then she says in a tiny voice, "Please don't be angry with me."

"Angry at *you*?" I bark out a laugh. "Sweetheart, I'm furious with my younger self—I want to go back in time and punch that kid in the nuts. And I am livid with the guy who messed with your head in college. It's taken everything I have not to find out where he is now, where he works, buy the company, and ruin him." I cup her jaw and soften my voice. "But I would never be angry with you. Not about this."

Her brows draw together. "Then why did we leave? Where are we go—"

"You don't trust me. So we're going back to my place, and I'm going to make love to you until you do."

Great plan, right? I think so too.

Her eyes go golden with heat. "That . . . could take awhile."

"Then it's a good thing my stamina is unparalleled. We're screwing until you trust me—or we starve to death—and that's final."

She sounds breathy. Excited. "Harrison would never let us starve."

I wink. "Exactly."

• • •

Two days later, Kennedy's still at my house. As I pet her awake, she tells me if she has one more orgasm—even a little one—she'll drop dead. So, I take pity on her and go for a run. When I get back, she's curled up on the chaise longue in the living room, wearing a pair of my blue-and-white-checkered boxers and a Green Lantern T-shirt. Her soft hair falls over her shoulder as she turns the page in a brief and sips her coffee.

And warmth blooms in my chest and down my arms—making my fingertips tingle. With the rightness of it all. What did Waldo say about relationships? *Satisfaction.* Having her in my house, wearing my clothes—it's so much more than satisfying. It's fucking joyous. Exuberantly fulfilling in a way I can't possibly describe.

I still want to live my life free—but I want to live it free *with her.*

Kennedy must feel me watching, because she peeks up. "Everything okay?"

I nod, slowly smiling. "Yeah—everything's perfect."

I kiss the top of her head as I walk past, heading up the steps to take a shower. When I walk out of the bathroom with the towel around my waist, I hear voices coming from downstairs. One definitely Kennedy's, the other too deep to be Harrison. Still dripping, I walk down the stairs—and listen.

". . . you know his family. But you need to understand that we're his family too. Don't fuck with his head."

That's Jake—talking to Kennedy in my living room. There's no hint of a threat in his voice; he'd cut his tongue out before he'd ever threaten a woman. But he has this way of putting things that makes the simplest sentence sound like a warning.

"You think I could do that, Mr. Becker? Fuck with Brent's head?" Kennedy sounds almost surprised.

"Watching the way he's turned himself inside out over you the last few weeks—absolutely."

There's a pause, and I imagine the look on her face, her stance—the way her eyes probably narrow, her arms cross, and her hips cock—like when she's in court, sizing up her adversary. "You're very protective of him, aren't you?"

"Yes," Jake says simply and without hesitation.

And then Kennedy sounds defensive. Maybe even . . . offended—on my behalf. "Why? He doesn't need it. He takes care of himself just fine. If you think patronizing him is helping—"

Jake's deep, rumbling laugh cuts her off. "I have no doubt that Brent is fully capable of handling his own shit. It's not about that."

"Then what's it about?"

Now Jake pauses. And I know he's analyzing the angles, choosing his words to efficiently convey his position. "I never had brothers . . . not until I met Brent and Stanton."

That's when I make my presence known. Stepping from the hallway to the living room, still wrapped only in a towel. Which Jake doesn't appreciate.

"Jesus—I'd rather not go blind from an accidental glimpse of your nut sack. How about putting some clothes on?"

I shrug and lob an arm around Kennedy's shoulders. "Clothes are senseless at this point. What brings you by, big guy?"

His black eyebrows lift, and reproach reflects in his steel-gray eyes. "I've been calling—is your phone broken?"

I tease, "Mom, you look different. Did you change your hair?"

He flips me off.

Then I give him the real explanation. "I've been busy—a lot of sex has been happening."

Kennedy pinches my chest—and it fucking hurts.

While Jake's face remains blank. "Congratulations."

I raise my eyebrows. "So what's up—why the house call?"

I've barely seen him at the office this week. He's been in court a lot, working a murder case. And he's been really busting his ass over it, because he truly believes his client is innocent. That's an uncommon, double-edged luxury we aren't often afforded.

"We're having a barbecue this afternoon. You're invited," he tells me. Then he turns his rare, charming-Jake-Becker smile on Kennedy. "You're invited too."

• • •

That afternoon, Kennedy and I head over to Jake and Chelsea's place for the barbecue. Their house has a great layout for entertaining—a built-in pool, a gorgeous garden, and an outdoor kitchen Jake just installed.

Sofia smiles warmly at Kennedy, the bond of being a woman in the legal profession overcoming any lingering animosity from their showdown in court a few weeks earlier. The fact that Kennedy is here with me, that she's important to me, probably helps too.

I introduce Kennedy to the McQuaid brood, and her head is practically spinning by the time I get through Riley, Rory, Raymond, Rosaleen, Regan, and down to the littlest, three-year-old Ronan.

We enjoy the clear sky, the hot sun, and a few beers, until Jake sets a platter of burgers and hot dogs in the center of the red-and-white-checkered tablecloth and we all sit down at the picnic table to eat. While the pleasant hum of kid chatter fills the lower end of the table, Riley McQuaid sits down with a huff in the chair across from me, her mouth fixed in a pout and unhappy blue eyes throwing sharp glances in Jake's direction. A palpable silence flows between the teenager and her father figure—it's heavy and awkward.

So, of course, I have to mention it.

"Everything okay here?" I ask, looking to each of them.

Jake takes a bite of his burger. "Yep."

Riley's eyes narrow. "If you consider living under the fascist rule of a dual dictatorship 'okay,' then yeah, I guess it is."

Jake's mouth pulls up at the corner. "Fascist? That's cute."

I lean into Kennedy and whisper, "This sounds juicy." Then I lift my chin at Riley. "I thought we'd moved passed the angry-nobody-understands-me-teenage phase and were happily settled in the responsible-working-part-time-young-adult stage. What gives?"

Riley and Jake go silent—a Mexican standoff if I ever saw one.

Chelsea, doll that she is, fills in the blanks.

"Riley and Jake had a disagreement yesterday. She had a friend over. A friend who is a boy. In her room. With the door closed."

And it all becomes so clear.

I turn to Jake. "Did you flip out?"

He shrugs, face deceptively blank. "I don't flip out. I just got the drill from the garage. Problem solved."

"Solved how?" I'm already grinning at what I'm sure will be an entertaining answer.

And I'm not disappointed.

"He took off my door!" Riley shouts. "I have no door! I'm sixteen years old with five little brothers and sisters, and *no door*!"

"Like I said, problem solved," Jake says evenly.

"I have rights, you know," Riley counters.

Jake's smile is patient. "Yes, you do—and not one of them includes having a door. Or a window, for that matter. You might want to keep that in mind, and quit while you're ahead."

Riley grinds her teeth, but goes quiet. And I just bet she's sticking her tongue out at him in her head—or, more likely, flipping him the bird. I know the feeling.

"Come on, Riley," Stanton says, "don't be like that. It could be worse."

"I don't know how," the teen grumbles, folding her arms.

"You could be Presley—that's how." Stanton's referring to his fifteen-year-old daughter, who lives most of the year in Mississippi with her mother. She's been considering colleges in the East, and he's been positively giddy with excitement.

Riley's face loosens with curiosity. "I texted her the other day, but she hasn't gotten back to me. Where is she?"

"In her room, without Internet, TV, or phone, where she's gonna be for some time."

At our questioning gazes, he elaborates. "It seems she tried sneakin' Ethan Fortenbury up the oak tree outside her window to her bedroom."

I notice eleven-year-old Raymond frowning deeply.

Then Jake reads my mind and tells Stanton, "You seem surprisingly calm about that development."

The former teenage father waves his hand. "Jenny and I have been anticipating it for years. Had it all planned out. The little shit, Fortenbury, showed up and found Jenn waiting for him by the tree. Her—and her shotgun."

I whistle.

Stanton winks at Riley. "So you see, darlin'—it could always be worse."

Riley sighs and shakes her head. "None of you understand us."

"*Au contraire*, Fresh Prince, they understand all too well—that's your problem," I tell her wisely.

But she just looks confused. "What's a Fresh Prince?"

I groan. "I feel so frigging old. Thanks, Riley."

Kennedy pats my hand. And her eyes sparkle as she teases, "You are old. It's good that you're finally realizing it. We should hang out with these kids more often."

It's the first time she's ever referred to us as a "we." A unit. A couple. And as fucking girly as it makes me sound, I like the words on her lips.

"*We* should, huh?"

Her smile hits me right in the gut. It's warm and sexy, tender and naughty all in one. "Yeah, we should."

We gaze at each other for a few moments in that annoying way new couples do—in our own little shining bubble of lust. Then little Ronan McQuaid pops it.

"Daddy!"

He throws himself across Jake's lap fearlessly, secure in the knowledge that strong hands will always catch him.

"Up, Daddy, up!" he demands.

Without rising from his seat, Jake scoops the toddler under his arms and tosses him high over his head, catching him as he squeals. And Jake's smile is so wide and big, a weird mixture of happiness and envy surges through my chest. He sets the kid on his feet and Ronan toddles off toward the swing set. Finished eating in record time, the rest of the kids follow suit—leaving us six old people at the table alone.

Stanton asks, "Daddy, huh?"

Jake's eyes flash to Chelsea, warming to liquid mercury when he catches the adoring look she saves just for him. "Yeah."

"When did that happen?" I ask.

Chelsea puts her small hand over Jake's immense one and explains, "This weekend, Regan and Ronan sat us down for a talk."

"Regan did most of the talking," Jake interjects. "But Ronan nodded a lot."

Chelsea continues in a soft voice. "They said they knew that Robbie and Rachel were their parents and that they were in heaven, but they don't remember them—not like the other kids do. And they said all their friends got to have mommys and daddys . . ."

When she trails off, Jake finishes for her. "And then they asked if we would be their mommy and daddy."

"Wow," Stanton mutters, and Sofia's eyes are brimming with sentiment.

"Yeah." Chelsea sighs.

"Did you cry?" I ask Jake. Because I'm man enough to admit if I had been in his position, with those two adorable, chubby faces gazing up at me, I would've fucking lost it.

"It was pretty damn close," he admits.

Chelsea raises her hand. "I cried like a baby."

I nod and nudge the big hulk with my elbow. "So you're officially a daddy now."

His mouth quirks up into a slow, humble smile. "I guess so."

"That's awesome, man."

He nods. "It really fucking is."

• • •

A while later, Rory bounds up to the cleared table with a big red kickball in his hands and his twin brother, Raymond, close behind him. "We're gonna play kickball—you guys wanna play?"

With my arm resting around Kennedy's shoulders, I reply, "Count me in. I'm a champion kickball player."

"Cool."

The normally timid Raymond adjusts his glasses and aims his bold gaze at the hot girl on my arm. "You wanna be on my team, Kennedy?"

Kennedy smiles. "Sure."

I wrinkle my nose. "Ewww, why'd you pick her—she's a girl. She kicks like a girl too. I speak from experience."

Raymond shrugs. "She's prettier than you. And besides, you like her, so you'll probably take it easy on her."

"Not a bad strategy, Raymond."

"I'm all about the strategy."

Kennedy stands and takes the ball from Rory, spinning it in her hands and challenging me with those gorgeous eyes. "My girl kicks were enough to beat you back in the day."

I scoff, "I let you win. Even at eleven, I was a gentleman."

She laughs and leans down, closing in for a kiss. "And at thirty-two, you're a liar."

Just as I'm about to get a taste, Rory kiss-blocks me.

"Dude—no kissing. I have to put up with enough of that from those two." He jerks his thumb at Jake and Chelsea, who don't look the least bit ashamed.

Poor kid. The things he must hear from their bedroom.

Then he points his forefinger at me. "And you have to kick righty—no bionic leg allowed."

I shrug. "Makes no difference to me." I tell Kennedy, "Perfect male specimen that I am, I'll still beat your ass without it."

Mmm . . . beat her ass—now there's an idea.

She rolls her eyes. And it makes me hard.

"I'll play too," Sofia pipes up. "I love kickball."

Rory's head jerks back, frowning toward Sofia's burgeoning belly. "Are you nuts? You should be taking it easy."

Stanton throws up his hands. "Thank you!" He looks hard at his wife. "From the mouths of babes."

But Sofia isn't fooled. She looks closely at Rory. "Did Stanton tell you to say that?"

Rory smirks. "Nope. Jake paid me five bucks to slip it into the conversation, though. But even if he hadn't, you still couldn't play. I'm not throwing a ball at a pregnant lady."

Rosaleen comes tearing across the patio, snatches the ball from Kennedy's hands, and consoles Sofia. "You can be referee." She tilts her head toward five-year-old Regan. "Keep an eye on *that* one—she cheats."

Regan frowns and stomps a foot in response.

Then Ronan scurries up to Rosaleen, butting his forehead into her stomach and reaching for the ball. "Me!"

Rosaleen holds the ball up out of his reach. "You can't play, Ronan, you're too little."

His freckled face turns pink with resentment. "*Me!*"

Jake scoops Ronan up and over his shoulder. "Come on, buddy, let's go kill a watermelon."

But as Jake carries him away, the little boy stretches his arms out toward the ball, wailing pitifully, "Meeeeeeeeee!"

• • •

Raymond and Kennedy's team ended up crushing us. We were left two men down when Riley bailed for an "urgent" phone call and Regan got ejected for arguing with the umpire.

I could've pegged Kennedy twice—but when my competitive instinct and my dick went head to head over the issue, the dick won out. 'Cause he knew we'd be rewarded later on. And watching her ass in those tight shorts as she ran the bases just wasn't something I could bring myself to interrupt.

Rory called me a chump, and he was totally right.

But I was a chump who was getting laid—so that makes it all better.

Later, after I threw Kennedy into the pool and she in turn tried her damnedest to drown me, after the kids cannonballed in with us and we played a fierce game of Marco Polo, we said our good-byes and headed out.

I pull my car up to the curb in front of my townhouse and kill the engine. Kennedy's eyes are a satisfied kind of tired, and her cheeks and nose are pink from the hours in the sun. Her hair is pulled on top of her head in a messy bun, with a few loose golden strands brushing her neck.

It's almost scary, how beautiful she is. Even more stunning than the first time I saw her in that red dress, and I really didn't think that was possible.

"You're not even going to ask me if I want to go home?" she inquires with a smile and a raised brow. "Kind of presumptuous, isn't it?"

"I prefer to look at it as deductive reasoning." I hop out of the car, come around, and open her door. She takes my hand and I pull her straight into my arms. "Plus, you have to shower, I have to shower, there's a drought . . ."

"In California."

Ever so slowly, I lower my lips to hers—just a teasing touch. "We all need to do our part."

I feel her smile against my mouth. "You sound like my uncle Jameson."

This disturbs me. From what I remember of her conservationist uncle, he was a cross between General Patton and Cheech & Chong. An odd-duck, militant hippie who I don't want her thinking of while I'm kissing her.

So I ditch the bullshit and go for honesty.

"I don't really care about saving water." I skim my nose up her neck, scratching the delicate skin along her collarbone with my beard, leaving goose bumps in its wake. Then I whisper in her ear, "I just want to fuck you in the shower until neither one of us can stand." My tongue traces the shell of her ear, making her shiver in the best way. "Is that wrong?"

When she answers, her voice is shaky. "That sounds . . . not wrong to me."

I pull Kennedy tight against my side and smack her ass. "Let's get on that, then."

• • •

The first thing I'm aware of the next morning—before I open my eyes—is the sensation of soft, smiling lips trailing up my jaw, the tickle of breath against my neck, and the teasing brush of hair along my shoulder.

And this time, it's definitely not the cat.

Kennedy buries her face in the crook of my neck and inhales me. I stretch my arms back, grab her, then roll over so

I'm facing her, cocooned in my arms. I kiss her properly on the mouth—morning breath and all.

Then I notice what time it is. The sun is up—but just fucking barely.

"I have to go into the office," she says.

I smooth her hair down and smother her face against my chest so she'll stop saying silly things.

"Shhh . . . you're dreaming. Go back to sleep."

"Brent," she says with a laugh. "I didn't get any work done yesterday. I really *have* to catch up today."

Unhappy growls tumble around in my throat. Kennedy soothes them with gentle hands and a kiss for my mouth.

"I'll come back tonight. But I'm going to bring the boys with me."

One eye cracks open. "They have food and water. Cats don't need anything else."

"They need love. Attention," she insists.

"Cats disdain love and attention. It's beneath them."

She laughs again. "Not mine. I've been neglecting them—and if this is going to work out, I don't want them resenting you."

The woman knows how to deliver a convincing argument. "Fine. The cats can come."

A sweet peck of a kiss gets planted on my sternum. And then she slips away . . . like sand through my fingers.

I must have dozed off again, because in the next instant Kennedy's dressed. Her clothed breasts press against my back and she whispers good-bye as she kisses the bed-warmed skin at the nape of my neck.

I mumble back, still half-asleep, "Bye, baby. Love you . . ."

. . .

It's past noon by the time I drag my ass out of bed. I don't have to tell you this is completely fucking weird for me. My only defense is that Kennedy was a wildcat last night—completely wore me out. A few hours and one Red Bull later, I have enough energy for a run, and head down to my favorite jogging trail near the National Mall.

Afterward, I walk back to the townhouse, grinning like an idiot every step of the way. Because I'm thinking of a certain tiny blonde who totally owns me. I'm looking forward to hearing her bitch and moan about her day, watching her eat, listening to her laugh. She has such a great laugh.

Damn, I'm pathetic. I'm starting to annoy my fucking self.

When I get to my front steps, Jake, Stanton, and Sofia are there, waiting. Looking way too serious for a Sunday afternoon.

"Why the long faces?" I joke. "Who died?"

Not one of them cracks a smile, and a cold chill slithers up my spine.

Stanton averts his eyes and Jake watches me, ready and tense, like he's anticipating a reaction. Sofia steps forward.

"Brent, sweetie . . . something's happened."

18

The automatic doors to the emergency room slide open and I head straight for the reception desk. "Kennedy Randolph."

Behind the desk, the dark-haired woman's mouth hangs open slightly before she recovers. "Um . . . there's no Kennedy Randolph here."

She's lying. Even if she wasn't bad at it, spotting the automatic tells people do when they're nervous or hiding something is necessary for my job. This is the second hospital we've come to—and the receptionist at the first one wasn't lying.

One of Jake's contacts, a private investigator, called him after seeing the whole thing go down. He saw the pretty blond prosecutor get into a dark sedan with government plates, a driver at the wheel. And just a few blocks down the road, at an intersection, he saw that sedan get T-boned by an SUV—and flipped.

Intentionally.

Shots fired. FBI on the scene. Flashing lights and sirens. Injuries, medics.

Body bags.

So it's actually a relief that the receptionist is lying to me; it increases the odds that Kennedy isn't in one of those bags. Or wasn't when she got here, anyway.

I lean over the desk. "I know she's here, and I know why you're telling me she's not . . ." My voice wavers and my hands clench with frustration, panic—the urge to tear the hospital apart looking for her, or to go find the fuckers who dared to do this to her and tear *them* apart. "And you have to let me see her."

Even before she opens her mouth, I know she's going to shoot me down. "Sir—"

"I'm her husband."

It's not a smart lie; too easy to disprove. But it'll get me in—or at least get me to someone higher up in the chain who I can convince to let me in.

The desk lady's face softens. "Just a moment." She picks up the phone, turning her back to whisper into it.

Stanton, Sofia, and Jake watch me as I pace, fingers locked behind my neck, every muscle tight and straining. After a few minutes, a square-jawed guy wearing deceptively casual jeans and a button-down emerges from the door that leads to the bowels of the hospital. His eyes are quick, observant—but his face is deliberately blank.

"Can I help you?" he asks.

"Kennedy Randolph—" I start.

"Is not here," he finishes.

"I know she is."

"No, you don't."

"I'm her—"

"*No*, you're not."

It takes everything I've got not to grab him by the throat and squeeze the answers out. "Are you FBI? Are you with the Marshalls? Your department's job was security—keeping her *safe*." My cheek twitches. "Bang-up job they're doing, Skippy."

"I have no information for you. It's time for you to go. Now."

"Is she alive?" My voice sounds like a captive who's been tortured for intel, and is finally broken. "Just give me that, for fuck's sake."

I don't care about the rest—her hair, her face, her arms, her legs—they don't matter. I'll love her without them. As long as she's still breathing. As long as she's still her.

Stone-face gives me jack shit. "Information on an active case can only be given to immediate family. I'm not confirming that there is an active case, but if there was—you are no one's immediate family. So I have nothing for you. I won't be telling you to leave again."

I move forward, ready to get in his face, but Sofia's hand on my arm pulls me back. "Come on, Brent. That's not going to help. Let's go."

I let her pull me outside to the sidewalk.

"Fuck!" I push my palms against my eyes. "God fucking damn it!"

Was this what it was like for my parents after my accident? While they waited for the doctor to come out to tell them if I'd made it?

It's like there's a hot poker under my ribs, pressing against my stomach, my lungs, my heart. Burning me alive slowly, from the inside.

I drop my hands and turn toward the door. "I'm going back in to talk to that agent. I'll make him—"

Stanton steps into my path. "You'll get arrested. Not the way to go, man."

I grind my jaw so hard the sound echoes in my eardrums.

Jake puts his hand on my shoulder, and his voice is clear and calming. "Brent, pull it together. You have resources: take a breath and call them."

I've always hated assholes who use their money and connections to exert undue influence—and believe me, I've known a lot of them. But at this moment, I've never been more grateful for my last name. Because it opens doors.

I take my phone out and dial. "Dad? I need your help. Do we know anyone in the U.S. Marshal's Service?"

When he replies, my eyebrows go up. "The director, huh? That's convenient. Can you call him for me?"

• • •

Ten minutes later, Urban Cowboy walks back into the waiting room. "Brent Mason."

I stand, but when the four of us move to him, he puts up a hand like a traffic cop. "Just you."

I'm immediately engulfed in Sofia's strong embrace. "Call us as soon as you can—let us know how she's doing."

"I will."

Jake squeezes my shoulder, Stanton smacks my back. "Anything you need."

"Thanks."

Then I get into the elevator with Super Cop. As the doors close, he tells me, "She's all right."

My lungs collapse. Deflate. Like I've been holding my breath for a millennia—waiting to hear those words.

"Broken arm, two cracked ribs, some facial contusions, but nothing serious."

Okay. She's injured, but she'll heal. I'll help her heal.

Thank you, God.

As the elevator starts to rise, I feel his eyes on me. "My supervisor called, told me to get you upstairs straight away."

I nod. "Yeah."

"He said the director called him personally."

"That sounds about right."

He pauses for a beat and then asks, "Who the hell are you?"

There's only one way I can answer. I lower my voice and look him in the eyes. "I'm Batman."

And he actually cracks a smile. Then the elevator opens on the tenth floor and he leads me down a hallway. There are a few agents milling about, but only one door has an armed guard stationed outside. They nod to each other, the marshal opens the door, and I step in alone.

The lights are low, the blinds closed. Kennedy's propped up in a hospital bed, her left arm encased in plaster hanging in a sling. I stand there for a minute, reminding myself that she's alive; looking her over, taking in every mark, every bruise. Her face is a mess—bottom lip split in the middle, caked with black dried blood; her left cheek is scraped raw, already starting to turn purple; the eye above it is swollen completely shut; and there's a row of stiches at her hairline.

"You're here." Her voice is soft—raspy—like her throat is sore.

And then I'm sitting on the bed, cupping the uninjured side of her jaw. She leans into my palm, and my throat strangles so tight I can barely get the words out. "You're okay?"

She tries to smile, but can't quite manage it with her lip. Her good eye gazes back at me—that sweet, soft golden brown. "I'm okay."

My other hand gently—so gently—runs through her hair, over her shoulder, settling on her chest, soaking up the feeling of her heart beating strong and steady beneath it. I swallow hard and my eyelids burn, because she's my Kennedy and she's hurt . . . and I could've lost her. For good.

"Jesus, Kennedy . . . let me just . . ." I can't finish. Instead I pull her into my arms, chest to chest. I turn my face into her neck, breathing against her soft skin that still smells like peaches beneath the scent of hospital antiseptic. She's trembling, so I stroke her hair and rub her back and rock her slowly, resting my lips against her temple.

And I want to stay just like this. Where I know she's safe because my arms are around her, and I'll never, ever let anything fucking hurt her again.

"They hit the car hard," she whispers against my shoulder, her fingers clinging to my bicep. "I wasn't wearing my seat belt, and we flipped on our side. I saw their feet—I knew they were coming for me."

I press her closer and have to force myself not to hold her too tight.

Her voice goes shaky and I hear the tears. "And all I could think was that I'd never see you again." She pulls back just enough so she can look up at me. "That I'd never have the chance to tell you that . . . that I have loved you forever . . ."

The last word comes out on a sob, her face crumbling. ". . . but never as much as I love you right now."

I wipe her tears away with my thumb, kissing her softly—just a brush against her upper lip. And my voice is steady, solid, with the easiest words I've ever said.

"I love *you*."

Then I tuck her in against my chest, my chin on the top of her head. "We're going to have lots of time to say that to each other, Kennedy. Over and over again. Thousands of days to show it." I kiss her hair. "It's gonna be sickening."

She laughs.

And that's when I know for sure that she's going to be okay.

• • •

A little while later, after a nurse checks in with pain meds and Kennedy's sucking down some apple juice, I ask about the bastards who went after her.

"The agents shot them. They're dead."

"Good." There's a dark undercurrent to my voice.

I take the empty juice box from her and put it on the table. She lies back on the pillow, looking sleepy—the medication's doing its job. She touches her discolored cheek. "You can start calling me Bruiser now—there's a nickname for you."

"Bruiser's a name for someone who *gives* bruises, not *gets* them."

She traces the frown lines on my forehead, smoothing my scowl. "Too soon to joke about it, huh?"

"A millennium isn't enough time to make this jokeable."

Before she can reply, a sharp female voice cuts through the closed door.

"Do you think I'm concerned about hospital policy? I don't care if she already has a visitor, I will see my daughter *now*!"

Kennedy's good eye slides closed. "Oh no."

"Remove yourself from my path or there will be consequences, young man!"

"Oh *no*."

Mitzy Randolph steps into the room, looking unusually haggard in an untucked dark blue blouse, black slacks, her pearls askew, her hair falling out of its bun. I've never seen Mitzy's hair not flawlessly styled; I always figured the strands were too terrified to move.

Like a bodyguard, I stand but don't move an inch from Kennedy's bedside. Because, mother or no mother, if I hear one backhanded insult, I will lose my shit.

"Hello, Mother," Kennedy says quietly.

Mitzy's breathing is shallow as her eyes roam Kennedy's battered features. She moves forward slowly, as if she's in a trance. "Oh, Kennedy, your lovely face."

"It's all right." She tries for a stoic grin. "They're just bruises. Nothing permanent, no scars."

Her mother's lip trembles and her eyes fill, then brim over. I've never seen Mitzy cry—and from the look on her face, neither has Kennedy.

"My dear, precious girl . . ." Her voice cracks. ". . . what have they done to you?"

Kennedy's expression goes soft and she looks almost apologetic and at the same time, grateful that her mother actually cares enough to be bothered.

"Don't cry. I'm okay, really."

But her mother just shakes her head, weeping quietly.

I gesture to the door. "I'm gonna step outside a minute."

Kennedy's eyes flick quickly to me and she nods a silent thank-you.

Before I walk out, I glance back at them. For some people, this is how it works. You have to get smacked right in the face with the possibility of losing something before you wake up and realize how much it means to you.

Mitzy whispers softly and gazes down at her daughter like she's finally seeing *her*, not just all the things she wants her to be.

About fucking time.

• • •

Out in the hall, I spot the marshal who escorted me to Kennedy's room and motion him over. "You think they'll try again?"

His eyes narrow. "As long as there's money being offered, they might."

I nod, grab a pen from the nurse's station, and take a business card out of my pocket. I scribble on the back and hand it to him. "Any security arrangements that need to be made should be made at that address. When she comes home, she's coming home with me. And I'm keeping her there."

19

I keep Kennedy in bed for the next three days.

Unfortunately, it's not as hot as it sounds, because she's bruised and sore and her pain pills knock her out cold. But I take care of her—I fluff her pillows, cook her food. Okay, Harrison does the actual cooking, but I *bring* her the food.

I also help her bathe—and that's a fresh kind of hell.

Because with two cracked ribs, sex is off the table. I can't even eat her out, because I know making her come will give her just as much pain as pleasure. She tells me it'll be worth it, but I stick to my guns.

Until day five, when the sexy vixen takes matters into her own hands. Literally.

We were in bed, in the still darkness of night, and Kennedy proceeded to describe, in full, filthy detail, all the things she wanted me to do to her. Things she couldn't wait to do to me. Then she begged me to show her—to take my cock in hand and make myself come.

On her.

And I folded like a pornographic deck of cards.

On my knees, hovering over her, I panted and groaned, imagining that it was her hand stroking me hard. But her hand was busy between her own legs, rubbing her clit, driving her glistening fingers in and out, in time with my own fist. I painted her tits that night, and she impressively demonstrated that she was healed enough to handle an orgasm.

So of course I spend the better part of day six with my mouth attached to her pretty cunt—to make up for lost time.

But by day seven, she's antsy. Sick of television and too wired to work. I call the troops to my place for dinner. Harrison watches the McQuaid Monsters over at Jake and Chelsea's so they can come. Stanton arrives with Sofia, and the baby bump that could apply for its own zip code now. Brian and Vicki show up too. I introduce them to the rest of the squad, and we all eat pizza at the dining room table.

After dinner, we hang out in the living room—the guys watch the game while the girls talk baby announcements and bridal showers.

"It's going to be a brunch," Sofia tells Kennedy, about the bridal shower she's throwing for Chelsea. "Not too big, because Jake and Chelsea are antisocial."

"Ha!" Chelsea grins. "Let's see how social you and Stanton are after this little delight is born. Then multiply that by six."

"You really should come," Sofia tells Kennedy and Vicki. "It's going to be fun— mimosas and naughty bingo. Since they already have all their household stuff, everyone's bringing lingerie for the wishing well."

Jake's eyes light up. "Yes, you two should definitely come. The more the merrier—for me."

"When is it?" Kennedy asks Sofia, pulling up her calendar on her phone.

"The twenty-third."

Kennedy clicks her tongue. "I won't be able to make it— I'll be in Vegas on the twenty-third."

Spiders of unease scurry up my arms and across my back.

"What are you talking about?" I ask.

Kennedy meets my eyes across the room, and as casually as if she's giving the weather forecast, she says, "The trial starts in two weeks. They're handling the pretrial motions without me, but I'll have to fly out in a few days."

I put my beer on the coffee table and give her my undivided attention. "But . . . you're not trying the case anymore."

She frowns. "Of course I am. Why wouldn't I?"

I gesture to her arm, her swollen eye. "You're hurt."

"No, I'm healing. By the time the trial starts I'll be back to normal, except for the cast."

My heart beats against my chest—wanting to bust out and shake her.

I get to my feet. Because I argue better on my feet, and I have a feeling this is about to spiral into one hell of an argument. "Kennedy . . . that's . . . fucking crazy. Did the concussion knock you stupid?"

"Excuse me?"

"He tried to *kill* you."

She stands up slowly, her spine rigid and shoulders back. "But he didn't. And it's my case."

"They'll assign another prosecutor."

"No—they won't. Because I won't let them. Moriotti is

trying to scare me away, and I'm not going to let him. He doesn't get to take this from me."

My fingers press against my temples, and my voice rises. "Holy shit, Kennedy—he's not a schoolyard bully—he's a goddamn psychopath, with the means and motive to put a bullet in you. And you're going to walk into his territory to give him the opportunity? Why don't you just draw a bull's-eye on your forehead!"

I must sound as panicked as I feel, because her posture softens. Her voice fills with calming sympathy. "It'll be okay."

She reaches out to stroke my forehead, but I jerk it away.

"You don't *know* that! Fucked-up things happen all the time!" I point to Sofia. "She was in a plane crash, did you know that? With her whole family—and it was just dumb luck that they didn't die." I gesture to Chelsea. "And Chelsea's brother, he and his wife were just driving home and they were killed, Kennedy. They had six kids who needed them, and they *died*."

I rub the back of my neck, scrub my hand over my face, trying not to totally lose it. "And I was just a kid; a dumb kid who got his leg ripped off for no reason at all. Bad things happen even when you're careful—even when you don't deserve them."

"This is my job, Brent."

"It's a job you don't need! You have more money in your trust fund right now than you'll ever make as a prosecutor."

"That doesn't matter—"

My voice drops lower. "I get that—I do. You took this job because you needed a purpose. A reason to get out of bed every day." I grip her shoulders, bend my knees and look into her eyes. "But you have me now. We can be each other's reasons."

She gazes at me like I'm breaking her heart. No—like her heart is breaking for me.

There's a difference.

"You *are* my reason. And all I want in the whole world is to be yours." Kennedy puts her hand right on top of my heart. "But I have to see this through."

Goddamn it!

Something in me fucking snaps, because she's not *listening*. She's too damn stubborn. Too fucking fearless. And if I can't change her mind—it could get her killed.

"If you go, we're done," I say coldly.

"Brent—" Jake warns, but I throw up my hand.

Kennedy flinches. Then she searches my face, hunting for a sign that I'm bluffing. "You don't mean that."

"Yes, I fucking do. I'm not going to sit here and drive myself crazy worrying about you. I'm not going to spend the rest of my life mourning you after you get yourself killed. You do this, we're fucking done."

A small faraway voice that sounds suspiciously like Waldo whispers that this is wrong. Manipulative. But I tell him to go screw himself, 'cause I'm doing this to keep her safe.

"I've made promises to people, Brent."

Her expression is weighted with hurt. Maybe even a little fear. Like I haven't just dented her armor, but wedged a crowbar in there and cracked it wide open, exposing all her most vulnerable parts.

But I'm not going to feel bad about that.

"Then break them. Promises are broken every damn day—it's the way of the world."

"There are witnesses who have risked their lives to testify

against Moriotti. Who've gone into Witness Protection and given up everything, because I held their hand and told them it was the right thing to do. Because I swore I would put him away. And now . . . you just want me to turn my back because things are getting a little uncomfortable?"

My face feels hard, frozen—an ice sculpture image of myself. "Yes. I want you to turn your back and run the other way."

She shakes her head softly. "I can't . . . I can't believe you're making me choose."

"Well, I am. And if that makes me an asshole, I don't give a shit." My fingers squeeze her upper arms. "I'm asking you to choose, and I am begging you . . . to pick me."

The entire room goes quiet. I don't think anyone even fucking breathes.

Then Kennedy cups my jaw in both her hands. And her voice is hushed—the way you'd talk at a funeral. "I love you, Brent. I *really* love you, and I know you love me. But I won't be the woman you love anymore if I don't do this. And if we can just—"

I don't hear another word after that. Because I'm already walking out the door, slamming it behind me, leaving the frame splintered.

I wander the city for an hour—or three—because I'm afraid of what I'll say to her if I go back too soon. But when I finally do make it back, I don't have to worry about that.

The house is dark. Empty.

She's gone.

20

"How fucked up is *that*?"

Early the next morning, Waldo's eyes follow me like a spectator at Wimbledon as I pace back and forth in front of his couch, recounting my argument with Kennedy word for word. I barely slept last night—I was too busy replaying it in my head. And waiting for her to call. To tell me that she's come over to my side of sanity and she's dropping the case.

But my phone stayed mute.

Waldo clears his throat. "Throughout your impressive rant, you didn't utter a single word about Kennedy's perspective. Have you given any thought at all about what she may be feeling right now?"

Petulantly, I snort. "No."

I've been too busy being pissed off to analyze how she might feel about me being pissed off.

He nods. "Let's examine that. Kennedy is the one who was attacked and injured. She's the one who opened herself up to you when you fought so hard to regain her trust. The one who believed you when you professed your love. The one who watched you walk away when faced with your first challenge as a couple. How do you think she feels about all that, Brent?" His fingers thrum against the arm of the chair. "Afraid? Hurt? Devastated?"

Guilt trips from a seasoned therapist are a hard thing to resist, but I manage.

"She wouldn't feel *any* of that if she'd just do what I fucking tell her."

His lips hint at a smile, but not the good kind. He reminds me of Jasper, when he's got his mousey toy trapped between his claws—and he's about to screw with it. "But relationships don't work that way. You know this. Kennedy needs your support, not your direction."

I open my mouth to argue, but he talks right over me.

"Let's not waste our time here. How about you try being honest—and tell me what you're really feeling."

I rub at the frustration knotting the back of my neck. "Are you kidding, or just blind? I'm angry, Captain Obvious."

His gaze is steady and calm. Knowing. It's fucking annoying.

"You don't look angry to me. You look terrified. What are you actually afraid of, Brent?"

I throw my hands out. "I'm afraid she's going to get hurt!"

"That she's going to be hurt, or that you won't be able to prevent her from being hurt?"

I almost laugh. "Is there a goddamn difference?"

"Yes. One involves your concern for her. The other revolves only around yourself. The fear that you'll fail her. That you won't be able to protect her."

The truth is a relentless, ugly little beast. It scratches and gnaws, driving you crazy—until you let it out.

"I didn't protect her before, did I?"

I think about the night of the senior dance, Kennedy's face—muddy and bleeding. I think about years of poisonous taunts and hissed insults, which can break a soul as easily as sticks and stones break bone. "I left her to the wolves, and they had a feast. That's not going to happen again. No fucking way. I'm trying to protect her this time."

He nods. "You failed her before because you were selfish. An adolescent, thinking only of yourself."

"I know that!"

He spreads his arms—the big reveal. "And yet here you are—repeating yourself. Thinking of *your* wants. *Your* feelings. Like an irritable teenager all over again."

"I'm thirty-two years old—I'm a grown man, for Christ's sake!"

He leans forward in his chair. "Yes, you are. And for the last few weeks, you've been acting like one. So it's disappointing to see you regress overnight."

My teeth grind, and I jab a finger toward him. "You know something? Fuck you, Waldo."

Then I walk out his door too.

• • •

After that disaster, I go to the office, still pissed. Actually, more pissed, because he didn't tell me what I wanted to hear. Doesn't see my perfectly rational point that tucking Kennedy safely away in my house, in my bed—is the best, the *only* acceptable course of action. There are women who'd sell their soul to live in my gilded cage. But I don't want any of them.

As I stand in front of my desk, shuffling papers and banging drawers, Jake steps through the doorway.

"As far as temper tantrums go, yours is pretty pathetic. You should talk to Regan—she can give you some pointers."

"Fuck off, man." I don't even look up.

He folds his arms across his chest. "Can't do that, buddy. You're screwing up way too badly for me to just sit back and watch."

I slam my top drawer shut with a bang, then point at him. "Give me a motherfucking break! Like you'd be any different if it was Chelsea? How would you react if it was her walking into the lion's den?"

Jake's voice is low and lethally calm. "Chelsea can walk into any damn den she wants. Because I *am* the lion. And I'd make sure I was with her."

I breathe hard as he comes to stand in front of my desk.

"Your problem is you underestimated her. You threw down a marker you never intended to pay, and she called your fucking bluff. She's going, Brent—nothing you say is gonna stop her. So the only question left is, what are you going to do now?"

Then Sofia walks into the room. "Hey . . . guys? I think—"

I immediately cut her off. "*Et tu,* Sofia? Not now, okay?"

"I know, but listen—"

"Contrary to what you all think, I'm a big boy. This is between me and Kennedy. We'll work it out, and I don't—"

"My water broke."

There are few words in the English language that are capable of grabbing immediate and undivided attention. *Fire* is one. *Bingo* is pretty high on the list. *I'm going to come* is my personal favorite. But, much like the One Ring, *my water broke* rules them all.

Jake and I spin around and face Sofia, who's now leaning up against the wall. The bottom back of her green dress is noticeably saturated and liquid drips down her legs, leaving a trail on the carpet behind her.

"Wow—that's a lot of water. You could drown a puppy in that much water."

"I'll call Stanton," Jake volunteers.

Sofia holds up her hand. "No! He's in court, and I don't want him driving the Porsche to the hospital—he might kill someone or himself." She takes a deep, cleansing breath and assumes her drill sergeant persona. "Jake, go to court and bring Stanton to the hospital. Mrs. Higgens knows where he is. Brent, have Harrison bring the car around—then take me to the house to get my bag and then to the hospital." Her lips pucker and she exhales slowly—almost whistling.

Everything else disintegrates in the light of this monumental development. Because even though Sofia is chanting *everything is fine* to no one in particular, her face is tight and pale. She's shaking scared, and she's one of my best friends in the whole world. She needs me.

Jake and I move at the same time—him out the door, me sweeping Sofia up into my arms. Her hands clasp around the back of my neck even as she says, "I'm in labor, Brent, not an invalid. I can walk."

"Of course you can—but why should you have to when you have a manly man like me around?"

As I head down the stairs, I adjust Sofia's considerable mass in my arms. And of course, she notices.

"If you tease me about how heavy I am, I'll rip your beard hairs out."

"Tease? Me?" I grin. "I would never tease a woman about her weight—especially a pregnant woman." I make it down the last step, then add, "Although . . . I think my titanium prosthetic just bent under the strain."

She pinches me. On my neck, my arms—anywhere she can reach.

"Ow, Jesus! No pinching! Pinching is not cool!"

Sofia's got a lethal finger grip. Her older brothers, who teased her mercilessly, must've looked like Dalmatians growing up, 'cause I doubt she took that shit lying down.

But as I carry her out to the sidewalk, she's laughing. So my mission for now is accomplished.

And sixteen hours later, Sofia's mission is accomplished too. Because that's when our law firm's first baby comes screaming—arguing—into the world.

• • •

"Samuel, huh?"

I peer down at the bundle of sleeping, sweet-smelling baby in my arms. People always talk about how newborns have their mother's lips or their father's nose, but I never got that. They all just look like babies. Insanely cute, but pretty much the same.

"So, you guys are doing the *S* thing? As if Sofia and Stanton Shaw wasn't nauseating enough?"

Stanton tilts back in the pleather recliner beside Sofia's hospital bed. He picks a green grape from the bag on his lap and pops it into his mouth. "Nah, he just looks like a Samuel."

"He looks like an alien."

At Sofia's frown, I amend that statement. "An adorable alien, but still, he's got a head on him. How'd that feel coming out?"

Sofia smiles sweetly. "I hope you get kidney stones, so you can find out."

Then we sit in companionable silence for a few moments. Until Sofia gently prods, "Have you talked to Kennedy?"

My heart squeezes until my whole body throbs. My anger bled out sometime last night. Now I just ache for her.

"No."

Stanton pops in another grape. "Why not?"

"I'm still hoping she'll come to her senses."

"Do you love her?" Sofia turns to her husband with an open mouth. "Hit me."

He effortlessly lands a grape in her mouth.

I brush my knuckle across Samuel's perfect hand, imagining how it'd feel to hold a tiny newborn girl with blond hair. "Yes, I love her."

"Then fucking fix it, man," Stanton insists. "You had a fight; you said things you didn't mean—welcome to Relationship Land. But you don't break up over a fight. Not if you love her."

Sofia talks as she chews. "He's right. If we broke up every time we disagreed about something, Samuel's home would've been broken a long time ago."

Stanton nods.

Sofia's voice is sincere with experience. "It's scary, I know. Giving someone that kind of power over you—accepting that your happiness will forever hinge on theirs. But it's worth it." She reaches out and Stanton takes her hand, giving her a secret smile.

Words from two decades ago echo in my head and slip out of my mouth. "The ride is the only thing that makes the fall worth it."

Sofia's head tilts curiously and I shrug. "A smart, fearless girl told me that once."

Stanton grins. "She sounds like a keeper."

Damn straight she is.

• • •

In my head, I act out every sappy grand gesture teenage girls fantasize about. I stand outside her bedroom window with a boom box over my head. I run through the airport, catch her moments before she boards the plane, and profess my undying love. I completely redecorate my home office, put her desk right next to mine, to prove to her how much I want her in my life.

In reality—I don't do any of those things.

Because this isn't a movie—this is real life. And Kennedy and I are the realest thing I've ever known.

What she needs most from me isn't over-the-top gestures or expensive gifts I could buy her without a second thought. She needs the words. And she needs to look into my eyes when I give them to her, so she can see that I mean every single one.

I nod to the federal agent stationed at the gate of her house.

He lets me through and I march up the steps of her porch, knocking on her door. After what feels like forever and a day, it opens, and shiny eyes—one still swollen—stare up at me from her bruised, beautiful face.

A guilty blade thrusts up under my rib cage—because she's still hurting. And I've made her hurt more.

The words rush from my lips.

"We're not done. I didn't—" My voice cracks. "I didn't mean it."

Her face softens in fucking sympathy—for me. And the blade plunges deeper, twisting cruelly.

"I know, Brent."

I touch her cheek, because I can't not touch her for a second longer. "I'm sorry."

Her breath hitches. "Me too. I'm sorry I can't make this easier for you."

"No. I was an ass. You don't have to make it easier for me—I don't want you worrying about that. I love you, Kennedy."

"I love you too." She takes a deep breath—then her chin rises and her voice is stronger. "Don't ask me not to go again. I don't think I could stand it."

"I won't. The only thing I'll ask is"—my head dips, moving closer—"let me come with you."

Her face crumbles and she surges against me. I hold her as tight as I dare as her tears soak into my shirt, and she nods against my chest. "Yes. Please come with me."

21

On the first day of a big trial, some lawyers want their sole focus to be on the case. They think about it while shoveling oatmeal into their mouths. They rehearse their opening statement while sipping their coffee, and tape their notes to the mirror while they shave and straighten their tie.

But not Kennedy. Because this morning, in our Nevada hotel room, her focus is wholly on my cock.

She's on her knees in front of me where I stand by the bed, teasing the sensitive indentation on the underside of my hot, hard rod as she sucks me off. And it feels so fucking good I practically decapitate myself when my head rolls toward the ceiling. I dig my hand into her hair and fist it tight, holding her still, so I can pump into her mouth.

Goddamn.

It's the roughest I've let myself be with her the last two weeks—and she loves it. She hums around me, sending ripples of decadent pleasure through every nerve in my body. My chin touches my chest as I look down, watching my dick slide smoothly between Kennedy's rosy lips.

"That's it. Take it just like that," I rasp. 'Cause I'm feeling fucking dirty.

Her responding moan is almost my undoing. With a swiftness born of desperation, I lift her up, toss her onto the bed, and grab her ankles—dragging her to the edge. Then I bend my knees and drive into her.

"Oh god . . . Brent . . . Oh yeah . . ."

She watches me, those golden brown eyes burning like a bonfire of fall leaves.

The angriest of her bruises have faded to mere discoloration, and a smattering of tiny scabs remain from the abrasion on her cheek. But the split lip and swelling around her eye are fully healed.

I rotate my hips, pushing in deep, then changing to smooth and steady thrusts. I slide my palms up her calves, grasping beneath her knees and spreading her wide open. Giving me a perfect view of her glistening dark pink flesh.

It's times like this I wish my mother had mated with Dr. Octavius.

Words scrape up my throat. "Play with your tits. Pinch those pretty nipples like it's your fucking *job*."

Kennedy closes her eyes with a moan. And it's only a second before she does my bidding—her small hands squeeze her supple mounds, then her fingers tug at the mauve peaks.

Hard.

Oh yeah—that's my girl.

Her needy cunt tightens around me, trying to hold me

inside. And she begs, and Christ—there is no sweeter sound on earth than Kennedy Randolph begging.

For *more*.

For *faster*.

Harder, Brent. Deeper.

Then it's a sonata of breathy gasps, ragged groans, and the sound of slapping skin. The tendons in my back lengthen and strain, like the string of a bow stretched to its snapping point. Kennedy's toes curl and her tiny feet flex, searching for purchase in the air. With a series of grunts that grate my voice box raw, I come, fingers digging into her hips, holding her still—making her take everything I have to give.

Her hands ravage the sheets and Kennedy climaxes right after. Her contracting muscles clamp down, wringing every last drop from my still-pulsing cock. My head goes light, my vision hazy. It's possible I'm about to pass the hell out.

And I collapse on top of her, my bones turned to Jell-O.

When the aftershocks eventually ebb, she laughs. That twinkling, magical laugh that sings of contentment and tugs up my own lips in a responding smile.

Now that—*that* is how you start a fucking trial.

• • •

Once I'm actually able to stand again, we hit the shower. With Kennedy's cast wrapped in a plastic bag, washing her hair—and all her nooks and crannies—is a challenge. Naturally, I've been helping her out. It's the only decent thing to do.

And just a little while later, I'm in my suit—the navy one

with my lucky cuff links—assisting Kennedy with her first layer of clothing.

"Kevlar's a hot look for you." I secure the Velcro seam. "We are definitely taking this home with us."

Her golden hair slides off her shoulder when she turns my way. "You're kind of a kinky bastard, aren't you?"

"You have no idea. But don't worry—you will." I seal the promise with a kiss on her cheek. Then I hold her blouse while she slides her arms in.

"How are you feeling, champ?" I ask.

I've seen firsthand over the last weeks that Kennedy is stellar at compartmentalizing. Burying any pesky emotions like fear or doubt way down deep during the day. But at night, when we're alone, that's when the demons creep from their crypt and tell her that she's bound to fail—or worse. And I'm grateful to be here—to be the man who gets to hold her when she trembles, the one she whispers those worries to, the one who helps her shoulder that burden.

She'll never have to do it alone again.

"I'm good." She grins back, and the gleam in her eye tells me that's true.

I drop a peck on her nose and button her blouse, because the cast makes that difficult too. But as I look at the remnants of her injuries—still visible through her light makeup—it hits me. I turn her head, checking out the yellowish bruising in different lights.

"What's wrong?"

"The defense is going to ask the judge to recuse you because of the bruises, the cast. They'll say you'll prejudice the jury."

She frowns. "You think so?"

"It's what I'd do." I shrug.

Kennedy nods her head slowly, gazing at the carpet—seeing the potential exchange play out behind her eyes. "Okay. Then I'll be ready to argue that motion."

"Yeah," I kiss her forehead now. "You will be."

. . .

Kennedy walks into court like a general. The way I imagine Joan of Arc walked onto the battlefield—just daring the English to bring it on. I sit in the front row of the gallery, right behind her. Next to me is Connor Roth, the green-eyed, stone-faced marshal who took me up to her hospital room. He's been by her side ever since.

While she speaks in hushed tones to the other prosecutors at the table, I check out Moriotti, on the opposite side of the courtroom, next to his own team of attorneys. He's in his forties, short but stocky—powerful—with black, slicked hair that's just starting to gray at the temples. He looks like a typical scumbag, even dressed up in an Italian suit, which I know at a glance cost him the average person's mortgage payment. He follows Kennedy with his eyes, and when he notices the cast on her arm—the fucker laughs.

Rage shoots through my bloodstream like a speeding bullet, making me careless—thoughtless. I start to rise from my seat, intent on walking over there and ripping the motherfucker's head off with my bare hands. And I pity the bailiff who gets in my way.

A strong grip on my shoulder holds me back.

"Don't do it, Batman," Roth murmurs. "Getting thrown

out of court and locked up before the trial even starts won't do your girl any favors."

His words pull me from my gory fantasies, because he's right. It sucks—but he's right.

. . .

Three days later, I tell Kennedy I won't be in court that afternoon. When worry shadows her face, I'm quick to explain I have some of my own work to catch up on. It's a lie—Jake is awesome at holding down the fort, and even on maternity leave, Stanton has been picking up my slack from home. But it's just a little lie—the good kind.

Because if she knew where I was *really* going, that shadow of concern would turn into a full-blown eclipse.

. . .

The modern-day Mafioso is very different from the olden days of Al Capone, fedora hats, and Tommy guns hidden in violin cases. *The Sopranos* got it pretty right. If you didn't already know it, you'd never suspect that Carmine Bianco— the seventy-year-old, dark-haired, leather-faced guy in the back corner table of this neighborhood deli—is the supreme leader of a ruthless, multimillion-dollar criminal organization that the feds have been trying for two decades to pin a RICO charge on. He looks like somebody's grandpa, or an old benevolent uncle.

Except for the two massive bastards standing behind him—with gun belts strapped beneath their jackets.

We're the only customers in the deli, so when one of the big guys steps up to me a few feet short of the table, I automatically hold out my arms and he pats me down—checking for weapons or a wire. My whole life, people have commented on my youthful face, my boyish good looks, and have underestimated me because of them. I press that advantage now, and give Carmine an affable smile as I sit down across from him.

"Mr. Bianco, I'm Brent Mason. Thank you for agreeing to meet with me."

He puts his overflowing sandwich down and chews his mouthful, swiping a napkin across his lips with thick fingers. "You want a sandwich?"

I shake my head. "I'm good, thanks."

His eyes are sharp, gleaming like a switchblade as he takes me in—my gray suit, loosened tie, Rolex watch. "I don't know you. I don't know how you know me—but my money guy said I should meet with you, so here we are. What can you do for me, kid?"

His business advisor is an associate of an associate of one of my family's longtime brokers. So I made a few calls—because it doesn't matter if you're a mobster or a prince: money always talks.

"I guess you could say I have a . . . business proposition for you." My voice gives me away. It's hard—tight. I don't know if he ordered the hit on Kennedy, or if his boys clean up their own messes. And I can't ask; he wouldn't tell me either way. All I can do is deal with him, because when you want to get rid of a snake, you aim straight for the head.

He leans back in his seat. "I'm listening."

"Gino Moriotti. He works for you."

The old man's mouth quirks. "Allegedly."

"Of course, allegedly." I chuckle.

"What about him?"

Then I'm not chuckling anymore. "How much is he worth to you? How much money do you stand to lose when he gets put away—and I have no doubt whatsoever that he *will* be put away."

That gets his attention. He stares at me the way you stare at someone you think you've met before, but can't quite remember. Like he's trying to place me. Figure me out.

I give him a hand and lay my cards bare on the table.

"The lead prosecutor on his case—"

"The blonde." He points at me, nodding with understanding.

"The blonde," I confirm.

"She's cute."

"Yes, she is. She's also very important to me. When this case is finished, I'm going to take her back to DC. I'm going to marry her, have beautiful babies with her, and grow old with her. And I'm not gonna do that looking over her shoulder all the time, worrying that someone from your organization is going to try and settle a score." I let him absorb that.

Then I tell him, "I have money. I have properties I didn't buy, cars and carpets, antiques and jewels—and none of them means a damn to me if I don't have her. So—give me a number."

We stare each other down.

When he remains quiet, I add in a low voice—just shy of menacing. "Think of this as my big, fat carrot. You catch more flies with honey, y'know? But rest assured that my stick is pretty fucking lethal—and I'm not afraid to use it."

Laughter shakes his whole body, vibrating the table. "Aye, oh—listen to you. Somebody's got balls to spare, huh? Sounds like a threat." He turns to one of the ogres behind him. "You believe this kid, Tony?"

Tony doesn't believe it. "I don't believe it, Mr. Bianco."

"I musta misheard you. Right . . . *Brent*?"

And as quick as a snake strike, lethal energy radiates from him, like steam from a boiling pot.

And I don't give a shit—because I've done my homework.

I lean forward, looking straight into his eyes. "You're married, right, Carmine? To the same woman for over fifty years. There's just something about the girl next door—your childhood sweetheart. The prosecutor? She's mine. So . . . ask yourself if there's anything you wouldn't do to keep your wife safe. Any horror you wouldn't commit, any law you wouldn't break. Then . . . you tell me if I'm threatening you."

Thick, heavy silence blankets the room.

Then Bianco reaches down and takes another bite of his sandwich. As he chews, he tells me, "I like you, kid."

I shrug. "Most people do."

He takes another bite. "You gamble?"

"Sometimes."

He nods, swallowing his bite. "The way I gamble . . . you gotta try and tip the odds in your favor. Load the dice, weight the wheel, count the cards. But after you play your hand—if you lose, it's over. You cut your losses, walk away from the table. Turning around to take out the dealer only pisses off the casino. Brings unneeded attention, you know what I'm sayin'?"

And I'm pretty sure I do.

Bianco leans back in his chair, regarding me. "So . . . after

Gino's hand plays out, you marry your cute girl, have lots of blue-eyed lawyer babies—and don't bother looking over her shoulder. We're not gonna be there."

• • •

Three weeks later, the verdict is in. I'm right behind Kennedy when the foreman reads it aloud. And I'm the first person she hugs after Gino Moriotti is found guilty on all counts.

Kennedy and I go out and celebrate with the prosecutors and agents who worked the case with her. She drinks vodka. A lot of it. It's a great fucking night.

And then I pack up my warrior princess and take her home to my castle.

Epilogue

Six months later

"Welcome Saint Arthur's Class of 2000!"

The high school reunion: one of the most excruciatingly annoying experiences ever invented. You have to get all dressed up to see people you didn't actually like enough to keep in touch with over the past fifteen years. Men worry if anyone will notice how bald they're going—and the answer is yes. Women worry if they look the same as they did when they were eighteen. News flash—you don't. Or, if you do, that's some toxic fucking voodoo you're pumping into your veins, so you should stop right away.

Vicki and Brian begged off, using the ultimate ironclad excuse of their kids to get out of going. Kennedy was reluctant too. But after my relentless oral persuasion—and two orgasms—she gave in.

I think it will be good for her to face those ghosts, so she can see that even bullies grow up, and more important, get old. She says she doesn't need that, but I think deep down, she still carries a tiny open wound from those years. Coming back here, with me, might finally scab it over completely.

And to be honest—I want to be here with her. I want to show her the fuck off—her and the three-carat engagement ring I put on her finger last month. It's not just because she's drop-dead gorgeous either. I'd want her on my arm even if she was still wearing those old glasses and braces and big baggy sweaters. Because I'm proud of *her*—not just how she looks.

And—if everything goes like I think it will—I have an additional ulterior motive for coming back.

Cher blasts from the speakers as Kennedy and I step into the gymnasium, hand in hand. Since our boarding school costs a pretty penny, you'd think the event would have more elegance. Class.

But nope—it's the typical streamers, dimly lit, candles on the table, occasional strobe lights flashing like we're in a club, bad DJ, kind of setup. We get a drink from the bar and walk around—mingling with my old lacrosse teammates and even chatting for a few minutes with William fucking Penderghast. He's a big-time CEO now, with a Victoria's Secret model for a wife. Good for him.

But we both know I still got the better end of the deal.

"Holy shit, Brent Mason! Come here you handsome bastard!"

I'm accosted by a tan, blond woman in a sequined gown, wearing way too much Chanel No. 5. When she steps back, I see it's my old girlfriend—Cashmere Champlaine. It'd be nice to say she got what she deserved—that the years hadn't been kind to the face and body she valued so much. But that just wouldn't be true. She's still beautiful, with a tastefully medically enhanced face and a toned body without any obvious fat. I'd heard she'd married a professional football player a few years back, then divorced him. And married one of his teammates.

Her lips peel back in an aggressive smile, revealing glowing, straight teeth. She smacks the lapel of my suit. "How are you, stranger?"

"I'm good, Cazz," I answer coolly. "How about yourself?"

"I'm amazing! I'm running my own modeling business now out in LA! Everyone thinks they're going to be the next Giselle—though most of them couldn't get a hemorrhoid cream commercial without blowing the photographer first. What are you doing with your fine self these days?"

And here's where that ulterior motive comes into play.

"I got engaged recently."

Her smile turns forced and her eyes harden. "Really? How nice."

"It is." Then I pull Kennedy around from behind me. "My fiancée is Kennedy Randolph. You remember her, don't you, Cazz?"

Her pretense of good humor drops, melting into an ugly scowl.

"Hello, Cashmere." Kennedy stares her down, her eyes hard like topaz. It's similar to her court stance. Fearless.

"You have got to be fucking kidding me!" Cashmere screeches at me. "I knew it! I always *knew* you had a thing for her! Unbelievable!"

My voice is calm, and deceptively contrite. "Yeah, you're right. I always did. The thing is, I have a little confession to make."

"What?"

"I cheated on you, Cashmere. All through boarding school. All those nights when I said I had to practice late or my leg bothered me or I had to study—I was really with Kennedy." I look right into her angry eyes. "It was always her. Always."

When a stunned expression fills her face, I know she believes me. That my words struck her right in the heart. And Kennedy's final dragon is slayed.

"Are you . . . are you *serious*?"

"Totally." Then I shrug. "But it's no big deal, right? Kids are assholes. They only care about themselves—they don't give a damn how much they might hurt someone else. No hard feelings, right?"

Cashmere swallows whatever she was about to say, because we're surrounded by her old groupies—and every one of them heard. So she saves face as best she can.

She smiles tightly. "Yeah. No hard feelings."

"Great." I stroke the back of Kennedy's hair. "Oh—this is a good song. If you'll excuse me, I'm going to dance with the girl of my dreams. Later, Cazz."

I turn around and lead Kennedy away.

Once we're on the dance floor, with my arms around her, she smirks at me.

"Why did you do that?"

I press my lips against her hair. "I can't go back and change those years for you, but I can change how she remembers them. She doesn't get to think she was better than you—she never was."

Kennedy's sigh sounds content and grateful at the same time.

"Thank you."

She lays her head on my chest and we dance for a few minutes. Then her head pops back up excitedly. "Hey, you know what we should do?"

"What?"

"We should drive back out to the overlook." Her voice drops to sultry. Teasing. "We could . . . make out . . . like we did last time."

I brush my nose against hers. "Will you let me go all the way this time?"

She bites her lip, like she has to think about it. "I'm not sure . . . I'm a good girl, you know."

My hands slip down to her hips, squeezing. "But it's so fun when you're bad."

And hot. She's really fucking hot when she's bad.

Kennedy's head tilts back and her eyes sparkle. All for me. "You play your cards right, things could turn naughty."

Sweet. I'm a kick-ass card player.

"You know what else I just realized?" she asks.

My hands slide up her thighs, cupping her ass. "What?"

"You never settled on a nickname for me."

I kiss her softly, with the promise of more to come.

"But I did. The best nickname ever—and in a few months, I'm going to use it every chance I get."

Her head angles to the side, trying to guess. Eventually she gives up.

"What is it?"

I raise Kennedy's left hand to my lips, kissing the knuckles where her engagement ring sits. Where, very soon, a wedding ring will be.

"Wife."

Extended Epilogue

Once upon a time . . . at the Mason Potomac Estate

"**R**obert?" Vivian Mason's voice whispered. "Are you awake?"

She wasn't supposed to be. Her parents had tucked her into bed hours ago. Her mother had softly brushed back her blond hair and kissed her forehead, her mother's beautiful white dress glowing in the dim room like a star in the night sky. And her father had wished her sweet dreams, calling her his Little Fox, because he said she was smart like a fox. He was silly like that, always coming up with funny names for her and her little brother and sister.

But how could they expect her to sleep? It was New Year's Eve and there was a grand party in the ballroom below them.

"Robert!" she demanded, louder now.

"Yes, I'm awake!"

The silk sheets whistled as her best friend in the whole world, Robert Atticus Becker, emerged from them. Though they were both eight, Robert was already a head taller than her. Her rubbed the drowsiness from his ice-blue eyes, pushed a hand through his black hair, and stood next to her by the door.

"Did it start yet?"

Vivian smiled with excitement—because for as long as she could remember, she looked forward to the fireworks display that would soon light up the world outside. Like magic.

"No, but soon."

Robert took the lead, cracking open the door and peeking out, making sure the coast was clear. Then they crept down the endless hallway, Vivian's slippered feet and Robert's bare ones not making a sound. They stepped into the red bedroom and closed the door softly behind them.

This was where her grandmother kept her most treasured photo albums—the book shelves were lined with them. Her parents had had two weddings—one on an empty beach of white sand and swaying tropical trees—and another, fancier affair, with hundreds of guests in a building with intricate arches and marble columns. And there were photographs of all her parents' trips and travels. Before she was born, they'd even jumped out of an airplane together. But they didn't travel much anymore, not to anywhere the whole family couldn't go.

Her father once said that having her was their greatest adventure.

The two children climbed onto the velvet window seat. Vivian rose up on her knees, her palms against the cold panes, looking out to catch a glimpse of the guests below.

"I can't believe Samuel got to go to the party this year but we didn't." She pouted.

Robert shrugged. "He's older than us."

As the youngest of seven, Robert knew all about having to wait to do things his older siblings were already allowed.

"Just be lucky you're not Nat or Xavier—they have years to go."

That was true. Vivian's younger siblings were at this moment confined to the nursery, with Harrison and Nanny Jane keeping careful watch.

Vivian stretched her neck as the crowd of guests stepped out onto the veranda in their shiny jewels, floaty gowns, and sharp tuxedos. She could practically hear the tinkling of champagne glasses as white-gloved servants handed them out from silver trays. She spotted her parents then—her mother laughing at something her father whispered in her ear. There were few things Brent Mason enjoyed more than making his wife laugh.

Then slowly, her father turned, his handsome face tilted up, as if he was looking right at her. And she could've sworn he winked.

For a second she gasped. Until she remembered the room was dark and they were high above him—he couldn't possibly know she was there.

She saw her Uncle Stanton—tall and golden—walk up to her parents, with his arm around her beautiful Aunt Sofia. Beside her mother, she spotted Robert's parents. Vivian thought Aunt Chelsea must be cold, because Uncle Jake had her tucked against his broad chest, his big arms around her, shielding her from the wind.

Sounding slightly bored, Robert asked, "What do you want to be when you grow up? I'm going to be a Navy Seal—they have the coolest assignments."

Vivian sat back on her heels. "I'm going to be a writer, like my Aunt Vicky."

Robert's nose scrunched. School was easy for him, he could read something once and remember it word for word. But that didn't mean he liked reading.

"What would you write about?"

Vivian gazed down at the three couples below, who were such a huge, wonderful part of her life. "I'm going to write about three superheroes. Everyone thinks they're just normal people, but they have hidden identities."

Robert nodded his head. "Secret identities are cool. What will they be?"

Vivian's voice went soft as she imagined. "One will be a cowboy, one a knight, and the other, a prince."

"Will they kill people?"

Vivian's head whipped around to him. "No. They'll save people. Every day. And they'll have beautiful superhero wives who save them."

Robert squinted. "I don't know, Viv. Sounds kind of dumb."

She just smiled. "My stories will be amazing. Everyone who reads them will laugh and cry and know how it feels to fall in love. And they'll end the way all the very best stories end."

Robert leaned toward her, his attention caught. "How will they end?"

" 'And they all lived happily ever after.' "